Dying
By
Design

Charles Belfoure

Broken Pediment Publishing Co.

Broken Pediment Publishing Co.
4596 Wilders Run Lane
Westminster MD 21158
www.brokenpediment.com

ISBN 0-9722279-0-3

Printed in the United States of America

1

"We don't like the way the outside looks."

Aisquith didn't look up. He continued to gaze at the white cardboard model in the middle of the polished mahogany table. There was a smile on his lips, but rage gathered force in the pit of his stomach. In seconds it would move up into his throat. In a minute, he feared, it might spew out of his mouth, rivaling Linda Blair's letting in *The Exorcist.*

He had had this feeling before.

Aisquith had no children from two failed marriages, but he always imagined that this was the instinctive rage parents felt when someone threatened their child. Like a lioness attacking an enemy intent on hurting her cubs. His child was sitting in the middle of the table. He suppressed the urge to strike Mr. Dunwoodie, his chief tormentor, in his ample stomach. With the rage now in a holding pattern at the base of his esophagus, he looked up and beamed a great diplomatic smile.

"What exactly don't you like... about the outside?"

Dunwoodie and Mrs. Huxley glanced anxiously at one another. Aisquith's silence had rattled them. They both realized they had crossed the Rubicon of architectural criticism into outright insult.

Dunwoodie cleared his throat. A retired chief executive officer in his seventies with many idle hours on his hands, he was the ideal person to serve as chairman of the library building committee. He began the delicate process of damage control.

"You've done a wonderful job of designing the interior, Allan. Everything fits together perfectly."

"My goodness, yes," added Mrs. Huxley, quickly picking up on Dunwoodie's approach. "I've been a librarian for thirty-two years and I've never seen such a beautifully designed overdue book counter. I bet you've had some overdue books in your time." She cackled with laughter.

1

"Why, thank you. Yes, I've paid a fine or two," said Aisquith. This brought on another torrent of laughter. When Mrs. Huxley laughed, she reminded Aisquith of Miss Hathaway's high-pitched giggle on *The Beverly Hillbillies*, one of his favorite shows when he was a boy.

Dunwoodie, who looked like Sydney Greenstreet, but in Brooks Brothers clothes and tasselled loafers, also chuckled at his comment. Even when he merely chuckled, his belly shook like Jello. It was time to change the tone of the discussion. As if he had turned off a switch, the smile vanished from Aisquith's lips, and he gave them an icy stare. Seeing their discomfort gave him great pleasure.

"Then what *is* the problem with the design?" he demanded, gravely.

"It's the exterior of the building," Dunwoodie blurted out. It isn't at all what we expected."

"Evan, this building's scale and space attains a complete compositional unity. The exterior clearly expresses this."

Dunwoodie reacted as though Aisquith had responded in Navajo.

"Well, yes, I suppose... but it still looks like one of those airplane hangers you see at Dulles. It just doesn't fit our image of what our library is all about, Allan," he said in an upbeat of courage. "I'm sorry."

Clients always described the exterior of a building with a simile. It looks like an upside-down Christmas tree. It looks like a beer truck. Animal analogies were the most popular. The most noisome one Aisquith had heard was that a building looked like a giraffe lying on its side. He had worked for weeks on that design, re-examining it day after day, and had never noticed a giraffe.

Aisquith shifted uneasily in his seat and gently admonished them. "I don't believe you've grasped the meaning of the design."

Dunwoodie and Huxley shifted their eyes to the white model gleaming under the downlights of the conference room. They stared at it for long seconds, desperately hoping to find a glimmer of comprehension somewhere in its curvatures.

"I'm sorry Allan, I guess it's staring me right in the face and I'm just missing it," Dunwoodie whined. Mrs. Huxley kept staring.

Dunwoodie looked down at the model again, his face contorted into a confused frown as if he were looking at a Roswell alien.

He gave up and voiced his frustration in an exasperated tone. "It's just not what we expected. We wanted a library that's inviting to the community, not . . . an airline terminal."

The rage that lay in wait at the base of his esophagus now inched upward again, but Aisquith kept it in check and quickly took control. He was quite proud of this skill. In his younger days, he would have exploded at the client, branding him a jerk and a philistine to his face, but with age had come tact and a measure of patience.

His temples ceased to pound like kettledrums. He smiled again. He would now "educate" the client on the basics of good design, or rather his definition of good design. It was all a kind of Jedi mind trick where the architect implanted his design values into the mind of the client without him realizing it. Aisquith had always loved the part in the first *Star Wars* movie where Alec Guinness got past the Imperial Storm Troopers by making them say what he wanted. Very soon Dunwoodie would say, "This design establishes a serious discussion about the man-made environment and we must build it."

"What goes on inside the library determines what the outside will look like," Aisquith, said, deliberately moving down a few levels in architectural discourse. He had long since given up using the phrase "form follows function." It might have worked for Louis Sullivan but it always drew blank stares from his clients.

"Here, the circular stair becomes a design feature on the outside, a cylinder."

"But it looks like a silo with a slice off the top," Mrs. Huxley protested.

Aisquith instantly saw that the mind trick wasn't going to work. His child was in grave danger. He knew he had to put on the gloves and fight to the death. He jabbed quickly. "It anchors the entire front façade, giving it a distinct duality of solidity and movement."

"It still looks like an airplane terminal, and, besides, that's a lot of glass to clean. Our janitorial budget is quite limited," Dunwoodie replied, in a sharp practical uppercut to Aisquith's ego.

"The exposed roof trusses are a clear expression of the structure of the building and form the curve of the roof," Aisquith puffed, throwing a punch that hit nothing but air.

"But it's like a warehouse," Mrs. Huxley snapped, with a mean jab to Aisquith's rib cage.

They were standing their ground. Aisquith sensed he was losing the fight. But he had enough energy left to throw one more desperate theoretical punch. "These forms establish a correspondence between aspects of the site and a built structure."

Dunwoodie counter-punched. "I have a hard time figuring out where the entrance is? Can't you put in some columns or something at the front door?"

"The entry is… right here…can't you see it?" Aisquith whined as if he were a six-year- old. All theoretical arrows from his quiver were gone.

"Allan, you know, this is all just a misunderstanding on our part," Dunwoodie said with a newfound cheerfulness. He looked quickly at Mrs. Huxley, clearly hoping she would follow this new tack.

"Yes, we've been too caught up with the inside of the library and didn't pay any attention to the outside. We should have given you far more direction, I'm afraid," she chirped.

"EXACTLY," Dunwoodie boomed. "This is all our fault."

Now industrial strength flattery was injected. "You've done a magnificent job on the inside," Mrs. Huxley said. "The reading rooms are beautiful."

"We can work this out," Dunwoodie insisted, reaching across the table and patting Aisquith's hand gently.

Aisquith stared past them. He had been at this crossroads many times in his nineteen-year career. The signposts on the road were always the same. On the right the sign read artistic capitulation, which meant taking a dive and getting paid. The left sign read artistic integrity, which meant fighting for your design and getting it built the way it should be. The latter decision could mean no compromise and walking away with only a fraction of his fee.

As he had often done in his career, he turned right. As you know, I'm a reasonable man. "Just what *do* you have in mind?"

Mr. Dunwoodie and Mrs. Huxley glanced at each other and smiled. They sensed victory was at hand. Dunwoodie went in for the kill. "You know, Allan, our library has been in Ripton for over a hundred years. We like to think our values and traditions are best expressed in the colonial style."

Aisquith's heart sank. Colonial. The kiss of death for any project. The only architectural style Americans seemed to know or want. He had always been mystified by this passion. On his first trip abroad during his second year at architecture school at Columbia, he had seen countless European towns and cities that accepted modern buildings among their centuries-old buildings. America, only 225 years old, coveted *only* buildings from the past.

House plan magazines at supermarket checkout stands filled with nothing but colonial houses. Pilasters. Palladian windows. Dentiled cornices. God forbid if the roof is flat; everyone knows that flat roofs leak.

Aisquith's attention snapped back to the nightmare at hand. "Do you want a building that's inspired by colonial vernacular architecture?" This was a roundabout way of asking whether the building could be designed with the barest perceptible allusion to a colonial building.

"You wait right here," Mrs. Huxley said, startling Aisquith by leaping up from the table and sprinting to the door of the conference room. Still as thin as she was when she entered Smith, or Vassar, or some other Seven Sisters School, Mrs. Huxley looked as if she had never exerted herself in her entire life. Aisquith wondered if she really had been a librarian all those years. With her patrician good looks and expensive clothes, she seemed like a rich man's wife who killed time until her husband came home. Aisquith was still staring at the door when Dunwoodie started speaking.

"I bet I know where Sidney is off to," he said with a chuckle.

"Where?"

Dunwoodie didn't reply.   After a few agonizing minutes of silence there was the sound of hurried footsteps in the corridor. The door flew open and Mrs. Huxley reappeared with a stack of books in her arms.

"Here's your direction. I should have thought of this earlier. Shame on me."

She bounded in and let the books spill onto the table. They slid across the shiny surface. One thick volume fell into Aisquith's lap, jabbing him in his groin. He looked down and saw the title *Great Buildings of Colonial Williamsburg* staring up at him. It was quite fitting where it landed.

"Allan, we're looking for a real Colonial Williamsburg look. Just like this." Dunwoodie picked up one of the books on the table, fanned the pages, and found a specimen he admired. "The Doctor Barraud House is wonderful isn't it? I know it's a house, but if you could incorporate some of the same flavor into our building, that'd be super. Or maybe just blow it up to the size of a library. Can you do that?"

Aisquith nodded meekly.

"You can take all these with you, Allan," Mrs. Huxley said sweetly. "We'll check these out for you. You can have them for a month. That's enough time for you to redo the outside, mmm?"

"I don't have a library card," Aisquith muttered, desperately grasping at any excuse in the universe.

His tormentors roared with laughter. "Allan, you're a pip," Dunwoodie boomed, red in the face from laughing.

"No problem, Allan, I'll fix you right up with your own card," exclaimed Mrs. Huxley. "Now that we've provided a direction, we hope to see some new sketches real soon,"Dunwoodie bellowed happily.

Panic again seized Aisquith. Like a man about to be sucked under by quicksand, he frantically made a last-minute attempt to pull himself out. "I really feel this is the right design for this building. You really should reconsider this before I go and do another set of schematics," he whimpered.

The silence was deafening. Dunwoodie looked down at his tasseled loafers, cleared his throat, and gazed into Aisquith's eyes. "Allan, we all want to stay friends here. We'd really like to see another approach. " Dunwoodie's fatherly tone was reminiscent of Ward Cleaver talking to the Beaver.

Aisquith was about to reply when Dunwoodie let loose a punch that was definitely below the belt. "You know Allan, it is ... *our* money."

Aisquith's face turned red in a new surge of anger. He stood up suddenly from his red leather seat and started to roll up the drawings on the table. Alarmed, Dunwoodie looked over anxiously at at Mrs. Huxley, who had the fleeting thought that the architect would use the rolled drawings to strike them.

But Aisquith slowly put the rubber band around the drawings and then extended his hand to Dunwoodie, who stared at the hand in front of his face before rising from his seat.

"I'll start on another set of schematics and call you when I'm ready to present, Evan," said Aisquith in his best authoritative tone.

A look of relief came over Dunwoodie. He stood up and he eagerly grasped his hand and shook it so hard Aisquith thought his arm would come out of the socket.

"That's great, Allan, just remember …colonial, think colonial," he blustered. "Think of the time you visited Williamsburg."

"Yes, I will." Aisquith had never been near the place.

"Now don't you change a thing on the inside," Mrs. Huxley said cheerfully.

"Just the outside," added Dunwoodie.

"You can count on it," Aisquith muttered with a nod. He scooped up the books from the table and put them under his arm. With great difficulty, he then picked up the model and the roll of drawings. Dunwoodie opened the conference room door and heartily patted him on the shoulder as he went into the hall, as if Aisquith were a thirty-year member of the Maryland Club.

"So long, Allan. We can't wait to see the new drawings." Dunwoodie obviously imagined the wonderful cupolas, dentils, and string-courses he would see on the new set of drawings.

Carrying his doomed model, Aisquith walked across the parking lot that he knew would soon become the site of a new pseudo-colonial library. The late October afternoon was cold, crisp, and clear. Normally, Aisquith would have stopped to take in a deep breath of the cool night air; for it was his favorite time of the year. He was fair-skinned and hated the summer sun so he always eagerly looked forward to the coolness of autumn. But today, he dragged himself along like a beaten rebel after Appomattox. There was no air; he walked through a vacuum.

When he got to his Volvo station wagon, he dropped the drawings and books to the ground, flung the cargo hatch open, and threw in the model. He heard little bits of cardboard ricocheting off the side windows and ceiling. The books and drawings followed with even greater force, producing a loud crunching sound from within the car.

Aisquith slammed the hatch shut, then leaned against the back of the Volvo with both arms extended and head down like he was being frisked by the police. He stood frozen in the position for long minutes waiting for the sting of defeat to subside, but it didn't. Every second of the meeting ran through his head as if a film projector in his brain couldn't be turned off.

He desperately wanted to go home and cope with this defeat in the usual manner, by getting into bed with his suit on, pulling the covers over his head, and sleeping for eighteen hours straight. But he had another appointment that he couldn't miss.

Pushing off the back of the station wagon, he straightened up and walked slowly to the driver's side. He got in and drove off.

2

He was once a young man of great expectations.

But as Aisquith rode down the Jones Falls Expressway, he reminded himself that at forty-four, he was no longer that young nor could he expect anything great from life.

Nineteen years ago, the future had seemed so bright. Everything seemed to point to success. He had an impeccable architectural pedigree. The best Ivy League architectural education one could have. Three years as an assistant to one of the most admired architects in the world. By now he should have been one of the brightest young stars in the architectural firmament; instead his career was in a black hole. No matter how hard he tried, he just couldn't escape its cruel gravitational pull. He knew it was no one's fault but his own.

Instead of being a creative lion, he was a creative coward. For fear of losing his fee, he always gave clients what they wanted no matter how absurd. If they wanted a Mexican hacienda with a Gothic steeple and Egyptian columns, they got it. Nineteen years back this would have been unimaginable. But somewhere along the way, years before today, the seeds of his cowardice had been sown.

An only child, raised in Baltimore by his divorced mother, who survived as a miserably paid teacher, Aisquith's childhood was a threadbare existence. He simply accepted this as the way things were meant to be and that he would never have the nice things his friends in the neighborhood had. No nice home or bicycles or a father. It just wasn't in the cards. His mother, though, wanted something better for her son and understood that those with élite educations had a decided advantage in life. By taking on a second job and asking her father for financial help, she was able to send Aisquith to Chaucersburg Academy, a second-tier boy's school in Pennsylvania.

Until he left to attend the sixth grade there, poverty to him was like the shape of one's nose. That was what you were given in life and you learned to live with it. But the experience of attending school with those who had everything and to whom money meant nothing hammered into the boy an almost pathological fear of growing up poor. Most prep schools in the northeast had their quota of unfortunates that were academically qualified but belonged on a low rung of the socio-economic ladder. In his case the rung was the bottom one of a tall ladder at Chaucersburg. No matter how well he got along with the other boys, an invisible cloak of poverty enveloped him, setting him apart from the rest.

As in England, everyone had a place in the class structure at Chaucersburg. If one didn't know one's place there was always a reminder. One week after arriving, someone reminded him in no uncertain terms. But instead of being crushed, Aisquith knew his only way up the social ladder and out of lower middle-class desperation was an education. And the only education that counted in this world was an Ivy League education, and the one that counted most was from Harvard.

With the single-mindedness of a pilgrim walking on his knees to Mecca, he inched toward his goal. For the next six years, every paper he wrote, every pop quiz he took, was an opportunity to show the Harvard admissions office he was their man. By participating in the obligatory extracurricular activities and writing an admissions essay that Balzac would have envied, he actually made it. But what would he study when he got to Cambridge? Aisquith had one very exceptional talent. He could draw beautifully.

At first, he devoured every art class offered at Chaucersburg, often going back to the classroom in the evenings and weekends to work on projects. Looking back, those evenings were the best times of his life. But at Chaucersburg, anyone with an artistic bent was considered a fag or to have fag-like tendencies. Painfully self-conscious,

Aisquith heard the snickers behind his back and realized his talent was now a liability.

The worst reputation to have in a boy's school was to be suspected of practicing the unspeakable vice of the ancient Greeks. With great regret he scaled back his artistic pursuits and put more emphasis on sports, the real barometer of acceptance at a prep school. When he wanted to draw or paint, he found an empty room in the art wing on the weekends and closed the door.

In his third year his life took a new direction on a school field trip to New York City. In the name of culture, the entire eleventh grade was herded onto a bus for an afternoon performance of the American Symphony Orchestra at Carnegie Hall.

After the opening bars of the overture to "The Barber of Seville," Aisquith and six of his classmates could take no more and went out a side exit onto 56th Street, headed for a showing of "Oral Call Nurses," playing at an Eighth Avenue establishment they had spotted riding uptown on the bus. Walking down Sixth Avenue, they turned west on 53rd Street toward Times Square, but Aisquith stopped suddenly and looked east. Although it was his first trip to New York, from his limited knowledge of the city he knew that the Museum of Modern Art was on West 53rd. It was a place he had always wanted to visit.

He told his friends he wanted to take a quick detour to check out a store and would meet them inside the theater. The "plot" in a porno film was never that crucial; so he was pretty sure he could come in at any point and pick up the story line.

His classmates were momentarily puzzled, but because their hormonal levels were at record levels in anticipation of a triple-X movie, they quickly said okay and hurried on. Aisquith ran down 53rd to the museum and went inside the lobby. A Francis Bacon exhibit had just opened and the place was mobbed by culture vultures who would brag at parties that weekend that they'd already seen the exhibit. He bought a student ticket and followed the signs to the exhibit but was dismayed when he got there to see wall-to-wall patrons.

Deciding to let the crowds thin out a bit, he went to look at the museum's permanent collection. He was excited to see his favorite paintings he had only seen in art history texts, like Cézanne's *The Bather*. On his way to the upper level where the collection was housed, he passed the entrance to a small exhibit that caught his attention.

It was an architectural exhibition of American and international buildings done since 1970. Looking at his watch, he knew that he had very little time and that the movie was probably into its fifth minute and its tenth sex scene by now, but the photos on the wall interested him so he went in. He had the whole gallery to himself. Aisquith was quite impressed by the wonderfully inventive forms of the buildings. They were almost like great pieces of sculpture, but one could go inside them and attend a concert, pray to God, or actually live.

Besides the photographs, there were large beautifully crafted architectural models under glass, along with dynamic drawings of proposed buildings. One section of the exhibition showed the evolution of a building from a powerful line drawing on a piece of yellow tracing paper to a cardboard study model to photos of the finished product.

Aisquith forgot about the movie and became totally immersed in the buildings. He had always thought of architecture as something that only nerd engineers who knew calculus could do. That it was an art had never occurred to him, but the drawings on the exhibit walls changed his mind. The people who created these buildings were artists, not guys with plastic pocket protectors and slide rules.

Aisquith got to the end of the exhibit, then backtracked to look again at some buildings he especially admired. He had lost track of the time and rushed down to the museum bookstore to get the exhibition catalogue. He still had enough money left to go to the movie and sprinted across town to Times Square. His friends would think him weird if he chose art over x-rated sex and never showed up. He loved art but he also had the hormonal urges all teenagers are saddled with, so he didn't want to miss his first triple-x film experience, especially one that featured nurses.

For over a week after he left the Eros Twin-Sex, the movie Aisquith and the others had seen three times replayed continuously in his head. When it finally disappeared from memory, he refocused on the architecture exhibit at the Modern. He got out the catalogue and began to study the buildings in earnest, even sketching from the photos of some of his favorite buildings. The pure simple geometry of the powerful forms excited him. He especially loved the play of light and shade on them.

Aisquith next went to the school library and took out books on architecture regularly until he had read every one on the shelves. His friend Mark Collingsworth noticed his newfound interest and mentioned to Aisquith that he had an uncle who was an architect in New York. When Mark talked about his uncle's work, Aisquith noticed, it was always with great respect and admiration. One evening Aisquith's friends congregated in his room to bullshit about one thing or another. The subject shifted to Aisquith's interest in architecture. Aisquith was surprised to hear admiration expressed for architects by teenagers who never seemed serious or respectful about anything.

At 2:00 A.M., when they finally emptied out of his room, Aisquith sat on his bed for a while and began to realize he'd found a form of artistic expression that wouldn't brand him a pansy. Even before he knew what they actually did, he had great respect for architects. Just the technical expertise to put up a skyscraper or museum seemed quite a feat. It wasn't something any jerk in the street could do. It seemed everybody respected architects.

He decided to look into the career possibilities. With Mark Collingsworth's encouragement he called his uncle, Brian Collingsworth, of Collingsworth, Bailey, and Bamberger in New York, to ask him some questions.

Collingsworth, in his early fifties, was a plainspoken man who got quickly to the point. He told Aisquith what he thought the best and the worst parts of the profession were as well as the skills one must have to succeed. None of it made much sense to Aisquith. When asked about higher mathematics, Collingsworth roared with laughter and asked whether Aisquith knew simple arithmetic. That was all he would need. The public had this higher math prerequisite in their heads, he explained, because they didn't know what the hell architects really did.

When Aisquith said he loved to draw, that drew an enthusiastic response from Collingsworth, who proclaimed that drawing was the true basis of the profession. This was all the encouragement Aisquith needed to choose this path. He thanked his friend's uncle, who said if he needed a summer job, to give him a call and then hung up.

According to Collingsworth, there were two educational routes to an architectural degree. One could attend a five-year program at an undergraduate school and get a bachelor's degree in architecture. Or one could attend a four-year college, get a degree in anything, then apply to a three-year architecture program at the graduate level.

Since almighty Harvard, his goal, offered no undergraduate program in architecture, the latter was the way he would go. When Aisquith got to Cambridge, he took as many courses closely related to architecture as he could, even some in Harvard's Graduate School of Design that were open to undergraduates.

He also took up Collingsworth's offer to work summers to learn about the business but, more important, to make his application to grad school look good. He loved working in the architectural office. At first he did menial tasks like running blueprints and photocopying but his talents were quickly discovered and he was soon on the drawing boards. This was the pre-computer era when draftsmanship was still highly prized in the office. Aisquith's sure hand was greatly appreciated and admired.

From his summers of working and hanging around the GSD in Cambridge, Aisquith learned exactly how the architectural pecking order worked. As in the rest of life, an Ivy League pedigree counted the most. But to his delight the preferred path to an architectural school was the one he had taken by default. Getting any kind of undergraduate degree from an élite college, then going into a three-year program at an Ivy League school was indeed the most highly regarded route. A bachelor's degree from an architecture school was somehow considered déclassé. Even with an undergraduate degree in the field, you had to attend an Ivy League graduate school to assure the right level of polish and credibility.

Harvard, Yale, Princeton, and Columbia were the natural choices. He was accepted by all four. Picking Harvard would have been the natural thing to do, but Columbia was his selection. His connection with Collingsworth in New York meant part-time work anytime he wanted and he knew he'd need the money. Paying for grad school would be the same as paying Harvard, a patchwork quilt of grants, loans, and fellowships.

But Aisquith also had an artistic reason for choosing Columbia. When he applied to graduate school in 1979, a new aesthetic was sweeping the architectural profession: the pure, unadulterated modernism that Aisquith loved was being swept away by a craze for retro historical styles. Up until then, there was absolutely no acknowledgement of past historical styles at the top of the profession. A design that included an ionic column or a Palladian window was pure heresy, a crime worthy of castration by one's peers.

Architects never look back, Aisquith fervently believed, only forward for new inventive and exciting forms to stretch the creative envelope. But as he would soon painfully learn, the ordinary guy in the street hated modernism and yearned for the day when Palladian windows and crown moulding returned. That wish was granted in the eighties.

Columbia remained above such nonsense. Its ardor for modernism steadily increased. So Aisquith cast his architectural lot at Morningside Heights. He and his classmates howled with laughter at the new populist taste. Clients *always* had rotten taste but up until now architects had fended off their design ignorance. But this shift in taste was different. Architects who had toed the modern line now jumped ship in droves, producing Georgian shopping centers and Regency townhouses in the most recent real estate boom.

It was one thing for the average jerk in the street to like such stuff, but for an architect to go along with such a tidal wave of philistinism was as treasonous as renouncing America and swearing allegience to Iraq. Aisquith swore it would never happen to him.

The more modern the design, the better. No matter that his thesis project, a day-care center, was a mass of cold, jagged protruding shapes that would give four-year-olds nightmares. It was modern and abstract. As it should be.

Aisquith became a star at Columbia, drawing rave reviews from the visiting design critics who usually shat all over everyone's work. Even envious fellow students admitted Aisquith had enormous talent. For three years straight his work was featured in the *Columbia Journal*, an annual compendium of student work. *Architectural Review*, a highly-regarded British magazine, did a feature article on Columbia. Aisquith's projects took up most of the photos, even drawing the envy of his instructors who would have sold their mothers to have their work published there.

Aisquith knew he was good and he had a precise plan for attaining eventual architectural stardom. Like all architects, he wanted to set up his own practice but first he had to intern for three years before he could sit for his architectural license. This was galling. He wanted to strike out on his own right away. In his young, egotistical mind he felt he could design as well as any twenty-year veteran. A law school student could sit for the bar exam a few weeks after graduation and become a lawyer right away. He despised being compared with medical interns who slaved away at internships--eventually they would earn ten times what an architect could make.

As a close student of architectural history, Aisquith knew that all great architects once worked for great architects. Henry Hobson Richardson worked for Richard Morris Hunt. Stanford White worked for Richardson. John Russell Pope worked for White. There was an élite architectural family tree that spawned superstar talent. He was determined to be part of it.

His chance to become a member of the family came quite easily. Columbia's reputation drew the most famous architectural names as teachers. Teaching at an Ivy League school was an extremely important part of élite credentials; all the stars wanted to be visiting professors at Columbia. An international star was worth more than an American star. It was naturally assumed in America that anyone from overseas was more talented and more cutting-edge. No matter how busy their practices, the stars had to make an attempt to impart their architectural wisdom to the younger generation. Although they were great design talents, most were terrible as teachers, more interested in blowing theoretical air out of their asses than giving one-on-one attention to their admiring students.

Even "once-a-semester" guest shots attracted stars, though holding an endowed chair for an entire semester was more prestigious. The real Holy Grail of teaching was a deanship at an Ivy League school. The star lent luster to the school in name but in reality rarely had much to do with running the school. Messy quotidian details could be left to underpaid underlings.

Aisquith's work drew the attention of *all* the visiting superstars but one in particular. To Aisquith's good fortune, she happened to be the hottest international talent of all, Ranah Marhedi. An Iranian architect raised in London, she had just recently built her first design, a museum addition on the Thames. Young design superstars derived most of their fame from exciting, dynamic drawings and plexiglass models published in the right architectural magazines. They rarely got to build their visions. Their exciting designs remained only on paper. But in the world of high theoretical architectural hype, that was just fine. Ideas were the most important thing. No one seemed to care whether the things ever got built.

When Marhedi taught at Columbia, students crowded around her desk five deep, straining to her Oxbridge-accented English as she explained the deep architectural meaning of her work. She was an olive-skinned anorexic, almost six feet tall with raven black hair and dark brown eyes. Dressed head to toe in black, the official garb of international stars, she was so painfully thin she reminded one of a sixty-five-pound survivor of a concentration camp strolling through Avery Hall, home of Columbia's vaunted architecture school.

Many international stars who were awarded commissions in the United States set up offices in New York City and manned them with Columbia grads. In that world of architectural employment, the more famous the architect the worse they paid and the worse they treated their employees. One design superstar in fact did not hire grads but offered them "visitorships," the opportunity to volunteer services in return for working in the presence of his great talent. The IRS took the view that he wanted them to work forty hours for free and advised him to change his hiring policy or face a hefty fine or prison.

Marhedi walked up to Aisquith after a design critique in the spring semester of his final year and personally offered him a job. She told him she greatly admired his drawing and his design skill. He would have eventually gone to her to ask for employment and was quite flattered by her unsolicited offer. His stock among his classmates shot into the stratosphere. He soon found them hanging around his studio desk, two and three deep at times. And nothing was stolen from his work area anymore, a certain sign of respect in Avery Hall.

Aisquith started work the July after graduation. Others would have taken the summer off for a trip to

Europe, but he had his own agenda and dove into it. Marhedi picked up more and more work, mostly museums. Trendy museum directors chose the hottest modern architects for their projects, a way of saying to the public that they were hip and in tune to the most fashionable trends in architecture. An addition to *their* museum would be a piece of art in itself. The board of directors might hate the proposed design but would support the director's choice of architect because the director insisted it would bring more paying visitors to the museum and its supermarket-size gift shop.

In a short time, Marhedi was swamped with work from Cairo to Toronto, and Aisquith, despite his youth and inexperience, quickly became her right-hand man. It was impossible for her to design everything, so she shared design responsibilities with him. She became a napkin designer: when she had to do a fine arts center for, say, the University of Akron, she read the space requirements, scribbled on a scrap of paper a floor plan and a sketch of what the outside should look like, then left it on Aisquith's desk with a post-it-note saying "Work this out. I'll be back on the 16th."

Marhedi came to rely on him more and more as the workload increased. He had her design vocabulary down pat so she had only minor criticisms of his work. Sometimes she just handed him the program without even looking at it.

It was like ghost surgery. The patient thinks the experienced old surgeon will be performing the operation but once the anesthetic knocks him out, it's actually the young resident doing the cutting. The old surgeon pops his head into the O.R. once in a while and asks if things are going okay. Marhedi's clients never knew Aisquith was the ghost designer. They couldn't tell the difference. He didn't give a damn if Marhedi got the credit. If it meant advancing his career, he would do anything to please this superstar architect. His day in the sun would soon come if everything went according to plan.

Aisquith threw himself into the entire milieu of theoretical architecture. He started dressing from head to toe in black even on the hottest days in New York. Of the little money he received, he spent a great deal on dense, unreadable theoretical architecture tomes. In the arena of high architectural discourse, the more esoteric and unreadable the reading, the more valued it was.

Marhedi liked and valued Aisquith because he took a lot of the burden off her twig-like shoulders, but there was another reason. For theoretical architects like Marhedi, their designs usually remained beautiful renderings on paper, but once they started getting real commissions, the designs had to be actually built. The soaring, curving forms that seemed to defy the laws of physics had to be translated into a drawing from which a contractor could build.

Marhedi had no skill in this field. She had virtually no interest in the nuts and bolts of the profession and, until recently, never had to bother with it. But from his years working for Collingworth, Aisquith had learned how to put a building together, unlike the other Columbia and Ivy League grads in the office. Design was all that mattered in the élite schools. It was the fun, high-profile part of the profession; the messy business of making the building stay up would be handled by those poor devils who had attended the non-élite schools. But Marhedi never hired such people. It would have been like an English aristocratic clan allowing a plumber to marry into the family. So without complaint Aiquith took on the responsibilities of coordinating the construction drawings as well.

Although he loved going to work every morning and staying until midnight, he never lost sight of his dream of going out on his own. Most architects do work on the side, unable to resist the urge to be their own creative boss. During his three-year internship, Aisquith cultivated his own list of clients, preparing for the day he would make his break. It was like waiting for a prison sentence to be up. He would say goodbye to the warden, walk out the gates, and there would be a patron in a BMW or Mercedes waiting to take him home.

Usually a friend from Harvard days would recommend him to a friend who needed an addition or a small office renovation. Aisquith knew his contacts from Cambridge would be invaluable and he meant to preserve them. He did anything that was thrown his way in hope of another referral. He got paid far more for his moonlighting work than his actual day job salary. His poor childhood had made him frugal, so he salted away the extra income for the startup costs of his own practice.

At the end of the three years, he passed his architectural licensing exam. The day after he got the results he walked into Marhedi's office and quit. Since he had given no hint of dissatisfaction with his job, she was stunned. She had recently bestowed the title of associate on him, but he was too smart to be taken in by that. Architectural firms made employees associates as a way of flattering them without increasing their salaries. In fact, from "associates" they expected even more unpaid overtime.

Aisquith didn't believe in the two-week notice. It meant an agonizing wait to get out of a place that had become tiresome. Why hang around in awkwardness? So he cleaned out his work station and walked out the door with Marhedi following, begging him to reconsider.

Working out of a spare room in his apartment off Madison and 92nd, he quickly got his practice up and running. Marhedi's power and influence paid off for him. Within months, an office renovation he had done while moonlighting was published in *Abitare*, the influential Italian design magazine. Marhedi's work had been published there often, and he had made a contact with an editor who urged him to contact her when he went solo. Editors of all the important architectural magazines considered Aisquith an offspring of Marhedi, a genetic inheritor of her talent.

The same renovation was published in the other important Italian magazine, *Domus*. Aisquith had learned early from Marhedi the importance of milking one good project and getting it in as many magazines as possible. Her Paris country house design never got built but was published over and over all and added to her reputation. He could do the same.

3

As with most architects starting out, Aisquith's first major commission was a house. It was a dream come true. A brand new house for a Harvard-trained lawyer who could pay the standard fee of fifteen per cent of the construction cost.

Since it was his first shot at a house, Aisquith gave extremely careful thought to the design. Unlike many beginning architects, he resisted the urge to load every current design idea into the plan. Architects with their first major commissions could be like benchwarmers on a baseball team. When finally given a chance at bat, to make up for lost time and to prove what they can do, they swing for the fences and strike out. Aisquith knew there would be more chances. He developed a house with *one* strong design concept. It was an elegant horizontal composition of glass and beautifully stained redwood siding that blended into the two-acre lot in Kent, Connecticut. He smiled every time he looked at the design tacked to his wall. It was all but guaranteed to get into *Domus*.

Aisquith had met with the Gallagher's, a couple in their early thirties, at their apartment in Manhattan and also out at the site. They seemed to be the ideal client-- sophisticated and charming, and they read the *New York Times* "Home" section religiously on Thursdays. He went to their apartment on a Friday night to go over a few minor revisions, hoping to get the go-ahead to start the construction drawings that would be put out to bid. They had been ideal clients, accepting his design without question.

Shaun Gallagher was a successful Wall Street attorney who was starting to rake in real money. Tall, handsome, and self-assured, he now wanted the usual material things to show off his new-found wealth. His wife Winky was a strikingly attractive Seven Sisters grad who once had high hopes of doing medical research, but, given Shaun's income, now was one of those women she had hated so much in school, the wife who lives off the spouse's income. In a moment of self-reflection, she simply conceded that it was a natural feminine instinct to want to be taken care of by a man, so why fight it?

Aisquith unrolled the drawings and set the cardboard model on their coffee table and went over the revisions. When he finished, Shaun jumped up from the sofa. "Let's get the ball rolling, Allan. Start the construction drawings."

"Let's do it," Winky squealed.

Their words were sweet music. He needed to contribute to the euphoria. "You're going to be very pleased. This will be one very special home for you."

"Oh, Shaun, tell Allan what Daddy suggested," Winky chirped.

"Right, Winks, we'd like to have vinyl siding instead of the redwood," said Shaun, "a lot less maintenance and upkeep."

Aisquith couldn't believe he heard the words "vinyl siding" coming from the mouth of a Harvard man. It was as incongruous as a Kentucky coal miner uttering, "l'etat c'est moi."

"Vinyl? . . . on this house?," he gasped as if he'd been punched in the stomach.

"Sure and we found out we can get the vinyl in a custom color that matches the redwood color. We love the color you selected, it'll look great among all those pines." Shaun beamed.

"And it has an authentic wood grain finish, so standing far way it'll look just like real wood," said Winky in an authoritative tone that sounded suspiciously like Bob Vila in a Sears commercial.

"But it looks so goddamn fake," Aisquith blurted out.

The Gallagher's gave each other puzzled looks.

"It has the look and feel of real wood," insisted Winky.

"You know Allan, you aren't going to have to shell out $7,000 every five years to restain a 5,000 square foot house, I am." Shaun was beginning to look pissed off.

"Well, I wish you'd reconsider." Aisquith sounded like a child about to be punished and asking for a second chance.

"We've given it great thought. We've driven around looking at vinyl siding and we want you to put it in the construction drawings," said Shaun in an openly annoyed tone. A Harvard law grad was used to getting his way in life.

Aisquith knew there'd be a problem if he pressed the matter. He was ready to retreat but suddenly Marhedi and his Columbia classmates appeared inside his head, laughing at him and the wood-grain vinyl siding. Words came shooting out of his mouth like a machine gun.

"Shaun, you're making a huge mistake, it's in very poor taste and I think that..."

Winky shrieked. "You're saying we have no taste!"

"No, no, I didn't mean it that way, you have wonderful taste," Aisquith squealed. "Why, look how beautiful your co-op is."

The damage was done. Now Shaun weighed in with guns blazing.

"We like the vinyl siding and we want it on our new house," he growled.

Winky began to whine. "It's not as if we're changing your whole design. And it does have the look and feel of real wood, you know. It really does, honest."

"We are paying you and we hope you'll respect our wishes. It's our house and we can cover it with rabbit fur if we want to," said Shaun.

Aisquith immediately thought that choice would be much better than vinyl. He tried with all his might to control himself, but before he knew it "You just don't know what you're doing," slid through his lips.

A deafening silence engulfed the tastefully decorated living room. It was broken by a thunderbolt.

"Allan, we paid you for the design of the house and we think we can take it from here," Shaun said in a conciliatory attorney's tone. "You've done a great job and we really appreciate it."

Aisquith now realized the consequences of what he'd done and panicked.

"But I was supposed to prepare the construction drawings and oversee the project, I thought that's what we agreed to." He was a twenty-six-year-old man about to stamp his feet like a disappointed two-year-old.

"We had no contract or written agreement, Allan, and we can find a contractor on our own," said Shaun in a gentle voice that underneath meant "Go ahead and try to sue a Harvard lawyer."

Stunned, Aisquith rose shakily to his feet. The room was swimming around him as Winky thrust his designer black coat and black scarf into his arms and gently guided him to the door. He then found himself standing in the elevator. He couldn't remember if the Gallaghers had put him there or he had found his way by himself. The door opened on the first floor and he walked out through the lobby into the street like a zombie. The cold blast of January air across his face brought him out of his trance. Aisquith looked down at his empty hands. They had his drawings and the model. The house belonged to them now. It was as if his only child had been stolen before his very eyes and sold to a childless couple in Bolivia.

Then a realization came to him, so horrible that he took his hands and grasped the top of his head as if he had been struck by an ax. A large percentage of his fee was to be for preparing the construction drawings and specifications, detailed graphic instructions on how each part of his house should lovingly go together. But they had thrown him off the project. He now would only come away with a fraction of the fee he was expecting. The money he had counted on as his six-month rent reserve for his new office in Tribeca had vanished. He turned and faced the twelve-story building. He wanted to run upstairs, bang on the Gallaghers' door and beg their forgiveness, tell Winky he was sorry. But he knew the damage was irreparable. That was the last time he laid eyes on them and his drawings. Aisquith tried calling them at work and at home, but they never returned his calls.

4

For Aisquith it wasn't really the loss of the money that hurt most, painful as it was, but that the house design would never get published. Seconds after a house is completed and landscaped, the architect hires an architectural photographer at an exorbitant rate to take pictures. Timing is critical, for it's important to shoot before the client starts to make design decisions like covering vast expanses of glass with purple crushed velor drapes or tacking on a half-assed addition. Interior photos have to be taken before family pictures of the vacation at Seaworld and throw pillows cluttered minimalist interiors.

When he finished the renderings of the Gallagher house, he showed them to an editor at *Architectural Review*. She was thrilled by the design and promised it could go in the October issue next year. Now he couldn't even bear to pick up the magazine.

As the months went by the sting of his humiliation slowly wore off. Then one day at a self-serve gas station in Greenwich he looked on the other side of the pump and saw Donny German, a contractor who had done some work for him in the past.

German recognized him and shouted to him. "That's some house you did up in Kent."

"What the hell are you talking about?"

"The house for that lawyer and his wife; the one with the great ass."

Aisquith knew he was referring to Winky. Although she had no spatial perception, Winky had other admirable attributes.

"They brought me a set of drawings you did for them and I wound up building the goddamn thing."

Aisquith was silent.

"Don't you know which house I'm talking about, the one that looks like an aircraft carrier," said German in a puzzled tone. "Turned out great, though."

The last comment sent shivers down Aisquith's back. When a contractor says a house turned out great, it could mean only one thing--he changed the design to make it easier to build and increased his profit margin on the job. Contractors despised anything unusual in a design. If they had their way, every house in America would be a two-story colonial. And German was no exception.

The contractor finished pumping his gas and waved to Aisquith as he drove off in his Chevy Blazer, the car every contractor had to have to prove to the world he was successful. Aisquith got into his car and sat there staring at the dashboard. The renderings of his house came streaming into his head again.

Everything inside him told him not to go and see the house. But it was as if there was a tractor beam from a space station in a science fiction movie pulling him helplessly toward the house. It was useless to resist. He started his car and drove north to Kent. He thought of the house much like the biological mother who at childbirth gives up the kid for adoption and ten years later yearns to see what it looks like.

He knew the Gallagher's would have built on the two-acre lot because they had paid through the nose for it. They had found a buyer for their co-op, so they would have had no choice but to proceed.

He knew he couldn't just drive up in front of the house. The Gallaghers could happen to look out their window or come out to get their mail and spot him. It would be too embarrassing to get caught sitting in the car like a stalker. Instead, he would go around the block to a wooded lot that he knew backed up to their property. He would quietly and quickly walk through the woods and steal a look at the house.

Aisquith parked and started walking across the lot to the Gallagher's backyard. The property was thick with briars and sticker bushes which he hacked through with a stick like an explorer in the African jungle. As he walked, images raced through his head. Maybe they had built it exactly as he designed it, at least the exterior. Maybe all the changes were on the inside.

There could still be a chance for a photo. A photographer could take a passing shot from a car. Or early one morning when no one would be up he himself could stand down the road and take a wide-angle shot. He could get it published somewhere even if there were no interior shots.

Maybe he should go up to the front door and congratulate them on their new house. They'd be so surprised to see him, they'd let bygones be bygones. He smiled at this thought. Shaun and Winky would ask him in for a drink and give him a tour of the place. That's exactly what he'd do. They probably had received so many compliments about the house from their friends, they'd realized they'd been unfair to him. As he nodded his head at the thought of their reconciliation and seeing Winky's rear end again, Aisquith looked up and froze in his tracks.

He stood facing the house. A house so strange looking that he immediately thought he had walked up to the wrong lot. But as he was about to turn away when he caught sight of a roof overhang buried under the kind of low-pitched roof you'd find on a trailer. It was, goddamn it, his cantilevered overhang. Then, in horror, he focused on other details from his design. It was like picking out those Ninas in an Al Hirschfeld caricature in the *New York Times*. The ribbon windows that attenuated the horizontality of the house were still there, but now were broken up by green shutters and covered on the inside by forest green drapes. He started toting up the fragments of his design that had been hideously altered.

The worst abomination was the infamous vinyl siding in place of his beautifully stained redwood. But instead of mimicking plain board siding, it was the vinyl that imitated hand sawn shingles. It revolted him so much that he had to avert his eyes, as if he could no longer look at a horribly mangled traffic accident victim on the side of the road. He turned and started to run. The sticker bushes and low branches swatted him in the face like the clubs of an imaginary Indian gauntlet, wielded by his peers as punishment for producing such a monstrosity. There was no use explaining that it wasn't his fault. He absorbed the pain and stings as he stumbled back to his car.

He collapsed against the car, his cheek against the cold steel of the hood. Gasping for breath, he felt like crying but couldn't. He had always heard from women that crying relieved unbearable stress but for him the tears never came. The stress just stayed inside his chest like a football-sized tumor.

His mind plunged into an abyss of unbearable depression. He thought of the humiliation he'd suffer if his classmates found out that he'd done this house. Worse, Marhedi would be ashamed to admit she had employed a person who produced such a piece of shit.

Aisquith pushed himself off the hood and looked back toward the house. He swore then and there that even if they attached electrodes to his testicles he'd never admit he had anything to do with that thing. Suddenly he brightened and started fantasizing. Many great actors had an artistic skeleton in their closet; a truly rotten movie that they'd be ashamed of like "Mother Was a Zombie." After all, without failure, successes wouldn't mean as much. He couldn't remember whether Jean Paul Sartre had said that or he'd read it in a fortune cookie.

He had designed a wonderful house, but he couldn't put a gun to a client's head and demand his design be followed. He was glad he didn't have a gun in his hand now. He would have crashed through the tacky French doors he hadn't designed and blazed away.

At least the monstrosity was far away from New York. It would just sit there day after day radiating pure ugliness. There was nothing he could do about it. He couldn't throw a tarp over it. It wasn't a painting that you could rip up or a rotten novel that would go out of print and fade from public memory. Aisquith had always hated the architecture movie, *The Fountainhead*, where Gary Cooper blows up a building that wasn't built to his design. It seemed so corny. But now he had a new empathy for Cooper; only now he would revise Ayn Rand's plot so the client was inside when the building exploded.

With his loafers full of mud and his cheeks scratched and bleeding, Aisquith slumped behind the wheel of his Toyota Tercel. Staring at the dashboard, he suddenly realized that this tragedy was actually an epiphany. Now, more than ever, he would still stand up for his designs regardless of the economic suffering. He knew what was right and architecturally just and he would never capitulate.

On the very next job, Aisquith took a dive, producing a vaguely Greek Revival design for a small suburban shopping center in Glen Cove. The client loved it and referred him to a friend who needed a medical office building in New Rochelle. Thus came another dive that brought in another client and yet another dive. Like a drunk swearing it's his very last drink, Aisquith swore to the heavens each time that this would be the last dive. He might as well have vowed to pole vault over the moon. With each compromised design, he made more and more money. Money that bought him things he secretly thought he could never have. A Volvo, a co-op overlooking Central Park, trips to Europe. He got accustomed to having nice things.

But after two years and dozens of dives, he was unpublished and ashamed to face his colleagues. Sacrificing all the business contacts he had made in New York, he made a bold decision to return (or run away if one looked at it that way) to his hometown of Baltimore, an architectural backwater.

He'd be starting with a clean slate. No more dives. Aisquith would win the architectural glory that was rightfully his. Eventually he'd end his exile, move back to Manhattan, and again wear the black garb of the design star.

5

Aisquith pulled into the parking lot of Owings Mills Center, a high-rise office building in the middle of what had been a dairy farm. This part of Baltimore County was once all agricultural but it had been selected as the site of a new town. With white people moving out of Baltimore City in record numbers, the rival county government thought it could capture the escapees in the safety of the suburbs and harvest new property taxes.

Owings Mills New Town was a labryinth of subdivisions. When Aisquith had first driven out there he had looked for a town with a main street but soon found out that what the urban planners called a town center was actually an enclosed shopping mall with a few high-rises surrounding it.

Now he was there to show the developer, Gus Gavone, a preliminary design for an outlet mall in Carroll County, another once rural area to the northwest of Baltimore now engulfed by sprawl. Gradually blacks had moved to Owings Mills, and Gavone correctly--and profitably--anticipated a new white exodus to the surrounding farmland. One of Aisquith's clients told Gavone about him. Gavone gave him a small project to try him out.

To his credit, Aisquith had quickly established his practice in Baltimore and thriven financially. He took on all kinds of work, but especially commercial development, which was in a boom period. Gavone was the most important developer in the metropolitan area and this would be his first presentation to him. He wouldn't have dared postpone the meeting although Gavone had postponed it twice.

Aisquith arrived fifteen minutes early and sat for a while in his Volvo. He ran his hand over the leather of the passenger seat and smiled. He loved his Volvo. He complemented himself on shunning the trend to four-wheel-drive sport utility vehicles. He bought the Volvo because of a market research report that it was the choice of people with the highest education levels. And, on the practical side, the Swedes had driven Volvos in their miserable winters for generations and never needed SUVs.

He reached in the back seat and pulled out a black leather tube of drawings that contained Gavone's project. He didn't need to show an experienced developer like Gavone a model. Early on, he had learned that no matter how simple floor plans were, people were confused by them, although they never let on. A model was a three-dimensional representation the dimmest client, especially a woman (all women, he honestly believed) with a rotten sense of spatial perception, could grasp. He never told clients he was bringing a model. He loved to see their faces when he pulled the gem out of its carrying case. They held in their hands like a birthday gift, rotating it, poking at it, and imagining that all of a sudden they could shrink and walk through the cardboard building.

Aisquith got to Gavone's penthouse suite with time to spare and sat in the wood-paneled waiting area, replete with photos of the developer's completed projects. Design-wise, as he expected, they were nothing special. He hoped he might get a crack at a high-rise, but realistically knew he had to win his spurs with an outlet mall first. He still held to the credo that there weren't any small buildings, just small architects.

Aisquith was surprised when Gavone's assistant, an attractive woman in her mid-twenties in a very short skirt, came to fetch him for the meeting at the precise hour. He was sure he'd be kept waiting for a while. He knew the immense self-importance developers affected. The more insecure they were, the bigger the bluster and bombast. Aisquith had been impressed when he first met Gavone, who had quickly and concisely given him instructions on what to do on the outlet mall.

When Aisquith entered his office, Gavone remained seated and gestured silently for him to sit down. He would have been a great caricature of a developer bribing a politician in a political cartoon. He was obese and expensively dressed but disheveled as though his working-class origins didn't quite accept his $5,000 Armani suit. He had no neck. To Aisquith's amusement he looked like Jabba the Hutt in a business suit.

"So, whatja got for me today," he croaked, with a smile.

"I've done some plans and elevations of the stores for you. I've increased the net rentable footage," Aisquith replied, adopting a pleasant business-like tone.

The last three words obviously struck a positive chord in Gavone's heart, buried somewhere in all that fat. With a gleam in his eye, he sprung up like a frog leaping from a lily pad. "Pin it up right over there," he said, pointing to a large cork bulletin board at the far end of his office behind a conference table.

Aisquith had prepared to explain the design strictly in developer's language, meaning dollars and cents. He pinned up the floor plans and described them in great detail, emphasizing the extra rentable space he had squeezed out with space-saving tricks.

"That sounds great." Gavone scribbled numbers down on a scrap of paper.

"You're not including space for common area heating and cooling in those numbers?" He asked this sharply as if it were too good to be true.

"No, just pure rentable space. Now, suppose your big box tenant goes belly up, this plan is extremely flexible for creating any tenant space you need. You can offer a space as little as 2,000 square feet and as much as 12,000."

"I really like the dumpster location, a truck can get back there real easy." Gavone was beaming. "What's that space at the center on the sidewalk?"

"That's just a public space so people can sit under some trees and rest while they're shopping." Aisquith sensed danger; a predator was after his child.

"This is just an outlet mall, people are in a hurry. They want to run in and run out, so take it out," said an exasperated Gavone. "I can't get any rent out of it."

Aisquith stood his ground for a minute. He suspected that a street kid like Gavone respected moxy.

"It'll make your mall different from all the others. People will come because you're offering an amenity," Aisquith lectured. Architects often included public spaces that supposedly promoted a sense of community but always remained empty and unused. Countless plazas in front of office buildings had turned into repositories for derelicts and drug addicts. Still architects believed in them and kept churning them out.

"The only amenity the shopper wants is a parking space right next to the store," said Gavone said. "That's why every handicapped space is always stolen by the non-handicapped." This was followed by a great bellowing laugh.

"I suppose I can work it back into the interior space," Aisquith replied, miffed.

"Let's see the outside now."

Aisquith pinned up the elevations of the exterior, showing an imaginative screen of steel beams, metal panels, and huge graphics which hid the huge blank boxes that would contain such stores as Home Depot and Linen 'N Things. Facing the cork board, he closed his eyes and drew in a deep breath, then turned to start his presentation.

He opened his mouth to speak but stopped cold when he saw Gavone shaking in silent laughter. Aisquith was baffled.

"What the hell's so funny?" he blurted.

His response brought forth such an explosion of laughter from Gavone that Aisquith could smell the garlic bread he had had for lunch.

Convulsed with laughter, Gavone pointed to a conference table chair. "Sit down, son."

As Aisquith sat down, he half expected Gavone to clutch his throat and fall dead of a coronary. He imagined seeing the soul of his three per cent fee float from Gavone's corpse up to the heavens, never to be seen again.

"Should I put in their leases that they all get space helmets?"

"Space helmets? What are you talking about?"

"You know, like in the Jetsons."

"What?"

"I mean if you're giving me a Buck Rogers design, shouldn't everyone wear those fishbowl space helmets and aluminum foil space suits?"

Aisquith stared across the room at an autographed picture of Gavone and Jerry Vale on the wall. He got the point. Along with the animal analogies, any building that was ultra-modern might also be described by anyone over sixty as a Buck Rogers design in reference to the space hero of movies and radio in the 1930s. Aisquith, born in 1958, had missed the golden age of radio, but he knew about it. He always wondered why no one ever said it reminded them of Flash Gordon, another radio figure of that same era. For some reason, Flash never came up in design critiques, just Buck.

Now completely composed, Gavone placed his meaty hand on top of Aisquith's and smiled. "I like you, kid, I really do," he barked with sincerity.

Aisquith nodded solemnly.

"People say I treat architects like shit and they're right, I do. But I saw you had something when you showed me those plans. Instead of talking like some head-up-his-ass architect, you were speaking my language--money. I never heard that coming from an architect before."

"Well, I . . ."

"I really like you," Gavone bellowed as he pounded his bear-like paw on Aisquith's hand. "Forget about all that space ship crap on the outside," he said with a disdainful wave of his other fat hand.

"But this design that will make your stores stand out among the five billion others on Route 140," protested Aisquith.

"No one gives a shit, people just want to go in Bed 'N Bath and get a goddamn cheap pillow case. Only you dumb-ass architects think it makes a difference. Believe me, I've been in this business for almost forty years. The average jerk in the street doesn't give a shit about the outside. Besides, all that stuff on the outside will cost a bundle. This is a fuckin' strip mall."

"But you could do something a lot . . ." Gavone could see Aisquith was heating up so he tried to quell the flames before Aisquith exploded and said something he'd regret.

"Listen, relax. This is the first time we've worked together. We just have to get to know each other. The plans were terrific, you gave me far more space than I thought I could get out of the site. You just need some direction, that's all."

Aisquith suddenly pulled his hand from under Gavone's. The word direction put the fear of God in him.

"You know who uses these stores more than anyone else?"

Aisquith shook his head slowly.

"Women. Forget all this feminist crap about men sharing the shopping. Women still do all the shopping."

Aisquith nodded gravely.

"And you know what kind of style market research has shown women like best?"

Aisquith involuntarily grasped the edges of his chair with both hands, braced for a crash landing.

"Colonial. Exactly the same thing you did for my buddy. You know, Jerome's mall out in Henley. Give me the same thing but make it different. What's the name of that olden times place in Virginia that Disney or somebody did?"

"Williamsburg."

"Yea, that's it. Get yourself a book on it and you'll be fine. Just don't fool with the plans. Leave the inside alone. I love it. You and I are gonna do a lot of work together, you'll see."

6

Driving back to the office, Aisquith thought of the times he and his Columbia classmates had heaped scorn on the corny historical styles that America embraced. But in the span of three hours on this one day he had consented to do a colonial library and a colonial strip mall.

He could have walked out of both meetings.

Aisquith remembered his acting analogy after the Gallagher fiasco. Every important actor did schlock when starting out. An architect was no different. But after all these years, he couldn't even consider himself a B actor. The caliber of the work that he had done was more akin to stag movies.

There was a domino effect to taking dives. Each client referral lead to another until Aisquith actually had a lucrative practice with sixteen employees, accountants, and 401-K plans. He felt he had been thrown into a raging river of material success and couldn't escape the current. Or rather didn't want to escape the current.

Aisquith pulled his Volvo into the parking lot of the building that housed his office. It was a renovated textile mill over 600 feet long, built of brick and heavy timber. As industry died off in Baltimore in the mid-twentieth century, buildings like this sat vacant for years, then were recycled into new uses. This one, with its interior of exposed beams, curving walls, and glass block, now housed architects, graphic designers, software companies, and an occasional lawyer who wasn't self conscious about image. The only blue-collar workers who came here now were the night cleaning crew.

Aisquith had designed the renovation of the entire building. It provided a handy example to show visiting clients though the renovation hadn't turned out the way he wanted. He had hoped to hollow out an atrium in the center of the mill, but Arnstein, the developer, complained it took away from rentable space.

With rolls of drawings and his briefcase in his arms, he strode through the glass entry doors of his office. The reception area was conventional for an architect: a glass-topped table, filled with the last six months of *Architectural Record*, de rigueur Eames chairs, and a Scandinavian sofa. As he walked in, he noticed a balding man in his fifties sitting on the sofa. The man looked vaguely familiar but Aisquith couldn't place where he'd seen him before. Grace, his receptionist since his return to Baltimore, sensed he was in a bad mood and didn't greet him as he entered. As he passed her desk, she motioned to him to stop.

"Allan, Mr. Kelly has been waiting to see you," she whispered, tilting her frosted hair toward the visitor.

Aisquith glanced at him and turned to Grace with a puzzled look.

"Who the hell is he?'' he whispered back, visibly annoyed.

She shrugged her shoulders and went back to her typing. Aisquith knew there was no way to brush off the man, since he'd been seen coming in, so he approached him, still carrying everything in his arms. The man wore a light blue shirt with blue-and-red striped tie and a khaki jacket.

"Can I help you?" Aisquith asked in a bored tone.

"Mr. Aisquith, we've never formally met but I'm Chet Kelly from IBM in Eldersburg. You're doing some work there renovating our building." The voice was high-pitched and carried a note of anxiety.

"Oh, yes. I remember now," Aisquith lied, not wanting to hurt the man's feelings. All the anonymous workers at IBM looked the same to him whenever he visited there. "How can I help you?"

"Our group head showed us your new design."

"And how do you like it? Aisquith now turned jovial. He had never had a client's employee personally deliver a compliment about his design.

"You're taking away my office. And putting me into a cubicle." The voice was pitched even higher.

"That was the direction I got from management. Only enclosed offices for senior administrators and cubes for everyone else."

"But you can't put me in a cubicle. There's no privacy. I can't shut my door and I can't concentrate. And I can't make a personal telephone call anymore."

Aisquith suddenly realized where all this was heading and looked at Kelly's jacket to see if there was a revolver stuck in its side pocket. He looked in the man's bloodshot eyes and saw they were brimming with anger. When he had walked through the IBM offices, he had seen office after office filled with men like Kelly and an occasional woman, all hunched over computers. He recalled feeling glad he wasn't one of those drones.

Now he stood face to face with a possibly crazed middle manager and he was scared.

"You can't put me in a goddamn cubicle. I've been there for sixteen years. You can't do that to me," Kelly shouted. Grace had stopped typing earlier to eavesdrop. Now she had no trouble hearing details she would relate to her husband at dinner that night.

Though frightened, Aisquith didn't panic. He had seen those paramedic shows on the Discovery Channel and remembered how they dealt with lunatics until the police came. It was all in the tone of one's voice.

"Mr. Kelly, I think I can help you. There is some room for some extra offices and we don't need all those cubes." He tried for a soothing tone, like a hypnotist saying, "You are getting sleepy, very sleepy."

"Really?" Kelly's round face lit up with a smile.

"Yep. I talked to Fred Smirna about it the day before yesterday and he gave me the okay to add some regular offices. I think your group which is over . . ."

"By the east entry, past the copy room," Kelly shouted with glee.

"Yes, that's it. Past the copy room. Fred said they'd be getting offices. I'm working on the revision right now."

"So Fred'll be showing us the new design, soon?"

"Yep, probably the week after next."

"That's great. I knew they wouldn't put personnel with over fifteen years' experience in a cube. I'm sorry to barge in on you like this. But they never tell us anything."

"I can imagine. But it's no problem at all. I'm glad to straighten it all out for you."

"Well, I better get back. They only give us an hour for lunch and they dock us for extra time."

Kelly saw that he couldn't shake Aisquith's hand because his arms were filled, so he made a little bow and walked briskly out of the office.

"Thanks for coming," Aisquith shouted after him. He turned and faced an ashen-faced Grace.

"My fingers were ready to punch 911," she said in a hushed tone.

"And I thought doing that postal facility was dangerous," Aisquith sighed, shaking his head.

He went directly into his office, the only space aside from the conference room that had floor-to-ceiling walls, and slammed the door behind him. He flung his briefcase across the room and lay down on the leather sofa at the far end of the office. He closed his eyes and started to doze off. He had to take care of office business and couldn't go home to take his preferred depression catnap.

Aisquith enjoyed having his own enclosed office. He had hated the lack of privacy in the open office plan when he worked for Mahredi and could empathize with Kelly over losing his office and door. The studio was a tradition that had started in the offices of French architects in the nineteenth century when the staff worked in one big room with drawing tables. The master would walk around criticizing the work, making his employees do all the drawing and design and telling the client he did all the work himself. The layout had always reminded Aisquith of a late nineteenth-century sweatshop.

Aisquith had really hated the fact that he couldn't make a private telephone call, especially when he had to talk with his moonlighting clients. He whispered into the receiver like a pervert making an obscene telephone call with the extracurricular client on the other end saying over and over, "Can you speak up?" Finally he had no choice but to make these calls from a bar around the corner on Jane Street.

As he settled into a restful sleep, a sharp knock at the door awoke him. He rose from the sofa enraged, stomped over to the door, and yanked it open. Leaning against the jamb of the door as if he waiting for a bus was Grigor Vaslov, one of his project managers. Grigor could see that his boss was quite annoyed and was greatly amused by this.

"Yes, comrade?" He loved to kid the Russian émigré about the now defunct Soviet Union. Sometimes, armed with a barb that had occurred to him the night before, he couldn't wait to come in the next day to needle the Russian.

"Allan, that sonofbitch structural engineer you hire is moron," Grigor shouted in a thick accent. The sound of his voice brightened Aisquith; whenever Grigor spoke, the image of Boris Badanoff from the "Rocky and Bullwinkle Show" popped into his mind.

"Please, comrade. Calm yourself. We are all brothers in the fight for the socialist cause."

"Fuck you and fuck engineer."

Aisquith could see the situation could not be remedied by humor.

"Okay, I'll talk to him."

"I wait six goddamn weeks for details on tower."

"I promise you, on the soul of Lenin, I'll get you those details." Aisquith knew he had been lucky when Grigor showed up at his doorstep looking for a job nearly four years ago. He had a superb technical education and could detail any kind of building. The Commies didn't waste time on pie-in-the–sky design, but Grigor was, mirabile dictu, a good designer. He had won the Russian Institute of Architects gold medal for the design of Gulag 12. In fact most of his portfolio was made up of prison work. Aisquith hadn't thought this experience would ever come in handy, but when the firm applied for work for the Maryland Department of Corrections, it received the job because officials were impressed by Grigor's imaginative use of barbed wire.

"Okay, you talk to him today or I outta here," Grigor barked.

"Got it, my Bolshevik friend, on the eyes of Trotsky I swear I shall call."

Grigor gave him the finger as he walked away. Aisquith laughed. The defeats of the day receded for a few moments. He remembered with amusement the adjustments Grigor had to make when he started working for Aisquith. The chain-smoking Grigor couldn't believe it when the State of Maryland banned smoking in the workplace. "I thought this was a free country," was his bewildered response. The concept of risk from secondhand smoke risk seemed preposterous, "So don't breathe near me."

There had been even greater consternation when Aisquith informed Grigor that he could not pin up a picture of a 38 Double-D girl from *Juggs Magazine* in his workstation. "Everyone else has picture of family up, how you know that not picture of my sister?"

Aisquith knew he couldn't go back to sleep so he walked down the hall to the studio. The word studio suggested an artistic environment, but it was just one big room full of computer workstations looking much the same as an insurance company. The only sounds in the room were mouse clicks. His staff stared so intently into their monitors that no one noticed his presence.

They reminded him of zombies. But they were his zombies and he needed them to crank out the drawings. Aisquith still believed in hand drafting and despised the computer but had forced himself to learn how to use it to for architectural drafting. Many of his architectural colleagues in Baltimore were in their late forties and fifties and felt they were too old to learn the new technology. Aisquith's attitude was that everyone in every profession had to keep up with new techniques. Even surgeons in their fifties learned to use the expensive new medical equipment that jacked up the cost of health care. But Aisquith's main reason for learning was staving off complete helplessness in case the entire staff walked out on him. Most owners wouldn't even know how to turn the machines on.

Aisquith crept up behind Kurt Collins, an intern architect who had Walkman earphones on and his nose four inches from the screen. He lifted one side of the earphones off Kurt's head, yelled "Hey," into his ear and jabbed him sharply on the shoulder. It scared the hell out of him, the response Aisquith had hoped for.

"Kurt, I know you use a Zippo lighter when you smoke. Do you have any lighter fluid?"

Kurt was taken aback. " I'll . . . I'll see if I have any in my car, Allan," he stammered.

"Good boy. I'll meet you out in the parking lot."

Kurt gave him a baffled look and walked out of the studio.

Aisquith liked Kurt's work and hoped that he'd stay on with the firm, but the chances of that were slim. Turnover was high in any architectural office, especially among graduate architects like Kurt. Architects generally were rotten business managers and Aisquith was no exception. Instead of rewarding his staff with incentives, he expected them to slave away for the pure love of the art. And he paid them the industry standard, which was peanuts. An insurance claims adjuster with a high school education got paid more. Aisquith got to do the design, the fun part of the job, while guys like Kurt got stuck with the messy details of creating the construction drawings.

After three years of service, Aisquith had grown sick of working for Mahredi because she expected the slaves to have the same enthusiasm as she did though she made $150,000 a year. He had sworn he wouldn't do the same thing with his own firm but he had.

He trailed behind Kurt, again observing the heads glued to the screens. He had always had a secret desire to mount a television in the corner of the studio as they do in a bar, so they could be entertained during the day. That wouldn't have been so different from listening to a Walkman all day. He always watched, or rather listened, to the TV when he worked out of his apartment. He even thought of putting living room furniture in the middle of the studio so people could take a break and relax. It would be the comfortable chairs from Ethan Allen instead of the modern sculptures that gave you a chronic backache. But the architectural world had a certain code and the studio system was sacrosanct no matter how deadening to the senses.

Aisquith had always thought of himself as a Republican, but as a result of the computer revolution he had developed socialist leanings. As the machines of the industrial revolution had chained people to the tedium of the factory, the computer condemned them to a similar fate in an office. But after entertaining a few seconds of empathy for the workers he would sigh and think that's just the way it goes. As long as *he* wasn't stuck behind a computer.

Aisquith found Kurt waiting next to his dented Toyota Corolla with a blue and yellow can of lighter fluid in his hand. He motioned to him to stay there while he went to the Volvo and opened the rear hatch. He pulled out the remnants of the library model and walked over to Kurt. Throwing the model down on the blacktop of the parking lot, he motioned for the lighter fluid. The uncomprehending Kurt slowly gave it to him. Aisquith took off the cap and placed the can at the level of his groin and began to squeeze the can, producing a urine–like stream of lighter fluid onto the model. Embarassed, Kurt looked away.

"Too bad piss isn't flammable," Aisquith said with a laugh.

Pulling a pack of matches from his tweed coat pocket, he struck a match and tossed it on the model, producing a burst of flames. The white cardboard browned and curled, then blackened into a form that Aisquith found more interesting than the design itself. The sight of something burning always mesmerized him. He sometimes sat for long moments in front of his fireplace at home watching a stack of newspapers or rolls of old drawings burn to a crisp. Here, the cardboard base of the model was the last thing to burn. Finally all that was left of the model was a curled black shape that looked like a beehive.

"Allan, that's a great design. Why the hell are you doing this?"

"I don't want to be reminded of what could've been. You know, I bet it's more fun to destroy a building than to create one," Aisquith replied, still staring at his handiwork.

He looked up and saw Kurt's expression and smiled. "I was once a young man like yourself with great expectations, but I turned out like Miss Havisham."

"Who?"

"Dickens." Aisquith took a perverse pleasure from being better read than today's youth.

"Come on, let's go in and show me what you've been working on."

As they walked back to the building, they saw they had been watched.

Aisquith smiled and waved at the figure standing by the door. "Carlos, you've been observing my pyrotechnic skills, I see."

Carlos Ricardo was a tall, almost breathtakingly handsome Cuban who had been with Aisquith for six years. He was an excellent designer who could detail down to the tiniest connection in a building. The way a toilet paper holder was attached to a wall was important to him. He had neither a sense of humor nor a Latin devil-may-care attitude about life, but was stern as a Puritan schoolmaster. Aisquith had once made the mistake of addressing him as "muchacho."

Carlos was an associate in the firm. There were two kinds of associates in the architectural world, those who quickly realized the emptiness of the title and others, poor devils, who actually believed it bestowed on them some real importance. Carlos belonged to the former group. He made no reply, but when Kurt and Aisquith got to the door, he stepped in front of them.

"Allan, I need to talk to you. Right now."

Aisquith knew what was coming. He hated confrontation and usually ran from it at all costs. But this was one occasion where he could run but couldn't hide anymore.

"Okay, meet me in my office," he said, looking Carlos straight in the eye.

As the three filed silently into the office, Grace came up to Allan with a fistful of pink "while you were out," message notes. "Allan, you had a billion calls this morning," she drawled in unadulterated Baltimorese.

"Yea, yea, I'll get to them in a second."

"There's this attorney who called twice and said it was urgent that you call."

"Was it my first wife's attorney?"

"Well, he didn't say."

"Then it's not urgent," Aisquith snapped. There was no call that was so important it couldn't wait unless it was the one of the attorneys of his former wives.

Aisquith closed the door behind him, signaling to the office that something important was afoot. The door was kept open ninety-nine per cent of the time. He closed it when he fired someone or made a telephone call of an intimate nature to a woman.

Carlos walked to the conference table at the end of the office and sat down, signaling that he wasn't leaving until the issue on his mind was settled. Aisquith always admired Carlos' good looks and his taste in expensive clothes, which indicated that he did work on the side or had money in his family. He sat down across from Carlos and waited.

As expected, Carlos fired the first volley. "You've been dodging me long enough. I want to be a partner and I want your answer now."

"I've given it a lot of thought, but I still haven't made up my mind," Aisquith lied. He had decided against making Carlos a partner the minute he had brought up the subject six months before. Aisquith's deprived youth and the fact that he was an only child had made him especially greedy. He was never good at sharing either his toys or his profits.

But Carlos had been with him for six years and Aisquith had come to depend on him. Because of the high turnover in the business, a firm needed at least one steady and reliable hand to help run the show. Aisquith knew that Carlos was that one person. Little by little over the years, Aisquith had given up pieces of design responsibility because of the need to go out and beat the bushes for new work. He couldn't design everything as he had when he worked out of his apartment in New York, so he farmed out the lesser jobs to Carlos.

Aisquith was surprised Carlos had stayed this long. The Cuban had one of the best architectural pedigrees in Baltimore, including degrees from Cooper Union and Cornell. He was a first-rate designer, a cut above anyone in the city. Aisquith knew Carlos was destined for better things than slaving for him.

The ghost surgery that took place in Mahredi's office had been replicated in Aisquith's. Clients assumed that Aisquith designed every detail of a project and he did nothing to correct that impression. Yet Carlos was the true author of many of the designs.

"Don't bullshit me, Allan," said Carlos in a very calm voice. "I want to be a partner, now."

"You're the best worker I have, so if it's a question of money, that can easily be remedied," Aisquith said, adopting a fatherly tone.

Carlos bridled at being called a worker. It conjured up images of a migrant bean picker.

"You can't buy me off!"

Aisquith jerked his head toward the door. "You can leave anytime you want."

"I'll be damned if I'll start from scratch in another firm."

Carlos knew that Aisquith didn't want him to leave.

"I have been a beard for you too long and you know it," he said.

This was absolutely true but for some reason it felt like a punch below the belt. Aisquith stared at the inlaid cherry strip on the granite conference table. He just wanted to get Carlos out of his office.

"All right, you're a partner. Satisfied?"

Without a trace of emotion, Carlos rose from his seat and walked toward the door.

"A twenty per cent share," Aisquith added quietly.

The words froze Carlos in his tracks. He paused for a second, then, with his back still toward Aisquith, walked to the door, opened it, and left.

A second after Carlos' exit, there was a sharp knock on the door. Before he could say come in, Grace poked her head through the door.

"The foundation guy called again for you"

"So have him talk to McKinnon, he's the construction coordinator. He'll answer any questions about concrete." Aisquith sighed. He was already preoccupied with figuring how to cheat Carlos out of his share of the year's profits.

"Not that kind of foundation. This one's the Addington Foundation down in 'nnapolis." Grace sounded perplexed

Aisquith snapped out of his daydream. "What guy?"

"Attorney John Charles Carrollton of the Addington Foundation for the Fine Arts," she read from the pink message slip in a staccato voice

"Let me see that," Aisquith barked. He walked across the office and snatched the slip out of her hand.

"Hey, take it easy. Want the rest of the messages?"

Aisquith gazed at the slip and muttered no. He recognized the name instantly. Carrollton was a rich power broker lawyer in Baltimore and a member of Maryland's most élite family. Why would the most influential attorney in the state call him three times in one day? Like any professional, his first interpretation of this was that he was getting sued. It had been a rotten day, so what could be more natural than ending it with a lawsuit? And by a lawyer who was a friend and confidant to politicians and billionaires.

Architects lived in constant fear of being sued over a leaking roof or--the absolute worst case--a structural collapse. As a result of this litigious atmosphere, architects did everything possible to duck responsibility. They added disclaimers on drawings and specifications, shielding themselves from the specter of liability.

The worst result of liability phobia was that the typical number of construction drawings increased ten-fold so that they matched the thickness of the Manhattan phone book. Each and every square inch of the building construction had to be documented for fear of the building contractor blaming the architect for omitting something. Unfortunately, as the drawing set increased, the architect's fee did not. Aisquith had once been astonished by a set of drawings for a huge museum built in Manhattan in the 1890s. His set for a county library that was one-tenth the size had four times as many drawings.

In the old days architects went to construction sites to answer questions and guide the construction crews. Aisquith rarely set foot on a building site. He only visited after the workers had gone home for the day. He hated to be told to his face that he had left out a dimension or a detail. No matter how careful he was, something always was omitted and the contractor was the first to let him know, usually *after* he'd gone to the client like a schoolboy telling on a classmate.

Aisquith believed in getting unpleasant things over with quickly. He sat back in his leather recliner executive chair, took a deep breath, and dialed Carrollton's number.

A woman's voice answered and informed him that Mr. Carrollton had left for the day. It was only two o'clock. Only lawyers cut out that early and never felt guilty about it, Aisquith thought.

"I'll call back tomorrow at nine," he said in a cheerful tone.

"Mr. Carrollton's usually in between ten and ten-thirty," was the terse reply. Lawyers probably never feel guilty about coming in late either.

"Damn," he muttered as he hung up the phone. He would have to wait another twenty hours before he could find out what this was all about. His spastic colon was already starting to gurgle from the stress of waiting. His stomach had a nervous system of its own. When it sensed stress it sent signals to his colon that meant onslaughts of diarrhea.

Aisquith sat still for a moment until the gurgling subsided. The events of the day had worn him out and he was ready to go home. He loved being the boss because he could go home whenever he wanted. But in fact he hated going home. Since his wife Allison left him three years ago, he found it more difficult to walk up the curving stone sidewalk to the empty house in Roland Park. Often he sat on the wooden bench on the deep porch that wrapped around the house for a half an hour before going in.

He had once loved the turn-of-the-century shingle-style house they bought together. He remembered the moment they looked at each other in silent agreement that this was the perfect house. The four bedrooms were to be filled with kids, family, and houseguests, but that wasn't to be.

Aisquith had been a loner most of his life and he didn't mind being described as one. He cherished his solitude and didn't care that he had few friends, but both of his ex-wives had cared a great deal. After his second marriage ended, he decided to revel in his natural solitude and succeeded for a while. He spent entire weekends alone in the great rambling house, never venturing outside. One of the third-floor bedrooms, once a servant's room, now served as a small studio where he could sit and draw to his heart's content.

He had reached far back into his memory and made the revelatory discovery that the happiest time of his life had been spent drawing and painting by himself. He had always been ashamed of the apartment in which he and his mother lived, never giving the boys at Chaucersburg details about his home. He left it at telling them it was a four-bedroom ranch house on two acres. But in truth his bedroom in the forlorn little flat had been a wonderful place where he often lost himself amid his drawings of soldiers, ships, and wild animals. At those times, he forgot about his threadbare life. His secret envy of the neighborhood children and all their material possessions disappeared for a while. Now, the third-floor bedroom in Roland Park was surrogated into that childhood sanctum.

One day, while drawing a still-life of a shoe, Aisquith realized that he'd been foolish to abandon drawing and painting for what he perceived as a more manly and more practical art form. Maybe as an artist he could have achieved the real fame that he could never have as an architect. A wasted opportunity was one of the saddest things in life. He wondered if this was for him the beginning of the mid-life crisis many men experience in their forties. Take Pete Norris, an architect for twenty-five years, who had become a barber and opened his own shop in the Fells Point section of Baltimore. Aisquith always found Pete in good spirits, as if he'd been paroled from prison.

Aisquith didn't want to go home to an empty house today. He picked up the phone and hit the speed-dial button. A woman's voice said hello.

" So what are you up to tonight?"

"Haven't heard from you in quite a while, Sir Christopher Wren."

"It hasn't been that long."

"Indeed it has."

"Well, I was just thinking about you."

"Mmm, then something's troubling you."

"No, not at all," said Aisquith, annoyed by her female intuition.

"You're in luck. I'm free tonight, so we can go out to eat, you can spill out your troubles, then we can make abbreviated love and finish up by 11:30."

"Sounds good to me," Aisquith said.

Taylor Henneman was exactly as her named implied, an Ivy League-educated psychiatrist from a Waspy family with utter disdain for the entire world. Unlike most people with that attitude, she seemed never to be troubled or depressed. Taylor by all appearances was a thoroughly happy, self-fufilled person. Aisquith was amazed that people would pay over $100 a session to tell her their troubles. He imagined her laughing in their faces when they confided that they were bisexual or cross dressers.

They had met at a party during the final days of Aisquith's second marriage and he had been attracted immediately to her beautiful figure and long blonde hair. But he was most fascinated by her combination of great intelligence and large breasts. Until Taylor, he had believed the bigger a woman's breasts, the lower her I.Q. Taylor was attracted to him as well. Aisquith was tall and quite handsome but like many women she was impressed by the fact he was an architect, believing it to be a romantic profession as opposed to being a computer programmer. Aisquith had impressed many a female in a bar or at a party when asked, "So what do you do?" His two wives had reacted the same way until they gradually found how little money he made for the enormous amount of work he had to do.

When his marriage finally ended, he called Taylor and they went out to a movie on a first date, then went silently back to his house to make passionate love. With an unspoken agreement that there was to be nothing serious between them, they saw each other every few weeks. Aisquith went out with other women, but Taylor, despite her prickly personality, intrigued him. She was well read, had great taste in clothes, and read the *New York Times* cover to cover each day, not just on Sundays. In sum, she was a sophisticated New York woman in a place like Baltimore.

She made him think of the women he could have had if he'd stayed in New York.

Aisquith left early to get in his depression nap that had been interrupted at work. He woke up around six o'clock and read the *Times*. He'd gradually stopped reading the *House & Garden* section on Thursdays because he kept seeing the work of his classmates from Columbia, but he continued to read the Sunday *Times*. He started reading the *Arts & Leisure* section and came across an interesting article on an exciting stadium design for Rutgers University. Three paragraphs into the piece, to his astonishment he discovered the architect was Kent Chapin, a student two years behind him at Columbia whom he thought was a complete moron with no talent whatsoever. Aisquith flung the paper across the room and went upstairs to take a shower.

They met at Alonzo's, a restaurant in Roland Park. As usual, Taylor shamelessly chattered on about her patients, breaking every ethical rule in sight. She was one of the very few people that Aisquith knew who enjoyed going to work. She found her patients' lives fascinating. With great exuberance and without revealing names, she described a city councilman who was a cross dresser, a Baltimore Oriole whom she suspected of being a flasher, and a TV weatherman who insisted on wearing snowshoes when he had sex with his wife.

Aisquith listened throughout dinner. He disliked revealing his inner thoughts to Taylor because he felt it made him seem weak, but it was really out of fear that Taylor would be telling her date of the next night about *him*.

After coffee, they drove in separate cars to Taylor's house in Homeland, an affluent neighborhood only minutes away for the sexual finale of the evening. As they undressed and started foreplay, Aisquith for the first time realized what hard work it was to make love to Taylor. He was amazed that this hadn't occurred to him before. She was like the man on the airport tarmac, giving those precise hand signals to guide a jet into exact position.

"Move your hand up just a bit."

"Okay."

"Run your hand over my breasts in a circle . . . No, no, now you're rubbing too hard, my breasts are a little tender tonight."

"Sorry."

"Just put your leg up a little closer. Yea, that's good . . . Take it easy, take it easy, you're not milking a cow here. Now, swing your leg . . . "

"Goddamn it," Aisquith yelled. He rolled over and sat up on the edge of the bed.

Taylor bolted upright and brushed the hair from her face. "What the hell's wrong with you?"

"Now I know what sex with Hillary Clinton must be like," said Aisquith in a dispirited voice.

"You bastard, you've been pissed about something all night."

Aisquith was silent for a few seconds. "I've never designed anything worth a damn."

"All architects feel that way."

"How do you know? Ever have any on the couch? I mean professionally."

"No."

"Didn't think so, no architect could afford your fee."

"Come on, out with it. What happened today?"

"Nothing, it's just that architects with real conviction get their buildings built without compromise."

"And you're saying that you don't."

"I don't know how. I'm so used to taking dives on all these projects. I just can't bear to lose the money. I automatically try to do something that'll please the client."

"And not yourself."

" For the longest time I always blamed the client, but it's really me that's the problem. I'm a goddamn coward."

"That's an important realization on your part," she said in her soothing psychiatrist's voice.

"Hey, don't patronize me like you do your goddamn patients. Leave me alone, I should've never brought it up."

"Come on, out with it. You'll feel much better," cajoled Taylor.

"Did you ever see "A Long Day's Journey into Night," the O'Neill play about his screwed-up family?"

"You're talking to a Yale graduate."

"There's this one part I always remember, when the father who's a famous actor admits that he squandered all his talent by buying the rights to this one play and playing this one role over and over again because it brought in a fortune. He could have become a truly great actor but he made the decision to go for the money instead. That's how I feel."

"You want to do that ultra-modern junk you see in architecture magazines or in the Sunday *Times*, don't you?" Now Taylor's tone was almost motherly.

"I don't want to do this pseudo-colonial horseshit all the time."

Taylor let out a shriek of laughter that startled Aisquith.

"Once I had a patient who was a painter who felt that his work was shit, not avant-garde enough to win critical acceptance. He was a portrait painter and I thought his stuff was really good, but he wanted to do more abstract work. His clients only wanted portraits that were super realistic. You know, Norman Rockwell-looking. He always wound up doing realistic, flattering portraits because he never could bring himself to turn down the money. He once told me the more famous a painter was, the more abstract and unrealistic the portrait could be. The more unknown he was, the more realistic the picture had to be. Picasso could do a portrait that had three eyes and two mouths but he couldn't."

Aisquith was impressed. "That's exactly how it is being an architect. He's a very perceptive guy. So, is he a patient anymore?"

"Well no, he ended therapy a couple of years ago and then I found out that he shot himself in the head last August."

"That's terrific. I bet that made you feel good."

"Hey, you win some and lose some in this business."

Aisquith picked his underwear off the edge of the bed and started to get dressed. "You know, I was a fool not to become a painter like I originally wanted. I could've done whatever I wanted on a canvas without someone looking over my shoulder telling me what to do. I probably would never have sold anything and starved to death, but I would've had creative freedom."

Taylor let out another shriek of laughter. "Allan, you're a pistol. Hey, you leaving already?"

Aisquith finished buttoning his shirt and slipped into his topsiders. He walked toward the bedroom door and turned to her. "I have to get up early tomorrow.

Taylor, who had been sitting up in bed with the sheets pulled up to her chin, let them fall way, revealing her pendulous breasts. "So, you'll give me a call sometime?" she whispered with a seductive smile.

"You know I will, *Hillary*," he called over his shoulder.

7

As usual, Aisquith loathed going to a construction site when the crews were still working, but this time he had no choice. The client, Rapid Financial Group, asked him to go out and look at their bank that was under construction. The president of the company, Alvin Edgar, had visited the site and felt there wasn't enough concrete around the night deposit box. Rapid Financial had had problems with thieves attaching chains from trucks to the boxes and dragging them away, so the more concrete, the harder they were to steal.

Aside from hating to answer questions, he couldn't stand the general contractor on this job, Paul Wiggs. If there wasn't enough concrete around the box, it was because Wiggs had misread the drawings or purposely short-changed the bank.

Architects and contractors got along like lions and hyenas. Aisquith sincerely believed that God intended them to be mortal enemies, like the mongoose and the cobra on those nature shows on Public Broadcasting. The architect, with his advanced degrees and aesthetic pretensions, lived in a completely different solar system than the typical semi-literate contractor who had attended vocational school and cared only about making a profit.

It was class warfare, pure and simple. This was most apparent on site visits. The construction crews especially hated the architect coming out to the site in his Pierre Cardin suit. On large jobs, where one had to wear a hard hat, the sight of the immaculately dressed architect slumming with the ultimate working class symbol on top of his expensive haircut was a real irritant. The workers snickered and laughed at him behind his back for no reason other than that he represented the college-educated class they envied and thus hated. Aisquith knew all this. What irony. He, who had switched his interest to architecture in prep school to avoid being called a pansy, once heard a bricklayer call him a queer under his breath. To construction workers he had as much masculinity as a hairdresser.

Early in his career he had made a mistake in the construction drawings on a day-care center, a careless error in detailing a roof overhang. The contractor made an enormous issue of it in front of the client, exclaiming," Well, I don't have no college degree, but I know when a roof overhang don't work." Aisquith never ever told a contractor he was a Harvard graduate, for if that were known and he made a mistake on a job, there would be no limit to the ribbing. To look like an idiot in front of a construction crew with an average tenth-grade education was probably the most humiliating experience one could have as an architect.

Aisquith believed in class discrimination and hated the fact that everyone in America considered themselves middle-class. The educated élite should always boss the rabble around. As a committed Anglophile, he disliked America's egalitarian ideals and often wished that the nation had retained Britain's rigid class system when it won the Revolution. Then a contractor would know his place in the animal kingdom.

As Aisquith drove up to the construction trailer, he looked in the rear-view mirror and saw a dark blue Mercedes-Benz right behind him. Recognizing Wiggs' car, he was reminded of another aspect of contractors that really annoyed the hell out of him. They always drove better cars than architects because they made a lot more money than architects. It undermined his entire notion of class structure. A guy who majored in carpentry in vocational school should not drive a better car than a Harvard graduate.

Aisquith made sure he parked in Wiggs' reserved spot next to the trailer and slowly got out of the car as if he were crippled with arthritis. Wiggs pulled along side and leapt out of his car like a mountain goat.

"Hello, Ass. I see you're making one of your rare guest appearances today. What's the special occasion?"

Wiggs was a new breed of contractor that first appeared in the real estate boom of the mid-1980s. He was trim and well dressed in contrast to the contractor of old with white socks and belly hanging over his belt. He had a summer home on the Eastern Shore and went skiing in Vail twice every winter. He was so successful in the 80s that in the early 1990s he had more work than he could handle and didn't even notice the recession that was raging through the nation.

"Hello, Paul. Alvin asked me to take a look at the night drop."

"And wwwwwwhy did he want you to do that?" Wiggs replied in a mocking tone.

"To see if you put enough concrete around it."

"If there's not enough concrete, then it's because your drawings didn't show the right amount," Wiggs said with a laugh.

"We'll see." Aisquith silently prayed that what Wiggs had just said wouldn't be true.

The two men walked slowly toward the building, about twenty yards away.

"I'm glad you're here though. There's two change orders I'd like to go over with you."

"What?"

"Change orders. You know, when the architect has overlooked something and I have to charge extra for the added work. I'm sure you've heard of them."

"Hey, you had four months to go over the drawings before construction started," Aisquith snapped.

"Don't worry, it's no big deal, only about $6,000."

"You got to be kidding, I'm . . . " Aisquith stopped dead in his tracks and stared wide-eyed at a straight stone wall bisecting the interior of the bank from front to back.

"What the hell's wrong with you?" said Wiggs. He had been walking ahead of Aisquith and turned around when he realized that the architect wasn't right behind him. He walked back to Aisquith. "You look like you've seen a ghost."

"That wall is straight."

"Yep, it's straight. You know, you're a pretty perceptive guy."

"It's supposed to be curved, damn it."

Wiggs gazed at the wall in question. "Oh yea, in the beginning, it was originally a curved wall. Now I remember."

"What do you mean it was curved in the beginning. Why isn't it curved now?"

"That's because we made a change in the field. We straightened it," answered Wiggs in a matter-of-fact tone.

Aisquith was crushed. The curving wall through the flat-roofed brick and stone bank was the unifying element of his design. The curve gave the building energy. The wall had divided the banking area from the space the community would use. Neighborhood groups could hold meetings, rehearse plays, or hear guest speakers. The wall itself was to be a gallery space on the bank side of the building for artwork of local school children and local artists to exhibit their tacky oils of still-lifes and out-of-proportion portraits.

Now the wall just slashed through the bank like the Berlin Wall. Aisquith turned and faced Wiggs.

"A change in the field, eh?"

"Yea, I changed it right before we poured the footing."

"Christ, I don't want to be in your shoes when Alvin hears about this."

"What the hell are you talking about? Alvin gave me the okay to do it straight."

To Aisquith, this was far worse than hearing one's wife had cheated on him or hired a hit man to kill him for the insurance money. It was the worst betrayal in the world.

"Alvin okayed this?" Aisquith literally suppressed a scream..

"Yes, Allan, he did." Wiggs spoke as if talking to a retarded child.

"And no one told me?"

"I guess not, we did it three weeks ago." Wiggs laughed heartily.

"But the curve was the essence of the whole design." Aisquith knew he sounded like a whining three-year-old.

"It looks okay to me. It has essence being straight. And it's still made of stone. I tried to tell him how much he could save doing it in brick. But he stuck with the stone. You should at least be happy about that. Anyway, I didn't see that it made that much difference."

"You sonofabitch, it makes all the difference to me, don't you understand, you goddamn ape?"

"Well, it's a done deal. Why don't you ask Alvin to tear it down and build a curved one?" Wiggs's grin was wicked. "I could prepare a change order for it."

Aisquith knew Wiggs was mocking him, but a hundred times worse was the fact that the client made a change without consulting him. Once a breach like this happened on a construction site, it was carte blanche for the general contractor all the way. The architect was just a bystander now. The client had no further need for the architect, exactly what Wiggs wanted.

For the architect, a critical detail was often the linchpin of the design. For Aisquith the bank was now ruined. Anger welled up within him but he succeeded in putting a lid on the volcano that was about to erupt inside his chest. Wiggs wanted him to go into hysterics but he wouldn't give him the satisfaction.

"You'll never bid on another job of mine or anyone else's," Aisquith said through gritted teeth.

Wiggs laughed. "Take it easy, Ass old boy, it's only a fuckin' wall."

"Never change my design, you bastard, never!"

"Yea? That's not how the owner feels. It saved him a ton of money."

"And you a ton of work."

"That's right." Wiggs smiled and shook his head slowly, "Fuckin' architects, always building monuments to yourselves."

"Keep your hands off my design," said Aisquith, remaining calm. He turned and walked back to his car.

"Hey, come back. I've got $6,000 of change orders for you to sign," Wiggs shouted at the back of Aisquith's

Harris tweed coat. "And don't kick up too much gravel when you pull out. That's a Mercedes next to you."

"Hyena, hyena, hyena," muttered Aisquith under his breath as he drove off. His fingers gripped the wheel of the Volvo so hard, it could have snapped into pieces. Vivid fantasies raced through his mind as he flew down the Jones Falls Expressway. A movie projector might have been beaming a film through his eyes. In front of him, instead of the road, he saw himself denouncing the bank president as a barbarian as he strangled him. The image repeated over and over.

As the ride wore on, the image faded and his anger subsided. He didn't care what they did to his building anymore. They could put an igloo on top and he wouldn't give a damn. The client never understood the subtleties of design. Throughout his career, hundreds of details that gave a building character and elegance had fallen by the wayside. The client just didn't get it. Expecting a contractor to appreciate a beautiful detail was like giving a string of exquisite pearls to an ape.

He had hoped a wealthy, well-educated client would be different, but he realized that a Harvard MBA didn't guarantee good taste. But what did he expect, really? Architects just didn't know how to communicate. They spoke in a code of abstractions that was totally incomprehensible to the average guy. No wonder the public always wanted Georgian houses. That was a language they understood.

Aisquith noticed it was almost ten o'clock on his dashboard clock and realized the events of the morning had made him forget about Carrollton. He was almost relieved to shift to an impending lawsuit instead of dwelling on Wiggs and the bank. He pulled into a space and slowly walked to his office. For the first time in a long while, he looked up to study the mill buildings in the complex. Aisquith's grandfather had worked in a mill like these in South Baltimore, operating a drill press. That's all his grandfather had done, day in and day out. He didn't understand how the old man could get up in the morning for forty-three years and face that drill press every day. He remembered how pleased he had been when he heard his grandson was admitted to Harvard and even more pleased when he became an architect. The old man never understood exactly what an architect did, but it seemed like an élite profession he could boast about to his cronies. Aisquith's grandfather had once taken him to his mill when he was a boy and showed him the machine he used every day. Aisquith noticed the wood plank floor was worn down about an inch right in front of the drill press and realized that his grandfather's feet ground out the dip in the floor over his four decades of servitude to the Nesby Tool and Die Company. Even then, Aisquith was aware that his grandfather was glad his grandson would never have to stand in front of a drill press or any other mind-numbing machine.

After the events of the last thirty-six hours, Aisquith wished he could have a simple, tedious job like operating a machine six thousand times a day. The problem was that they probably now had an industrial robot to do what his grandfather did.

Aisquith strolled through the reception area without saying a word to Grace and went into his office. Since yesterday, he had tried to figure out who would hire a power-broker attorney like Carrollton to sue him. None of his clients past or present traveled in that élite social circle. Let's get this lousy thing over with quickly, he thought. It was time to face the music. He dialed the number and waited for the secretary to put him through. The seconds he was on hold passed like hours. Finally, a deep patrician voice answered.

"Mr. Aisquith, so good of you to call me back," said Carrollton. He must have known full well that no one would leave a call of his unanswered, Aisquith thought.

"No problem at all. I'm sorry I missed you yesterday afternoon," he said in his smoothest voice.

"Sprat Simpson was in the squash invitational yesterday at the club. I had to be there."

The élite always had dumb nicknames like Webby, Ducky, or Bitsy. Aisquith's disdain for these people stemmed from his pathological envy of them because they all belonged to the Maryland Club. He, with his own élite credentials, had never been asked to join Baltimore's unofficial power fraternity.

"Well, I'll get right down to brass tacks, Mr. Aisquith. We're looking for someone to provide architectural services to execute a design for the Addington Museum that's to be built on the Patuxent Cliffs. It's in St. Mary's County and overlooks the Chesapeake Bay."

Carrollton's statement was met by a long silence. The kind of silence that comes after someone calls with tragic news of a family member killed in a plane crash.

"Mr. Aisquith? Are you there?" Carrollton spoke loudly into the phone as if he were calling someone in Antarctica.

Aisquith felt a part of him floating up to the ceiling. He blinked his eyes and returned to earth, realizing he had not said anything for the last fifteen seconds.

"Mr. Aisquith, are you there?"

"Yes, I'm here Mr. Carrollton. Would you kindly repeat what you said?"

"Certainly. We need an architect to design the new Addington Museum. Can you come in this afternoon about three and talk about it?"

Aisquith didn't bother to go through the pretense that he had other engagements. If his mother's funeral were at three, he'd be in Carrollton's office.

"Yes, and where's your office?"

"One Charles Center, on the eighteenth floor?" said Carrollton.

"Yes, I'll be there and thank you very much for ..."

"Great. See you then," Carrollton said jovially as he quickly hung up the phone.

Aisquith kept the receiver to his ear for almost a minute while he stared into space as if hypnotized. He wondered if he would awake from this dream and find himself under his goosedown comforter in his bed in Roland Park. He couldn't believe what had transpired in the last four minutes. He slowly put down the receiver. By what magic had this just occurred?

Aisquith was well aware of the Addington Museum commission. Angus Addington was an oil tycoon who grew up dirt poor in East Baltimore but scraped up enough money to start a kerosene business just before World War I. His business took off in the war economy, so successfully that he was thought of as a profiteer by some. The business grew into a chain of gas stations after the war, just when American started buying cars in great numbers. Addington had become a millionaire by the age of twenty-eight.

The son of a Scottish immigrant bricklayer, Addington discovered that a way to acquire class to go along with his wealth was by collecting art. Through a Jewish business acquaintance, he met the Cone Sisters, Baltimore's premier collectors of modern art in the 1920s. They were friends of Gertrude Stein, in turn a famous friend of Matisse, Picasso, Braque, and many other modern masters in Paris after the war. Through Stein, Etta and Claribel Cone acquired an amazing collection that filled every square inch of wall space in their luxury apartment in Baltimore. Addington, who knew nothing about art, met the spinster sisters at their home and asked for some advice on what to buy. The sisters made a list of artists and their addresses for Addington to contact while in Europe. He was skeptical of the artistic worth of the strange looking paintings on their walls, but the businessman who put him in contact with the Cones insisted they were true connoisseurs of art and that he should trust them. He did and amassed a collection second only to the Cones'. Filled with paintings by the masters of the twentieth century, the Addington collection also included many statues and pottery pieces from Greek and Roman antiquity as well.

Like the Cones, Addington adorned with art every square inch of walls in his mansion in north Baltimore County. At his death nine months ago at the age of ninety-eight, the big question was who was to get the collection. Major museums across the country licked their chops and fell over themselves in hopes of persuading Addington's eighty-nine year old widow to give them the riches. Instead she decided to follow her husband's wishes and build a museum on land he owned on the western shore of the Chesapeake Bay. The view of the bay and the lush green Eastern Shore of Maryland was supposedly breathtaking. The old man was said to have spent many hours sitting in a lawn chair, staring out at the bay, even staying until nightfall so he could gaze up at the great expanse of stars that stretched above him. When he fell asleep his chauffeur gently carried him back to the car and drove him home.

The search for an architect to do the museum had not been publicized, but all of Baltimore's architectural community knew about it. Everyone expected a well known out-of-town architect to get the job. Any really important commission in the state was farmed out to what was considered a more sophisticated and talented architectural firm, usually from New York. So it was accepted as a given that no local firm would be considered.

Puzzled rather than elated, Aisquith couldn't quite accept this thunderbolt of good fortune. Maybe it was another hoax played on him by his friends from the local American Institute of Architects chapter. Though it had happened two years ago, the thought of the prank still made him bristle with embarassment. A woman called the office claiming to be Blaze Starr, the legendary Baltimore stripper. She wanted Aisquith to design a home for her in Carroll County outside of Baltimore. Some of his colleagues remembered his telling them that as a boy he had greatly admired the performer's artistry, not to mention her zaftig breasts. Arriving at the agreed meeting time in a cornfield which the woman claimed she had just purchased as a home site, he waited two hours for her to show up, reasoning that she must be one of those celebrities who are chronically late. When told of the prank a week later by his friends over drinks at the Owl Bar, he went into a rage and had to be physically restrained from smashing his highball glass in Zak Trencher's face.

Carrollton hadn't asked him to bring a portfolio but Aisquith knew he should. How else could the selection committee decide among all the candidates? He knew the competition would be stiff, especially from the out-of-town firms. Flattered by the opportunity to be considered, he would put up an impressive show.

Aisquith strolled through the studio. As usual all faces were glued to the screens. He headed to the office of his ex-marketing director, Ellen Tate, to update the firm's portfolio. Most architectural firms had a marketing director, almost always a woman, who beat the bushes for publicity opportunities. They were supposed to look for new work as well, but hunting for new projects was mainly man's work, usually tapping into the old boys' network for referrals. Aisquith secretly found marketing directors useless except when they gathered material for submissions to awards competitions. Most architects would sell their first-born for an award, especially one from the AIA. Aisquith had received one award from the local chapter his first year back in Baltimore, but to his chagrin his only awards after that were from less prestigious organizations like *Builders World Weekly* and the Concrete Block Institute.

Ellen had taken leave to have a baby but decided not to return due to the tug of maternal feelings, supplemented by her husband's healthy income as a tax lawyer, six times her salary with Aisquith. Contrary to AIA advice, Aisquith had never bothered to hire a replacement. Ellen's office was now piled with files and other junk like an abandoned lot. He looked up on a shelf and pulled down the office portfolio, a calfskin book filled with looseleaf sheets of photos of his projects. Because most of his work came from direct referrals, meaning the job was already his, he rarely had to show his portfolio. Still, he kept it current, adding professionally made photos taken minutes after a building was finished.

He continually edited the portfolio, taking out projects that seemed great twelve years ago but now looked hopelessly out of date. As he turned the acetate sleeves, he wasn't really ashamed of the work but experienced again the gut-wrenching feeling that he was just a mediocre architect incapable of moving to a higher level of quality. He sometimes wished he were a complete hack with a third-rate education who didn't know any better. He had no one to blame but himself for what he saw before him.

He was glad he had escaped from New York. He hadn't seen Marhedi in years. She had been a guest speaker at a Baltimore AIA lecture series two years ago and he made sure he was miles away that night. The few times he returned to New York, Aisquith was scared to death of running into her on the streets. The first thing she would have said, he knew, is that she hadn't seen any of his work in the magazines. What could he have said? Didn't you see the March issue of *Vinyl Siding Digest*?

Getting published in a real architectural magazine was as remote as sprouting wings and flying to the moon. He had long given up submitting work to the top publications, but his ego forced him to pursue builders' magazines at least. He needed published pieces to put on the walls of his reception area; if they were from the National Asphalt Shingle Association then so be it. Just by glancing at the walls prospective clients were reassured that they were using an established architect.

Aisquith inserted a new sheet with a photo of a recently completed marina in Ocean City and walked back to his office. The project wasn't that impressive but there was one detail, a cantilevered stair that looked great, so he had made sure the photographer took shots of it from different angles. Aisquith used this salvage technique with many projects that had gone down the tubes aesthetically. He always tried to preserve one good detail from the client's ax, then photographed it, making it seem that the detail was representative of the quality of the entire building. As he passed through the studio, Kurt stepped right in front of him. Aisquith halted and stood eye to eye with the young intern.

"Allan, is it true you're on the short list for the Addington?" Kurt whispered.

Aisquith was always amazed how quickly information spread around the office. No matter how secretive he was, things always got out as if announced on CNN. The one and only time he had slept with his former receptionist, Lindy, six years ago was known throughout the office two seconds after she reached orgasm. He really believed someone had followed them to the motel and shot Polaroids. There was no use trying to hide this news. In fact, it would be good to confirm the rumor. The mere existence of the idea might lift office morale. Aisquith thought the concept of morale was pure bullshit, something owners of firms deluded themselves into believing. But this time he'd play along. He smiled at Kurt and kept walking. When they reached the doorway of his office, out of earshot of the others, he said, "Yep, I'm going to present this afternoon," with a wide grin. He realized he was getting a real rush breaking the news to the kid. Aisquith had nothing against breaking good news. Telling Carlos he would be a partner had been a single exception.

"That's terrific. I sailed past those Cliffs last summer, it's an incredible site. You can do some great things up there."

Instead of answering, Aisquith just looked at Kurt. The excitement he saw in his eyes suddenly sent him back twenty years when he first worked for Marhedi. He had once been just as enthusiastic as Kurt, full of hope and confidence in the future, living on a salary that qualified him for food stamps. At that second Aisquith remembered dropping a package containing an entry to the Progressive Architecture Award competition in a corner mailbox on Sullivan Street in Manhattan. He had been absolutely certain he would win, just like the suckers that buy a lottery ticket every week. A wave of sadness came over him as he realized how much he envied the lowly intern's zeal. Suddenly he was ashamed of burning the model in front of Kurt. He should have done what he normally did, burn it in the alley behind his house in Roland Park.

"Earth to Allan, earth to Allan," Kurt intoned like an alien being.

The image of his vanished youth disappeared from Aisquith's mind as if a projector had been snapped off.

"Yes . . . we could do something that invokes permanence and presence," he said, feeling the need for Columbia arch-speak. "Do you want to be on the design team?" He knew full well what the reply would be.

"God, yes!" Kurt almost shouted. "I could start the site analysis for you and . . . "

"Whoa, Trigger. Let's first see if we get the project first. Today is only an interview."

"Right, right," Kurt said, obviously afraid that he'd made an ass of himself.

Aisquith patted him on the shoulder. "We just have to be patient, son," he said, sounding like Ben Cartwright advising Little Joe on the Ponderosa. Kurt nodded and walked back to his computer screen.

Aisquith went into his office and set the portfolio down. It was one-thirty and he had time to go home to change into his most expensive suit for the presentation. Aisquith had dressed all in black when he lived in New York. If he had dressed like that in Baltimore, people would have thought him a cat burglar or worse, a fag hairdresser. His daily uniform even down to his underwear was now exclusively Polo by Ralph Lauren. He felt the way an architect dressed told people about the quality of his designs. A sophisticated dresser meant a sophisticated design. An architect wearing a powder-blue leisure suit meant a rotten design.

With the portfolio in hand, Aisquith bounded down the front stairs of the mill into the parking lot. Just before he got to his car, he stopped to feel the cold wind wipe across his face and hair. He closed his eyes, tilted his head toward the overcast sky, and smiled. When he opened his eyes a shower of golden brown leaves from the two oaks by the entry rained down on him. It felt wonderful just to stand still and savor the autumn. Yesterday life had seemed hopeless, but within twenty-four hours he had found a brand new lease on life. He took pride in never kidding himself and knew realistically that he had no chance to win the Addington job. But at this moment he had hope. A man needed hope to go on in life, didn't he?

8

Any law practice with partners over the age of sixty had to have an office lined with dark wood paneling and prints of hunting dogs and sailing ships. Aisquith had plenty of time to examine the wall of Carrollton's reception area. He had arrived fifteen minutes early and now was entering his twentieth minute of waiting past the appointed hour. He knew the office design had been done by Jansen Associates. Because Baltimore was such a small town professionally, every architect knew everyone else's work. They all silently sized up each other but rarely uttered unkind words about a design lest they be judged; everybody, without exception, at one time or another produced something that really stank.

The average person coming into the reception area would glance at the paneling, then pick a magazine to read. But an architect's eyes instinctively went to the corner of the ceiling to see if the molding joined properly. Aisquith constantly caught himself picking out details wherever he went. He knew that Carrollton had probably forced the architect to use all this mahogany paneling, including sticking it on the ceiling. Aisquith had mellowed in one way. As he had aged, he had become ever more tolerant of competitors' work even if it was terrible, assuming the client had ruined what had started out as a good design. In his younger days, right out of Columbia, he ripped buildings apart with savage ferocity and smugness, automatically branding the architects hacks.

"Please follow me, Mr. Aisquith," said the middle-aged receptionist, snapping Aisquith out of his reverie.

They walked down a wide corridor with more mahogany paneling and fox hunting pictures to an eight-foot-wide set of mahogany sliding doors. The receptionist deftly parted them and before Aisquith's eyes appeared a sea of middle-aged men in dark suits, with heads in various stages of baldness, all seated around a conference table as long as an aircraft carrier.

He stood at the doorway in frozen astonishment until from his right side came an extended hand that was connected to Carrollton's lean, well tailored figure. Aisquith instantly recognized him from his pictures in the newspapers.

"Thank you so much for coming," Carrollton boomed in a stentorian voice fit for the stage. Without waiting for Aisquith's reply, he started the introductions. "These fine fellows are the building committee," he exclaimed with a sweep of his arm.

"Meet T. Franklin Middleton III, the co-chairman of the committee. We call him T3." The entire room erupted in booming laughter as if a laugh track had been turned on. Without saying a word, T3 rushed forward with his arm extended and crushed Aisquith's knuckles in a handshake. As he made introductions around the table, Carrollton gently guided the bemused Aisquith into a richly upholstered leather chair at the head of the table.

"Sit here next to C. Z. Kensington II, C2 doesn't bite." The room again burst into laughter. Here was a whole new world of men whose names began with initials and ended in numbers.

Aisquith kept his portfolio on his lap, thinking it amateurish to place it on the highly polished tabletop. There was a pause in the air. He quickly took it as his cue to say something.

"I can't tell you gentlemen how honored I am to be considered as the architect for the Addington," he said, confident in using the word gentlemen, because there was a one in a billion chance there was a woman in the room.

C2 leaned toward him and clapped a meaty hand on his shoulder. "You know Allan, we looked at many architects, not just from Baltimore you know. What's the name of that guy that did the museum in Spain that looks like all these beer cans exploding?"

No one seemed to remember and Aisquith didn't want to remind them right at this moment.

"Yes, we worked up a complete list of criteria for making our decision, Allan," Carrollton said from the opposite head of the table that seemed six miles away. Aisquith had a hard time making out his features.

Aisquith sensed this was the moment to present his work. He slowly brought the portfolio from his lap to the table. "Well, I'd like to show you some…"

"But when all was said and done, you were our choice," said Carrollton, grinning from ear to ear.

The portfolio fell back into Aisquith's lap and onto the plush carpeting. "I beg your pardon?" he stammered.

Carrollton saw the shock in his face. Aisquith never could manage a poker face.

"*You* are our choice to design the Addington, Allan. Congratulations."

Aisquith's brain started swimming. It was if he'd been awakened abruptly in the middle of the night. He desperately tried to gather his thoughts. The words finally spilled out.

"You mean you've made your decision already? But this is the first interview. I thought it would be a long, involved process of selection. You haven't even seen my work yet."

Carrollton threw back his head of wavy salt and pepper hair and bellowed with laughter.

"Oh, we've done our homework. A few of us have been down to that little maritime museum you did in St. Michaels. Very nice job."

C2 chirped in. "I really liked the widow's walk you did so you can look out over the harbor. My wife loved it."

"Well, thank you," Aisquith replied, confused and elated at the same time by the compliment. The museum they referred to was just a renovation of an existing institution, full of ship models, crab pots, and oystering equipment. He had thought it nothing special. There was a substantial addition but he had been forced by the town's historic review commission to design it to blend into the surrounding nineteenth-century architecture.

"I didn't realize the selection process worked this way. But I'm honored and delighted by your decision. I can give you a very special building on the Cliffs. It's a very special site." Aisquith was emerging from his fog.

"We know you won't let us down, Allan," Carrollton said. He rose from his seat and walked down to where Aisquith sat.

"I can start right away," Aisquith blurted. Grateful to get a commission, almost to the point of getting down on their knees to kiss the client's feet, architects often said this to get off on the right foot.

"That's what we like to hear," Carrollton boomed. He turned to the board members, who nodded their heads in unison like the bobble-head dolls one sees in the back windows of cars.

"With the help of a consultant, we've prepared a program to help you get started on the design. It'll give you a handle on the size of the collection and the different galleries and functions we need," said Carrollton. At that moment a portly man who he introduced as G4 got up from his seat and handed Carrollton a bound book as thick as the yellow pages.

"Thanks, G4," Carrollton said. "Unfortunately, Allan, we haven't chosen a director of the museum yet. Normally, you would work with him on the design. But since we don't know when we'll get one on board, you'll have to go it alone. G4 worked with the consultant and will answer any questions you might have. It's very important to move on and not hold you back."

G4, now back at his seat, waved his hand at Aisquith in welcome. He glanced over to place his face, but G4 looked identical to all the other sixty-year-old men around the table.

"We know it'll take some time for you to digest all this, but we're anxious to see your ideas," Carrollton added in a kindly manner.

Like all architects, obsequious servants, eager to please, Aisquith couldn't keep his mouth shut. It was an instinctive response to promise too much. "I could get back to you in a month with some drawings, " he said in a loud and confident voice.

Lawyers would say, "I'll let you know when I can start on this case," but architects routinely made absurd promises to look good. Throughout his career, Aisquith had sacrificed quality by cranking out designs to meet unrealistic deadlines. A job of this magnitude would normally take months even to do a preliminary design.

Carrollton paused. It was clear he knew that Aisquith had made a foolish promise. This pleased him and he intended to take full advantage of it, "That's great. Why don't we set up a date to meet right now while we have everyone here? You said a month from now?"

As if on signal, the twenty or so men around the table pulled out their Palm Pilots from the breast pockets of their suit jackets in perfect unison. It was a like a choreographed number in a musical comedy. Panic shot through Aisquith from his head down to his spastic colon. In the past when he had announced a tentative time when he'd have drawings ready, he had always been able to stall later for a more reasonable deadline. Now it appeared he was on the spot.

"How's does November 18 work for everybody?" Carrollton asked, clearly aware that the members would all cancel whatever appointments they had on that day for his meeting. In unison, twenty voices responded,"Great."

"Allan?"

Aisquith looked in his leatherbound appointment book and saw nothing penciled in for the 18th. As the seconds ticked off no excuse occurred to him. "That'll work," he said solemnly.

"Fine. Now I bet the first thing you'll want to do is visit the site," said Carrollton.

"Yes, that's the very first thing to do."

"G4 will call you with the directions."

"I've heard there's an incredible view of the bay from up there. The duality of the site is quite unique."

"I suppose so. Mr. Addington always loved the Cliffs. That's why he wanted to build the museum up there," Carrolllton replied, puzzled over what the hell he meant by "duality."

Aisquith, who considered himself a master of small talk in business settings, found himself tongue-tied. The stunning news he had received in the last ten minutes had knocked the wind out of him.

G4 walked up next to him, put his hand on his shoulder, and almost shouted in his ear," We'll be looking forward to the 18th, Allan. I'm here to help you. Please call if you need anything."

Aisquith managed a wan smile. He turned to Carrollton to say goodbye. "Thank you again for this great opportunity, Mr. Carrollton." He wondered if Carrollton has a Waspy nickname like the others.

"We know you won't let us down. You'll be sending us a contract as soon as possible?

In all the confusion Aisquith had forgotten that he would be paid for his efforts. The size of his fee for a project of this magnitude suddenly dawned on him. Architects are paid a percentage of the construction cost of the building. Aisquith did the math in his head on a $100 million museum and a surge of new energy raced through him.

"I'll fax you a copy of the contract first thing tomorrow, so we can discuss it over the phone," he replied, with a 400 per cent increase in enthusiasm in his voice. Then a sea of charcoal grey and navy blue suits surrounded him and he couldn't see Carrollton any longer.

"You should have a drink with us at the club," a voice boomed from the crowd.

"You're going to be the envy of every architect in Baltimore." Another faceless voice.

"In the nation!" Still another.

Through the swarm of expensive suits and cologne, Aisquith saw Carrollton walk out of the conference room. In all his dealings with design and building committees, there was always one man that controlled the show and had the final say on what the building would look like. From today's events, Carrollton was that man.

9

With the sun shining on them, the waves of the bay below sparkled like a carpet of diamonds. Aisquith looked up at a cloudless sky of an indescribable blue. He felt he could start running, spread his arms, and fly up into the heavens. Spinning 360 degrees, he inhaled the magnificent view, understanding why old man Addington had spent so much time here. Just standing on top of the Cliffs for one minute was an energizing experience.

All his past defeats were forgotten. The slate was wiped clean. This was his new beginning. Aisquith felt like an actor who had worked in B movies for years whose big break had finally arrived. He had more than paid his dues in the last nineteen years and he of all people deserved some good luck. He believed that talent and skill weren't enough to succeed in this cruel world. You needed some luck to make it in life.

Maybe he had gotten all his failures out of his system in his first forty years and would have an uninterrupted flow of success for the next forty years. In sports an athlete is washed up at thirty-six. Architecture was the exact opposite, the best years could come when one was as old as the hills.

He turned his gaze from the bay and saw Kurt taking pictures of the site. Given the size of his fee, he had the money to arrange aerial photos of the Cliffs as a basis for his initial conceptual sketches, but he told the intern to go ahead and take his own ground shots. He saw the excitement in Kurt's face. He had the same feeling. Getting a new commission was always exhilarating, but this was even more thrilling because of the amazingly beautiful site.

Patuxent Cliffs was a geological aberration. The tidewater shore of the Chesapeake Bay was almost all flat, but for 1,000 yards in this one location the land inexplicably rose up in a sheer rock-faced wall sixty feet in height, towering over the bay. It reminded Aisquith of the storied White Cliffs of Dover along the English Channel. At the bottom of the Cliffs a jumble of treacherous-looking rocks made him think of the coast of Maine. At the top of the Cliffs there was a beautiful meadow of grass and wildflowers that unexpectedly came to a rocky outcropping at the edge of the sixty-foot drop.

Aisquith had decided to bring Carlos, his new "partner," along to bask in the success of the new commission. Kurt continued to beam with admiration and delight, but Carlos seemed less than impressed. He had been standing at the edge about fifty yards away and now walked back toward Aisquith.

"It's incredible isn't it, muchacho?" Aisquith said, no longer caring about political correctness.

"There's something wrong here," Carlos spoke in a schoolmarmish tone that irritated the hell out of Aisquith.

"What could be more perfect?" He was determined not to have Carlos rain on his parade.

"There's something wrong here," Carlos repeated.

Aisquith now regretted bringing him along and got angry.

"What the hell are you talking about?"

"Forget it," Carlos growled back and walked back to the car parked at the other end of the meadow.

Aisquith gazed at the back of Carlos' blue windbreaker and cursed himself for giving in and making him a partner. He had done all right without one for this long. But then, if the museum was successful, and Aisquith had every good reason to believe it would be, a partner would come in handy to handle the new work he'd be getting. He didn't want to wreck a beautiful afternoon thinking more about Carlos, so he put the matter out of his mind and walked over to his intern. Kurt had been like a racehorse champing at the bit since Aisquith returned to the office with the news that he had won the commission.

"So what do you think?"

"It's almost too beautiful a place to build on," Kurt replied with a perceptible sigh in his voice.

Aisquith was empathetic to Kurt's reaction. In normal circumstances, he, too, wouldn't have wanted to build on this site, but, with a multi-million dollar fee at hand and the opportunity to do a high profile project, what could he do? The site was really too beautiful to be ruined by a building but he was too cowardly to tell the board to pick another site. They would think he'd gone insane and simply pick another architect.

He launched into some serious arch-speak. "A site like this is an invitation for a reciprocal relationship between the built environment and the natural environment."

"There definitely has to be a real harmony with nature and a programmatic appropriateness," Kurt countered, starting to get a real rush from this theoretical blather.

"The demands of the program and the site must be balanced. You're absolutely right about that." Aisquith relished the opportunity to speak theoretically. He missed the old days at Columbia when high-octane arch-speak went on into the late hours of the night. On this site on this beautiful day he felt young and intelligent again.

"But does the presence of the site get greater weight in the scheme of the design?" Kurt asked in a deeply grave tone. He sounded as he might if asking for the death toll in an accident. Kurt had been very discouraged since graduating from architecture school. Instead of thriving in the creative atmosphere of the atelier, he found himself a poorly paid Autocad slave chained to a computer monitor. Spending eight hours a day in front of a screen killed his eyes. He never learned how buildings were put together since he only ever drew tiny portions of them. He'd waited almost two years to talk like this.

Aisquith spewed on. "A museum is for the contemplation of art but the view from the Cliffs can be part of the architectural experience too. The form of the building must be sublimated."

"You mean keep it low to the ground?"

Aisquith decided to speak English again. "Yep, even if it means digging it into the earth."

"I like that a lot," Kurt squealed, like a five-year-old getting a Star Wars figure for his birthday.

"Visitors will walk through the galleries and wind up at the end of the building where they can take in the view. A huge window wall could stretch across the rear façade that leads to a sculpture garden overlooking the Cliffs."

"Cool."

Aisquith took out his pocket sketchbook and Pentel and started jotting down his thoughts. He felt the strongest ideas were expressed by simple bold lines. He first drew a line representing the ground level, then drew lines rising dramatically out of the earth, but hugging it like waves.

"The museum will flow out of the ground. There's a lot of room up here so maybe we can make the rear of the building convex so it embraces the view," he said

"That's a great idea." Kurt's enthusiasm clearly was genuine, not ass-kissing.

While he was drawing Aisquith felt a great surge of exhilaration. He looked up into the cloudless sky, felt the early November sun on his face, and closed his eyes. When he opened them, he saw a hawk soaring in a graceful arc high above him. He watched intently as the bird glided along effortlessly. It then swooped down out of sight below the edge of the cliff.

"God, what a beautiful sight," he exclaimed.

Kurt followed Aisquith's gaze at the sky and smiled. "It's a ring-tailed hawk. There're a lot of them along the bay."

The hawk swooped up, then down below the cliff again. "Why does it keep flying down there?" Aisquith was like a fascinated schoolboy.

I bet its nest is among the rocks on the face of the cliff. It probably dives down over the water for a fish and brings it back to the nest."

"You think so?" With sketchbook in hand Aisquith started trotting toward the edge for a closer look.

"Wait, Allan," Kurt shouted when he saw Aisquith going near the edge.

Aisquith laughed. "I won't fall over."

"Stop. If her nest is right below the edge, she'll attack if you get too close."

Aisquith slowed to a halt and stared at the edge. The hawk plunged down past the same spot again, this time emitting a shrill screech. Aisquith slowly backpedaled toward the spot where he had been standing.

"I don't need my hair combed by a pair of bird talons, thank you," he said when he was back next to Kurt.

"Birds are insanely protective of their young." Kurt sounded like a narrator on a nature show. "They've been known to kill animals as big as a wolf."

Aisquith thought that was bullshit but didn't reply. He opened the sketchbook again and resumed drawing but suddenly stopped to look at the hawk again. Maybe this was a sign from God telling him something very profound but, because he was an atheist, he couldn't decipher the message. Careful, he thought . . . let's not go too far. Next he would think the bird was the Holy Ghost on a special mission to see him. He decried the absurd stories religious fundamentalists believed in. Here he was, almost believing in one himself.

The only epiphany Aisquith experienced was a vision of how his building should look. It would blend into the landscape so it wouldn't intrude on this magnificent place. It was a stroke of brilliance, he thought. It would show his humility and respect for nature. And one and all would respect him for that. When Wiggs had wisecracked that all architects care about is building self-monuments Aisquith had winced because he knew the contractor was absolutely right. Given this opportunity, many an architect would let fly with a colossal structure engulfing and smothering the site. He didn't have to. This wouldn't be his last chance to design, far from it; there would be plenty of opportunities to come.

10

Aisquith had forced himself to learn the computer but couldn't bring himself to design on it. He was strictly a hand operator who loved to draw on yellow tracing paper with a soft lead pencil. He sat at his drawing board three days after his revelatory visit to the cliff site. Tracing paper lay before him ready for the first mark of his pencil, like a blank white canvas waiting for a painter's initial brushstroke.

On the hour's ride back to Baltimore from the Cliffs, Aisquith had vowed to change his work habits. In the past, once a client had rejected his initial design, he cranked out a compromise in an assembly-line manner without really taking the time to refine the design. Why bother, he reasoned, when it was something he really wasn't proud of? He never invested any more time than was necessary. The job became simply a way to pay the bills. What he lacked in artistic accomplishment he made up in profit on a project.

Most architects were hopeless as businessmen, spending far too much time on a job than the fee covered. Their artistic sense often obliterated any business savvy. In the first year of his practice, Aisquith spent an incredible number of hours on a design for a medical clinic in Tarrytown, doing countless drawings, renderings, and a complete model, only to have the group of internists dismiss the design with a wave of their leader's hand. Aisquith had blown all the fee on the preliminary design. When he went back to ask for more money he didn't have a contractual leg to stand on. The doctors laughed when he whined that he'd done so much work. "And you'll continue to do more until we're satisfied with the design," was the client's retort. Aisquith lost his shirt on the job but learned an important lesson in business he never forgot.

With the Addington job the fee was enormous, giving Aisquith plenty of time to refine the design until he had it the way he wanted. When he saw the preliminary budget of $85 million in the front of the program Carrollton had given him, he first thought it was a typo. He called Barton, or G.

Hamilton Barton IV as he had discovered was his real name, and Barton verified the number. "It's not much, Mr. Addington was a frugal man," said Barton gravely.

Carrollton had no problem with his six per cent fee of $5.1 million. After the euphoria of the meeting at Carrollton's office where he learned he had the job, Aisquith had despaired in advance about haggling with Carrollton about the fee. He was ready to go down to three per cent but the lawyer agreed to six per cent without discussion. "I see no problem with the contract, Allan. The main thing is to keep going on the project."

"The drawings are being prepared while we speak." The classic architect's lie. Not a line had been drawn at that point.

Although the fee was a king's ransom compared to what he usually got for a job, the money really wasn't the important thing to him this time. This commission had but one purpose: to put Aisquith back where he should have been nineteen years earlier, as a cutting-edge architect who always got published and was universally admired. With this one design, he would put things right in his life. The hundreds of mediocre, compromised designs would be a distant memory.

Instead of going to his drafting table the day he got back from the site, Aisquith let the initial concept he sketched that afternoon sit for a few days. It was a test to see whether the idea still held up or was a dead end. In the meantime, he holed up in his house to study the huge volume--the program--Carrollton had given him. Today, as he opened the sketchbook and looked at the drawings he smiled with delight, then picked up the soft lead pencil to start.

He slid the site plan of the Cliffs under the tracing paper and started laying out the entire complex. He began with the entry from Calverton Road, snaking a curving drive that would lead to the museum entrance. Because the museum was off the beaten path, most visitors would arrive by car or by tour bus so a parking area had to be sited. He hated parking lots but he had to have one. Instead of putting it smack in front of the building as at a shopping mall, he decided to set the parking just inside the entry gate at the bottom of the hill that led to the meadow atop the Cliffs. A shuttle bus would take visitors from the lot up to the museum. A sea of cars would not mar his design. Other museums and historic sites like Monticello had done the same thing.

When explaining an idea to a client, it was always good to cite a precedent. In general, Aisquith found clients accepted an idea if other people had already tested it. He had learned never to justify a design idea by simply telling the client that it was right thing to do for this particular situation. Instead, he defended the idea by cloaking it in a practical rationale. The board, or rather Carrollton, might object to the parking being so far away. Aisquith would not only explain that the most prestigious museums did the same thing but suggest the admission price could be increased to include the shuttle ride and bring in more income. Economic justifications always seemed to work. When he included a huge skylit area in a shopping mall in Annapolis, he didn't say that it gave the mall a sense of place but explained it was a good location for a food court that would be a major attraction for patrons who'd spend more money than ever on greasy food. A spacious lobby in a cinemaplex that evoked the grand spaces of the old movie palaces he admired became a location for arcade games for bored teenagers.

He still wanted the front of the museum to hug the ground, but he knew a museum needed a grand entry--a statement to the public that this is an important place with a collection worth the $15 admission price. So when the shuttle bus brought the patrons to the entrance, they would get off and descend a huge spiral ramp down three levels to get to the entrance. It made for a dramatic entry, almost like the Guggenheim Museum in reverse, and it also worked as a ramp for the handicapped. Aisquith guessed that Carrollton would never go for a sunken entry unless something spectacular was going on around it. Voilà!, the ramp would spiral around a great courtyard which would be an excuse to put its big Henry Moore piece in its center. Once inside, the visitor would start to ascend the galleries, eventually ending up at the rear window wall at ground level, looking out at the spectacular view of the bay.

Aisquith drew one full sketch, then overlaid it with tracing paper as he refined the design of the entire site. The shape of the museum from above looked like a wedge, starting out narrow at the entry and widening toward the bay. He adjusted the curve of the drive to the museum and repositioned the huge parking area many times.

Outside the rear glass wall, Aisquith started working out a sculpture garden with a path that brought the visitor to the very edge of the Cliffs. He would never let them destroy the view by putting a railing along its edge. It wasn't his business if a kid fell off. When designing residences for young couples with small children, he had always been peeved when a mother would object to a raised floor area, fearful that her kid would fall the enormous distance of two feet and break every bone in its body. In Europe, there wasn't this phobia about eliminating every risk in life. They built stairs and porches without railings and didn't go to the expense of putting rubber padding under playground equipment. So what if a kid broke an arm falling off the jungle gym. It was all part of growing up.

Working, Aisquith lost all sense of time. It was the same time warp he experienced drawing and painting in his third-floor studio in Roland Park. He looked up at the window and realized it was pitch dark outside. He went into the corridor and saw that everyone had left even Kurt, so he knew it must be very late. Arching his back, he stretched his arms above his head and smiled. He walked to the receptionist's area and looked at the clock and saw it was 9:30. He had worked eleven hours straight. It felt like fifteen minutes since he had started drawing. He was not the least bit tired and returned to his desk, drawing until three o'clock the next morning, finally falling asleep with his head on his arms on his drafting board.

When he awoke at seven, Aisquith groggily lifted his head off his board. He pulled off a piece of tracing paper that had stuck to his cheek. He always thought that this would be the most appropriate way for an architect to die—to be found dead, slumped over his drawing board.

He peered bleary-eyed at his work. The sketches pleased him. Moving beyond the site plan, he had begun to work out the floor plans that showed the lobby and the all-important museum store, which, according to the program, was to be about the size of a Walmart. The plans for the rest of the levels showed the galleries and the circulation path the visitors would follow to get to the view at the rear of the building.

He took renewed pride in his draftsmanship. All architects said they could draw, but few had a real fine arts background like his. Most could draw a building in perspective, but frequently the result was dead and technical-looking, with no poetry at all about it.

He had started to draw a view of the five-story lobby from the perspective of a patron standing just inside the entry doors. To heighten the sense of drama, he put a sky bridge on the third level with another right above it at an angle, making an enormous "X". Both bridges would be suspended from the roof structure by long steel rods, giving the effect that they were floating in mid-air. Leafing through the inventory of art, Aisquith saw Addington had purchased a Calder mobile in 1961. It was more than large enough to hang in the lobby and could be seen up close from the bridges. A huge saw-toothed skylight could crown the top of the lobby.

The drawing was done in a Pirenesian fashion with dark shadows, bold arches, and streams of light pouring from the skylight onto the lobby floor. Aisquith knew he could never present this rendering to the board. He surely would hear the same comments about the Pirensian style drawings as always. "It kind of looks like a dungeon or it doesn't seem user-friendly." Instead, he'd get Paul Bolton, one of his project architects, to do a proper perspective showing a lobby teeming with culture-starved patrons yearning to get into the galleries--especially the museum store. The sky bridges would be filled with people marveling at the Calder.

Aisquith's feeling of having trapped himself into a month's deadline gradually subsided. He knew he could make a decent presentation that would show the board only the very basic design. He would then have plenty of time to refine it. The most important thing to him was that he had a strong, bold concept to run with. He could pass off to Carlos design responsibility for all the other projects in the office. The Cuban would jump at the chance because of his promotion. Carlos would have free reign to design what he wanted and Aisquith simply didn't care what he did.

Rubbing his eyes and stretching his arms, he yawned mightily. He gathered his coat and walked out of the office. It was only 7:30. He was glad to get away before others came in to start the morning.

11

Aisquith had spent two weeks working night and day to refine his drawings, which he now would hand over to Garrett Keegan, the project architect he had chosen to run the Addington job. Keegan had handled large jobs before at other firms. Aisquith needed an experienced man to guide the eighteen-month project along from the beginning to the end if possible. Given the high turnover in architecture offices, that probably wouldn't be possible, but for now Keegan was as excited as Kurt about working on such a high-profile project. Soon he would start putting the drawings into the computer to create a presentation set for the board.

Kurt, who would be Keegan's right-hand man, Aisquith, and Keegan stood before the corkboard wall in Aisquith's office. The drawings he had done by hand were finished and tacked up on the wall. As he had divined on his first visit to the cliff site, the museum would rise up out of the earth like a wave, cresting about fifty yards from the edge. He had visited the site many times since that first day, often staying until nightfall and sometimes just walking around the meadow for hours. He imagined himself down in the earth five stories, then rising up into the galleries until he came to the edge. Starting at the spot where he had drawn the entry on the site plan, he traced the ascent countless times, imagining what the galleries would look like, how the paintings would be viewed, and how they would be lit.

With the basic concept in place, he had designed the exhibition spaces, creating a way to flood even the subterranean galleries with natural light. Going page by page through the building committee's program, he carefully made sure he included every requirement in the initial design. He kept in mind that the program had been prepared by a consultant in the absence of a director and assumed the committee would rely heavily on the consultant's comments.

When he finished a drawing, Aisquith pinned it up on the board in his office and critiqued it. Pacing up and down in front of the drawing, he decided whether the design looked right. If his gut feeling said to trash it, he ripped it off the board, balled up the tracing paper and threw it into the wastebasket by his drafting table. Some days the basket was filled with yellow tracing paper balls. This pleased Aisquith, because it meant that he was taking his time with the design instead of cranking it out as he usually did. This time he had no fear of starting over.

With the elevations of the outside of the building he exercised even greater care. Though it was only for an initial presentation, he still worked hours on the detailing. He decided to clad the wave-like roof in copper. In a few years' time it would weather to a green patina and blend into the meadow. The base of the museum that rose out of the ground would be done in rough-faced granite to give it a rugged texture. He worked out the detail for the way he wanted the windows to wrap around the corner at the rear of the building, the pattern of the glass on the rear window wall, the proportions of the doors, and the spacing of the seams of the copper roof.

Now, with Kurt and Keegan, he walked along all the drawings like a general inspecting his troops. Giving them a final critique before sending them off to the computer, Aisquith took his red Pentel and made tiny adjustments, stepping back like a painter judging his canvas. He finally turned to Kurt and Keegan and nodded.

"Okay, boys, let's take the herd to Missouri," he said in his best John Wayne imitation.

Garrett, who was in his mid-forties, appreciated the quote because he had seen the movie "Red River" many times. Kurt drew a blank.

As Garrett took down the drawings, Aisquith said, "Make me two sets of prints. I need one for myself and the other to mark up for the model maker."

The presentation meeting now was less than two weeks away. Though the purpose was only to show the basic concept in broad strokes, drawings wouldn't be enough. He needed to present his idea in a bold manner and a model was the best way to do it. Even the dimmest member of the committee must instantaneously grasp his idea. There had to be a model. Not his usual white cardboard model, but one made of plexi-glas. Aisquith marked up a set of prints with dimensions and send them out to a model maker in New York to do a model showing the basic massing of the museum rising out of the meadow.

Aisquith's hand drawings had quickly become computer-generated drawings, showing with crystal clarity all the spaces of the museum. All the rooms were labeled with their names and the alloted square footages. The corridors were shaded a light grey to distinquish them from the galleries. Kurt printed out the drawings as he completed them and Aisquith continued to mark them up with his red Pentel in the unending effort to get the design exactly right.

Kurt didn't mind the changes at all, in fact he embraced them. This delighted Aisquith. If only all interns could be as subservient as Kurt. Most interns hated changes, especially at the last minute, because they were stuck with the tedium of fixing them.

Two days before the presentation, the model arrived. Like an eight-tiered cake at an Italian wedding, it was paraded around the office to cheers and applause. Measuring four feet square, it showed the museum sweeping out of a dark green plateau. The edge of the model was the rocky wall of the Cliffs dropping straight down to the bay. The sight of it took Aisquith's breath away. He couldn't stop staring at it. He was like a father mesmerized by the sight of his first-born through the window of the maternity ward.

A new father gazing at his flesh and blood dreamt of the wonderful things his offspring would accomplish when grown. Aisquith thought instead of the all the great things that would happen to *him*. His mind raced uncontrollably at times. After publication of the design drawings, he would get a call to lecture at an eastern architecture school, where students would listen in rapt attention because of his Ivy League credentials and publication in the right magazines. Then, after the building was completed, there would be an offer to be a guest design instructor for a semester at Harvard or Yale. He could go to New York and never have to cross over to the other side of the street when he saw a Columbia classmate coming toward him.

After everyone had left that night, he walked around the model for an hour, admiring its beauty yet finding a dozen things wrong with it. He thought of ways the museum could be shot for the photo that would go in *The Architectural Review*. There could be an aerial shot showing it rising up from the luxuriant green grass with the rich cerulean blue of the Chesapeake Bay beyond. There'd be the shot of the lobby with the sky bridges and then shots of all the galleries, ending with a view out to the bay from the sculpture garden.

The next day, Aisquith had the final set of drawings plotted out and mounted on foam core boards for the presentation. He took a last look at the model and placed the cover over it. That night, he slept like a log, dreaming he was gliding completely naked above the Chesapeake Cliffs. Taylor Henneman and his long dead mother were standing in the meadow below yelling up at him and waving their arms. He couldn't make out what they were saying so he just laughed at them and soared out over the bay.

12

Aisquith knew the presentation was going quite well. Experience had given him a sixth sense about such things. The client's subtle body language and slight flickers of expressions were all indicators of how well he was doing.

Aisquith had always been amused at the generally held view that architects had to be good in math. He remembered Collington's reaction when he asked him about it. The old man had been right that architects only had to know arithmetic. The one real talent that architects absolutely had to have was the ability to talk in public with ease and confidence. The whole point was to sell the idea, no different than a door-to-door salesman selling a vacuum cleaner. Architectural theoreticians, most of whom were tenured academics who didn't have to earn a living in the real world, hated hearing that. To them, an aesthetically brilliant concept would sell itself. Truth and beauty would win over the client. He'd like to see them try to win over Gavone.

Aisquith felt like Superman with x-ray vision. He saw through the stony visages of all the committee members, including Carrollton, and knew he was scoring point after point with them. His floor plans made everything so clear for them, from the ease with which the visitor ascended the galleries to the grand finale of the sculpture garden overlooking the bay. He explained the galleries and what they would exhibit, where the storage for the collection was located, how the loading docks worked, and how the huge elevators could move paintings from floor to floor. Refraining from arch-speak, he stayed with plain English, backing up every design decision with a rock-solid practical reason. As he talked he took in the almost imperceptible nods of approval from his audience. The sky bridges, the monumental lobby, the shuttle bus from the parking lot-- all seemed to be acceptable.

Aisquith paused to ask for questions. Only Carrollton responded with a few sharp, perceptive queries, not at all like the stupid questions Aisquith usually had to field. It never failed that after seeing plans, a client would ask where her ironing board would go or if his fly fishing equipment would fit into the mudroom closet. The questions or comments were never about the basic concept of the design. Aisquith felt clients missed the forest, not for the trees but for the twigs.

Carrollton's questions were holistic in nature. He seemed genuinely to want to understand the raison d'etre of the whole scheme. Aisquith was energized by such intelligent questions and answered them at length. Carrollton nodded his head vigorously at the answers, the first time anyone around the table had made an open show of approval. The twenty other men also nodded in approval, again as if on cue.

Aisquith was on a roll. He moved on to the cross section, with a cutaway view of the entire site that showed the relationship of the museum to the Cliffs. He noticed many around the table squinting in puzzlement at the drawing but he had anticipated that. In a few minutes, the model would clear up any confusion. He moved quickly, explaining the path of the visitor up through the museum to the sculpture garden.

Driving to the meeting, Aisquith had decided not to show the elevations of the museum but instead to let the model do the talking. When he finished explaining the section, he motioned to Kurt, who was sitting in the rear corner of the conference room with Keegan, to bring the model to the front of the room. Kurt came forward and gently placed the model as if it were an unexploded bomb on the table and disappeared from view. With a dramatic flourish, Aisquith placed his hands on the dark green cover and looked up at the committee with a broad smile.

"Gentlemen, this model I've built will show you better than any drawings can what the outside of the museum will look like and especially how it relates to this beautiful site."

Like a Las Vegas lounge magician, he yanked the cover off the model. He heard a gasp, a "wow," then a whistle. All at once the members rose from their seats and gathered around the end of the table to get a closer look at the model. Aisquith knew he had momentum and continued before anyone could make a comment or ask a question.

"Instead of setting a tall building form on top of the Cliffs, I lowered it and merged it with the terrain. I wanted to create a dialogue between the museum and this incredibly beautiful site you've given me to work with." He couldn't refrain from throwing in some arch-speak at the end. Then, with sweeping gestures of his arms, he explained once again how the visitors entered and made their way through the building.

"The galleries are arranged on both sides of a circulation spine which acts as the major organizing element of the whole scheme. The end of the spine culminates in this fan-shaped section that brings the visitor into contact with the vista of the bay. The overall design concept strongly relates to the edge of the Cliffs."

He paused to gauge their reaction. There was a buzzing throughout the room as well-tailored arms reached out to touch the model. It fascinated Aisquith that a client's first impulse was to touch a model, as if it were real. He knew the members were intrigued by the design. If they hadn't been, he would have been hit with a wall of silence. It was time to wrap it up. Many an architect blathered on after his point was made.

"So gentlemen, if you have any questions, I'll be glad to fend them off now," he said, to great laughter. Carrollton came up to him on with his hand extended.

"This is quite impressive for a preliminary presentation. Don't you all agree?" He seemed to be asking the mahogany ceiling. There came a roar of agreement. Heads nodded vigorously all around the table.

"Yes, this was a helluva presentation," Carrollton added in a loud voice. Aisquith was surprised he'd use a word like hell in a sentence.

"This is a lot to digest so the committee will meet to discuss the design, but this is all quite well done."

"Please take your time to go over it all." This was tactical dissembling. He wanted the okay to proceed right then and there. To Aisquith there was nothing to discuss.

The committee members gathered around him to shake his hand and congratulate him as if he'd homered in the seventh game of the World Series. Then they started peppering him with questions.

"What's the roof made of again?"

"Shouldn't there be a small parking lot next to the museum for VIP's so they don't have to take a bus?"

"Will the restaurant serve fast food or what?"

"Can't someone walk off the edge of the Cliffs?"

As Aisquith began to answer their questions, he realized Carrollton was right next to him.

"Allan, can I talk to you in the hall in about ten minutes?" he whispered. Aisquith just nodded, unable to say anything because all he could think of at that moment was the impressive scent of Carrollton's cologne. The committee members continued circling around him, slapping their hands on his shoulders, and telling him incidents from their life stories.

"You know, I always wanted to be an architect. I took some courses at Princeton but my dad forced me join his insurance company," Barton said, shaking his head sadly.

"I always wanted to go into architecture, but I just didn't have the math skills," bleated another voice from the crowd.

"When I was at Amherst, I was really thinking of going to Yale to be an architect but a friend of mine told me you don't make much money at all. That can't be true. I shouldn't have listened to him," this from another regret-filled voice.

With the patience of a saint, Aisquith graciously listened to every boring story down to the last man, then told Kurt and Garrett to wait for him out in the lobby. He gathered his belongings and went into the hall to look for

Carrollton. He knew he wouldn't be waiting in the hall after all this time, so Aisquith went down the hall to his office where he found him talking on the phone. Carrollton looked up when Aisquith tapped on the open door of his office, which was the size of the entire first floor of his house in Roland Park. Carrollton wound up his call and with a wave of his hand motioned Aisquith to come in.

"Ah, Allan, I was wondering if I could meet you out at the Cliffs tomorrow afternoon, say about two?" he asked jovially.

Aisquith had a prior appointment but sensed this was important despite Carrollton's tone.

"Yes, I can make it if that's a good time for the committee?"

"It'll be just you and me tomorrow," replied Carrollton. He saw the confusion in Aisquith's face when he said this.

"I've some questions about the design, so I thought it'd be best to discuss them right at the site. Makes it easier for a layman like myself to visualize what's going on. And anyway too many cooks spoil the soup, eh?" He saw that Aisquith was still puzzled so he got up from his chair and walked over to him.

"I have a little trouble understanding the plans and I don't want the rest of the fellas to know, if you want to know the truth," he said in a semi-whisper. "You understand, don't you?"

Aisquith nodded with great empathy.

"The design is very complex. I bet most of the committee really didn't get it the first time either. I respect your honesty." Aisquith knew he sounded sanctimonious.

"Thank you, Allan," said a seemingly humbled Carrollton. "I'll see you tomorrow."

Carrollton turned and strolled back to his massive mahogany desk as a signal for Aisquith to leave. Aisquith was relieved. He had explained plans to hundreds of clients and knew that most of them didn't understand what the hell was going on. They pretended to know, especially the men who didn't want to look dumb in front of their colleagues, or, worse, in front of their wives. When the building was actually built, they were shocked to see what they had approved. The length of a hallway, a slope of a roof, or the size of a window brought the same old refrain, "Boy, I didn't know it would look like that." They could never remonstrate because he could show them their approval by initials on a set of drawings. Few ever admitted not understanding in the first place. No one wants to look stupid.

As Aisquith walked down the carpeted hall to the lobby, he realized tomorrow's meeting would be a one-on-one opportunity to get the go-ahead to move on with the design and refine the drawings. Carrollton obviously was the only vote on the committee that mattered and he would make the most of the meeting with him. He was jubilant as he joined Kurt and Garrett, throwing his arms around their shoulders. They were startled by the show of affection and hesitated over his offer of dinner, but Aisquith persisted and off they went.

13

Aisquith stood alone on the Cliffs looking out at the bay. The leaves on the trees over on the Eastern Shore had dropped, revealing a stark gray landscape as far as the eyes could see. He closed his eyes for a full minute, feeling both the warmth of the November sun and the cold breeze on his face.

He arrived a half-hour early, not to be punctual but to enjoy some time to himself. Walking in a wide circle a quarter-mile in length around the spot the museum would go, he imagined his plexi-glas model in life size on the site. Gazing up at the clouds floating by, he didn't notice Carrollton coming toward him until he was about twenty yards away.

Carrollton raised a hand in a silent greeting. He was dressed in a brown tweed jacket and a navy blue crewneck sweater. Aisquith was surprised by his informality.

"Hello," Aisquith said, with a wave of his hand. "What a magnificent day."

Carrollton smiled broadly and nodded.

"Mr. Addington loved this place. He had thought of building his retirement home here but his wife persuaded him to move to England."

"Wouldn't have been a bad place to retire, though."

"A week before he died, we talked about this site. You know, Allan, it was his greatest wish to put his collection here. Even in the terrible pain he suffered in his last days, he wanted to talk about his museum."

"He was an interesting man, I hear." Best to be polite, he thought.

"No, not really. He was a businessman down to his toes." Carrollton seemed eager to get down to business. "I want to thank you for coming out here on such short notice."

"No problem at all," said Aisquith, eager to begin his sales pitch. He had brought a roll of drawings in a black leather tube and was ready to pull them out.

"First off, Allan, I want to say how impressed we all were with the way you designed all the exhibition spaces. You understood all our intentions when it came to showing the collection. It's a huge collection and you've made it very accessible to the visitor."

"It was quite a challenge and I . . ."

Carrollton cut him off in a most unpatrician manner. "I was Angus Addington's personal attorney and advisor. So this building committee is really just a committee of one-- me. He entrusted me with the task of getting his vision built so everyone could enjoy his collection."

"Yes, I know and . . ."

Carrollton, visibly annoyed by the interruption, continued. "So you must realize that Angus had a particular vision of how his collection should be housed."

"He must have, to pick a spot like this for his museum."

"Yes, right. But I'm talking about the building itself or to be more specific, the look of the building."

An alarm sounded in Aisquith's head. He sensed trouble was afoot.

"The look? But this is the way the building should look in a place like this," he blurted out, forgetting his rule about holding his tongue. "It's a harmonious relationship between building and nature. A perfectly balanced duality," he protested. Suddenly the Cliffs, the bay, and the sky all seemed to be spinning around, making him dizzy.

"Angus had an image of a temple to the arts. A very formal home for his collection that would dominate the top of the Patuxent Cliffs. A structure you could see from miles away on the bay," Carrollton said.

Aisquith remembered survivors of an Oklahoma tornado describing the event on CNN. An incredible roar had lasted for a fraction of a second and suddenly everything in their trailer park was gone. His design had just vanished in the same manner.

Carrollton paused, waiting for a rebuttal. Aisquith stared at the lush green meadow at his feet and swallowed hard. To his surprise, words came out in a coherent stream.

"No one ever mentioned such a "look" to my recollection," he said quietly. "And if they had, I would've told them it was all wrong."

"I wanted you to come up with a design with no preconceived ideas. I thought your design would be more traditional looking, which would have been more in keeping with what Angus wanted. Frankly, I was surprised at what you came up with, given some of your recent work."

"What do the hell do you mean by that?"

Carrollton seemed amused by the response. "Some of your latest work has been more in a traditional vein, wouldn't you say? You've a reputation for being very accommodating when it comes to the client's aesthetic wishes." This was said through an icy smile.

"I had to do that, goddammit, so I could . . ." Aisquith stopped himself, ashamed at what he was about to blurt out.

Carrollton smiled again. He had trapped his prey and was now ready to move in for the kill.

"Let me finish your sentence, Allan. So you could get your fee, right? It was either making a comfortable living or standing up for your high-minded design principles. But you can't pay for that vacation to Bali with bullshit design theory, can you?"

Aisquith was speechless. The day was cool, in the low fifties, but the back of his shirt was soaked with sweat. Like a cat playing with a mouse before killing it, Carrollton continued mercilessly.

"Come on Allan. Addington left millions for the museum. We could have gotten a really great architect to design it. But I knew they'd all be troublesome. With minds of their own and only concerned about their creative reputations. They wouldn't have done what we wanted. They would have tried to force some abstract design down our throats."

"Why me?" Aisquith squeaked.

"Don't get me wrong, Allan. You're a talented guy but you're flexible. I know when push comes to shove, you'll see it our way. We're out here all alone to come to an understanding. So let's cut all this bullshit about rational harmony and spatial rhythm, okay?"

Aisquith felt beaten to a pulp. All he could muster was "I see."

"I thought you'd see it my way." Carrollton grinned from ear to ear. He turned away from Aisquith and walked slowly toward the edge of the Cliffs. Suddenly, a bird shot up from the edge into the sky and soared above the meadow.

"What a beautiful sight," Carrollton exclaimed. Aisquith, angry and defeated, was surprised by Carrollton's sensitivity. He would have thought Carrollton was the hunting type whose first instinct was to blast the thing out of the sky.

He looked up and watched the bird glide over them in lazy circles, never flapping its wings. He then realized it was the same hawk he'd seen with Kurt weeks ago. Carrollton, standing 30 feet away, turned and faced him.

"Addington loved classical architecture. Like the Parthenon in Athens. To him that's what a museum should look like. He'd been to the British Museum, the National Gallery in Washington, and so on, so he literally wanted a temple with huge columns in the front."

"Columns?"

"Right. I talked to Evan Dunwoodie. He said you're doing something like that for his library."

Carollton saw the shock in Aisquith's face and laughed.

"Come on, Allan, it's like that Sinatra song, "We'll do it myyyyy waaaaaaay" He was obviously delighted at his witticism. "And don't you forget the six per cent on $85 million."

Laughing, Carrollton looked up at the hawk and followed it as it plunged past the edge, then soared above them again. He spun around and walked toward the cliff edge.

"Why does it keep doing that?" he shouted at Aisquith. "What's down there?"

"I wouldn't go any closer," he yelled. Carrollton ignored him.

Aisquith looked up at the hawk again and saw that it was swooping lower and lower in wide circles. When he looked down at the ground again, to his horror he saw Carrollton on his hands and knees craning his neck over the edge. Then Aisquith heard an earsplitting screech. Like a jet fighter, the hawk started a dive straight toward the edge.

Aisquith screamed at Carrollton but was drowned out by the ear-splitting screech. He started running the 90 feet between him and Carrollton.

Peering carefully over the edge so as not to fall over or dirty his gabardine trousers, Carrollton saw in the crevice of a rock outcropping eight feet below him a rustling of brownish red feathers and a high-pitched peeping sound. Placing his hands on some rocks at the edge, he slowly leaned over and smiled when he saw a nest of fledglings about eight feet below him squirming around with their tiny beaks bobbing up and down.

Aisquith had barely gone ten yards when he saw a brownish blur descend upon the kneeling figure. The brown tweed coat suddenly disappeared over the grassy edge. Aisquith froze in his tracks and blinked his eyes, expecting to see the tweed coat reappear, but all he saw was the edge of the meadow against the choppy gray-blue water of the Chesapeake. He walked slowly to the spot where Carrollton had been, watching above him for the hawk, which now was nowhere to be seen. Just before he got to the edge, he got down on all fours and crawled like an infant for about six feet, then lay down flat on his stomach and stretched his neck over the edge.

He thought he'd find Carrollton crouching on a rock just below him. When he saw Aisquith peek over the edge, he'd jump up laughing, congratulating himself on the joke he'd played on him. But Carrollton was not there. He scanned the rocks directly below him and saw nothing. Then his eye caught sight of something far below him. Aisquith stretched further over the precipice and his eyes widened in shock. On the narrow rock-strewn beach at the base of the Cliffs was Carrollton. He was lying on his back with his legs bent at ninety degree angles and both arms extended above his head. He looked like a cheerleader leading a chant at a football game.

Aisquith stared in disbelief at the lifeless form below. He shimmied away from the edge and slowly rose to his feet. Dumbfounded, he stared at the grass at his feet. His museum had been snatched away from him by a bird! Literally, in one fell swoop God had swept away his life. Though not a believer, he shook his fist at the sky and cursed Him.

He stopped himself and remembered that it was a human being, not a commission, at the base of the Cliffs. He was a shit for automatically thinking about himself. Probably a by-product of being an only child, selfish to the core, as those with brothers and sisters often claimed.

Aisquith felt the sweat pouring off his body. Wiping his sleeve across his forehead, he started running back to his car parked down by the entrance on Calverton Road. He had to get to the cell phone he'd left in his Volvo. Maybe Carrollton wasn't dead but just unconscious. A 911 call could bring a helicopter in minutes..

His idea of exercise was parking his car far away from a mall entrance so he could get some walking in. Now he raced across the meadow, his heart pounding like a bass drum in his chest. As he ran, he thought how ironic it would be if the police found Carrollton's twisted body down below and his own amid the wildflowers, dead of a heart attack. The car was only 300 yards away but it seemed like he was crossing the state of Arizona to get there. He kept on going despite the pain in his chest. Each time he thought of Carrollton's lifeless body, he thought of his museum. He couldn't help it.

14

Not exactly the guest of honor, Aisquith stayed far to the rear of the crowd of mourners gathered for Carrollton's burial service at Greenmount Cemetery. As the Episcopal priest droned on, Aisquith looked around him. The cemetery, one of Baltimore's oldest, once had been far out in the countryside but now was surrounded by a black ghetto. Though the mourners were standing in the middle of a ten-square-block of land, they could still hear the thumping of rap music from a boombox somewhere in the adjoining streets. At first it seemed odd to Aisquith that Carrollton, with his Yale pedigree and tasseled loafers would be buried here, but he was from one of Maryland's oldest colonial families and every one of his ancestors rested in Greenmount. Carrollton, with his patrician sense of tradition, probably made sure in his will that he would reside here as well. Not just six feet under, naturally, but in a mausoleum the size of a two-car garage.

When the priest mercifully ended the service, a silence followed, interspersed with sobbing. As if by an unseen signal the crowd broke ranks and headed back to cars and limousines parked by the gate. Aisquith recognized none of mourners except some museum committee members, the governor of Maryland, the mayor of Baltimore, and two United States Senators, but he was sure everyone there knew who he was.

Most avoided looking at him as they might with a person with a hideous disfigurement like the Elephant Man. Some stole quick glances at him. A few threw decorum to the winds and gave him the most disgusted looks they could muster. For a second he thought one blue-haired old woman was going to spit right in his face.

The odd circumstances of the accident were at first disbelieved and a pall of suspicion was immediately cast over Aisquith. When the state police got to the scene, the hawk was still soaring above the meadow. One trooper pulled his revolver and took aim at the bird, but his partner advised him that killing an endangered species could jeopardize his pension. The gun was immediately holstered. Aisquith's innocence was proved when the state medical examiner called in an ornithologist from the Maryland Wildlife and Fisheries Department to verify that the cuts on Carrollton's scalp were indeed made by the talons of the hawk.

Aisquith kept his head down and started a dignified but hasty dash to his Volvo, which looked totally out of place among the expensive cars waiting at the gate.

"Mr. Aisquith," called a voice from behind. He froze in his tracks. Maybe it was a Carrollton relative who wanted to slap him in the face. He didn't have the nerve to start running for the car, so he slowly turned around and came face to face with Barton.

"Mr. Aisquith, we met at the committee meeting," Barton said in an anxious voice, hoping that Aisquith would remember him out of a roomful of almost identical middle-aged men.

"Of, course I do. I'm glad to see you again," Aisquith replied in the most courteous tone he could manage. He desperately wanted to get to his car.

Barton seemed relieved to be recognized. A smile came over his broad face for a fraction of a second then turned into a frown.

"That must have been a terrible thing to witness, Mr. Aisquith."

" I still can't believe it, Mr.Barton."

Barton gently put his hand on Aisquith's shoulder, then pulled it away, afraid he was being too forward. He cleared his throat nervously.

"Well, this may not be the most appropriate time to tell you this, Mr. Aisquith, but I've been elected by the committee to take Mr. Carrollton's place."

Aisquith halted his retreat.

"You mean you're going on without him?"

"Oh, yes, Mrs. Addington contacted us from her estate in England. She said to keep going."

"I'm really surprised. I thought this would kill the whole project."

"No, you're to continue the design. Mrs. Addington was adamant about that."

Aisquith smiled for the first time in a week.

"After your presentation last week, Mr. Carrollton told me he was meeting you at the site to discuss the design. I guess that's why you were both at the Cliffs the next day."

"Yes, we discussed some . . . revisions, I guess you could say." Aisquith spoke in a dejected tone. Details of the conversation before the accident suddenly came flooding back.

"Were they resolved?"

"Was what resolved?"

"The revisions to the design. Did you get to talk about them before he . . . ah . . .he . . ."

Aisquith smiled and benevolently finished Barton's sentence.

"Fell off the edge? No, we . . ." Aisquith stopped in mid-sentence and stared straight ahead at the rows and rows of tombstones and monuments stretched out in the cemetery. Suddenly his own obituary popped into his head. Dreaming of greatness when a student at Columbia, he had imagined an obit in the *New York Times* of at least 1,000 words, chronicling his architectural achievements and his place in the architectural pantheon. If he died right at this very moment, his life only rated a blurb in the *Baltimore Sun* death notices alongside one about a Baltimore Gas and Electric repairman. He'd die a nobody.

With that realization, all sense of right and wrong was sucked out of him. It was as if a large syringe was plunged into his soul and every molecule of decency extracted. He simply didn't care anymore. In that instant, he decided never to let anything stand in his way again.

"No, Mr. Carrollton only had a few minor revisions to the design. He was extremely pleased with the design. He said there was no time to lose and instructed me to move to the next stage."

"That's wonderful to hear. He did seem to like your design at the meeting," said an elated Barton. "John was in a great hurry to get the museum built, so please proceed. Call me when you're ready to present and I'll set up a meeting."

"Mr. Barton, I certainly will." He vigorously shook Barton's hand. When he reached his car he bounded into the front seat in a giant leap.

The fifteen-minute trip back to the office seemed to take only seconds. Aisquith pumped adrenaline so fast that time had no meaning. He had experienced the same feeling of timelessness when he stole an expensive pair of sunglasses from the Chaucersburg Pharmacy back in prep school. His exhilaration at not being caught had been incredible. But a feeling of guilt had quickly overpowered him and he lost his nerve for stealing again. Now, there was no guilt, just pure, unadulterated exhilaration as he drove.

He burst into the studio, placed two fingers in his mouth, and let out a shrill whistle. Despite their Walkman earphones, everyone in the room jumped up. The whole staff gaped at him from cubicles. He raised his arms above his head as if he were signaling a touchdown. Had he gone mad? His employees' opinion of Aisquith ranged from "He's a jerk," to "He's okay, I suppose." No one had ever thought of him as a funny and animated guy.

"Ladies and gentlemen, we've been given the go-ahead to finish the design. Which, I would like to inform you, they love," he said, sounding like a game show host.

This brought loud applause and cheers, not because the staff necessarily shared the boss's enthusiasm. Everyone knew a big job like this in the office meant a Christmas bonus this year. Kurt was characteristically boisterous, jumping up and down like a three-year-old. Carlos stood off to the side, leaning against the wall with his arms folded. His plate was full with all the projects Aisquith had passed on to him, so none of this really concerned him. He was both amused and disgusted by Aisquith's corny cheerleading. He rolled his eyes and walked away to his enclosed office, newly provided as a partner's prequisite.

"We'll be going all out for the next six months of the design development. We've been given the opportunity to do a very important building and I know we'll all do our best," Aisquith bellowed. There was an awkward silence. Suddenly Aisquith felt embarassed by his feeble pep talk. Basically self-centered artists, architects are rarely known as motivational speakers. The staff just stood, looking and waiting for more. Grigor half expected Aisquith to tell them to put down their work and all go out for drinks. They always did that in Russia when they got a design assignment for a new gulag. Architects of the old Soviet Union got completely tanked when presented with such good news. But Aisquith just put his hands in his pockets and looked down at his feet.

"Well, that's all. Thank you," he mumbled and quickly retreated to his office. The staff sat back down at their workstations. All except Grigor were relieved Aisquith hadn't told them to knock off for the day so they all could go out for a drink. Most felt awkward around him at rare social gatherings like the Christmas party. They couldn't wait to get out of the restaurant but of course had to wait until the Secret Santa gifts were exchanged. There probably wouldn't be a bonus this year after all, some thought, as they went back to staring into their monitors.

15

Over time in Baltimore, Aisquith had adopted the practice of securing approval of a preliminary design, skipping the refinement phase altogether, then cranking out the construction drawings as fast as possible. The designs had always been compromised so why spend time refining a weak idea? But now, with a generous fee and his newly found creative freedom, he could take his time to make the Addington museum design better.

He resumed revising his drawings meticulously and began working out the myriad details of the enormous building. He continued to pin up the drawings and pace up and down; continually making changes with a red pen, then shouting for Kurt to make them on the computer. He made cardboard study models of every part of the building, putting them away for a few days then coming back to them to see whether the ideas held up. The cycle of revisions went on and on, but he didn't care. For the first time in years, he felt like an architect. He would keep at it until he got it just the way he wanted.

A parade of consultants now worked on the project. Structural engineers to figure out the way to support the curving roof and sky bridges. Mechanical engineers to provide the heating and cooling for the Addington collection. Electrical engineers to help him design the lighting. Aisquith thought of himself as the quaterback, calling all the shots and guiding the team to victory.

He wanted to design the museum down to the tiniest detail, including the hooks in the coatroom and the paper towel dispensers in the restrooms. Nothing escaped his attention. He even put in a great deal of time detailing the benches in front of the lockers where the guards would change into their uniforms.

He lived and breathed architecture, and for the first time in years was truly happy. He had vowed to abstain from sex during the design process but the image of Taylor's breasts made him reach for the phone one night and two weeks of celibacy came to an abrupt end.

Whenever the image of Carrollton's lifeless body came to mind, he simply dismissed it by telling himself that it was meant to be in the grand scheme of things. He practiced no religion and had no philosophy about man's place in the universe. He rationalized right off the top of his head. Maybe the hawk *was* a bolt of lightning sent from above to destroy an evil being. No matter. He was actually quite proud that he had suffered neither compassion nor remorse.

The media took note of Aisquith and the museum, especially after the bizarre circumstances of Carrollton's demise. Besides the local newspapers and television stations, the national wire services picked up the story. Eventually Aisquith got the only media exposure that he believed really mattered when the *New York Times* ran a story on him and included a picture of the model.

When he felt the timing was right, he got in touch with some contacts he still had at the architectural magazines. All of them responded to his calls with variants of, "Why, I haven't heard from you in years?" By now most knew of the Addington commission and jockeyed to get the rights to publish the photos of the completed project. Now everyone was his best friend; some were even willing to make the three-hour trip from New York to Baltimore, a place they'd normally never consider setting foot in.

The most influential of all the editors and theoreticians, Colin Pigott-Smith, showed how intent he was to get his hands on Aisquith's work by actually taking Amtrak to Baltimore. To him, it was as remote as Nome, Alaska. Aisquith was quite nervous as he saw the Englishman step onto the platform at Penn Station. He feared he was rusty when it came to arch-speak. Except for the idealistic Kurt, he never found anyone in Baltimore erudite enough to enter into a discussion with, so he would be at a distinct disadvantage if he had to meet with New York and foreign publishers. He boned up on his arch-speak by buying the latest magazines and the densest theoretical tomes. "Materiality" seemed to be a buzz-word these days.

Aisquith purchased a new black ensemble for the occasion of Pigott-Smith's visit. He already had the right black shoes to go with it. While dressing that morning, he realized how easy it used to be to decide on what to wear each day. Anything, so long as it was black. Even on the hottest days in New York, he had worn a heavy black polo shirt.

He didn't have to stand on the platform with a crude handwritten sign with "Pigott-Smith" on it like some airport limo driver. He immediately recognized the editor, whose all-black outfit would have been a giveaway in any case. Though they had never met, Pigott-Smith instinctively walked toward Aisquith through the crowd. Aisquith was the only one wearing black in the station. Like two birds of the same species, they instinctively recognized each other.

"Allan, how good to see you, old man. What a trans-celebratory experience I anticipated in coming down here," the sixty-year-old Englishman bellowed.

Aisquith was duly impressed. Even greeting someone, the guy sounded theoretical. He reminded Pigott-Smith right off the bat that he'd worked for one of the world's most famous architects. "Colin, such a pleasure to meet you at last. Ranah constantly spoke about you."

"I saw her just a few days ago at the Theoretical Jamboree in Venice. She's heartbroken, she hasn't heard from you in so long."

"Well, sometimes friends drift apart."

They walked toward the exit to the street. There was a chic restaurant just three blocks ways. As they walked Pigott-Smith bleated. "The Jamboree was incredible. I wish you could've been there. The theme was solving the problems of the Third World with a holistic modern architectural vocabulary. How can we avoid planetary disaster through innovative technology? Not a mindless pursuit of technology for its own sake, but for a social end."

Aisquith couldn't just nod and say, "Mmm, yes I see." He had to plunge right in and test his arch-speak skills to see whether they were up to snuff. "We desperately need an architecture that celebrates the cyberworld's new measure of speed in a rapidly changing social and economic mileu, " he replied in a calm, relaxed tone as if he were saying,"Yes, it may rain today."

Pigott-Smith stopped in his tracks and clapped a hand on Aisquith's shoulder. Aisquith was suddenly frightened. Was what he just said a load of bullshit? Did he sound to Pigott-Smith like a hick trying to talk the talk?

"Exactly, my boy. Exactly. We have this platonic notion of a very static planet, when it isn't that way at all." Pigott-Smith spoke so loudly that a drunk sleeping outside the station door suddenly awoke. They resumed walking, passing an abandoned group of rowhouses.

"I'm starting to take in the zeitgeist of this city," said Pigott-Smith as he examined the façades of the buildings. "I find it problematic that so much of the work down here seems so retrograde when cities today are totally mobile because of the automobile. I'm so glad your work is setting a standard here."

They arrived at the restaurant and were seated at a booth in the rear.

Because Pigott-Smith was a natural-born motor mouth, Aisquith only had to interject some arch-speak here and there during their lunch. By the time coffee arrived with Pigott-Smith's oreo cookie ice cream pie, they were ready to get down to business.

"Allan, you know there's only one place to show your museum when it's done. *Architectural Review*. You're a talent of incredible sensitivity. Your work is expressive, evocative, and fluent. I think . . ."

Aisquith knew he was in for a tidal wave of flattery. Pigott-Smith was probably under instructions by his publisher to blow him in the men's room if necessary to get the exculsive rights to publish the museum. He decided to give the poor guy a break.

"Colin, I'd be honored to be in your magazine. You get exclusive rights."

With a mouthful of pie, Pigott-Smith sputtered out a sincere thank-you, spraying out small pieces of oreos across the table. Then he reached across and gave Aisquith a vigorous handshake.

With his mission acomplished, Pigott-Smith jumped on the very next train to New York. Aisquith knew he didn't want to spend a second more than he had to in Baltimore which to him was like visiting a Third World city and escaping without catching cholera.

As he watched Pigott-Smith board his train to New York, Aisquith knew again that besides actually getting his design built, the most important thing in his life was the approval of the architectural élite who happened to be in the theoretical vanguard of the moment. No other opinion mattered. Ten million people could say the museum was brilliant but Aisquith couldn't care less. The architectural arbiters had to give their blessing. And now he had that sewn up.

16

Aisquith watched the very last sheet come through the plotter and into his hands. As if it were a rare parchment, he gently put it on top of the 142 sheets that already made up the museum set. Kurt stood next to him, grinning.

"Ready to go to bid, Allan."

"Yep, it's ready," Aisquith replied, with a broad grin of his own.

"The bidders' list is finished too. I called Barton last Thursday to see if he wanted to add anyone to the list but he hasn't called back. That's weird, he always returns calls," said Kurt.

"He probably doesn't know of anyone. The committee doesn't have much experience in construction. They're all stockbrokers and CEO's. They've seen blue collar workers on TV but have never actually spoke to one in real life, I suppose."

Aisquith had designed the museum exactly as he wanted, but he knew that this was only half the battle. Just a drawing on a piece of paper and in models, it wasn't real until actually built. And he didn't construct the building. He had to rely on others for that. So he made sure that the contractors bidding on the job were of the right caliber to handle such a complex design. When word got around that the construction documents were near completion, his office was flooded with inquiries from construction concerns all over the country seeking to bid on the project. Many had experience with large buildings, but Aisquith carefully screened the potential bidders to develop a short list of those he thought also had the sensitivity and style to build his museum. It was as exacting as a yuppie couple interviewing 200 applicants to choose a nanny. He had to make sure his nanny wouldn't abuse his loved one when he wasn't around. He was intent on controlling the entire process all the way to the final nuts and bolts. He had seen too many good designs destroyed in construction. In many cases, after a design is completed, the architect is cast aside by the owner and contractor like schoolyard bullies stealing a kid's new basketball and going off to play with it. Aisquith looked down at the stack of drawings and smiled again. He gave the stack an affectionate pat and walked back to his office. At the door he ran into Grace.

"I just put a message on your desk. It's from Barton. He'd like you to call back as soon as possible," she drawled.

"Speak of the devil," he said as entered his office.

He picked up the phone and speed-dialed Barton. Although he wasn't as powerful as Carrollton, he was careful not to annoy the good-natured Barton, who reminded him of Friar Tuck in Savile Row clothes. He always returned Barton's calls immediately.

They were now on a first-name basis. "Hamilton, how are you? I'm returning your call."

"Hello, Allan, my lad. Thank you for calling back. I was wondering if you could find some time to come over to my office tomorrow morning." Since Carrollton's death all committee meetings had taken place at Barton's office on Pratt Street. The unprepossessing Barton, to Aisquith's amazement, was the chief financial officer of the fifth largest brokerage in the United States.

"I think I can work that out. We've just finished plotting the final construction documents and they're ready to be sent out for bid." Architects always felt reflexively the need to cite recent accomplishments to prove worthy of getting paid. Aisquith realized he needn't do this with Barton, who paid each invoice the day it was received, an occurrence as rare as Halley's Comet.

"That's what I wanted to discuss with you tomorrow. The bid." Barton's tone was jovial.

"All right," Aisquith replied, puzzled. Why was Barton interested in the bid? Until now, he had left everything in his hands. "I'll see you tomorrow at ten."

"See you then," said Barton.

Aisquith put down the receiver and absentmindedly fanned his Rolodex. He couldn't wait to start construction. It was the worst part of the whole process and he wanted to get it over with. Aisquith had once heard a story about Alfred Hitchcock. To the director the most enjoyable part of filmmaking was composing every shot of his movies on a storyboard. He hated the actual filming of the movie. Dealing with actors and technical and financial problems made him miserable. But it wouldn't be a movie until the idea was put on film, so the great auteur had to endure the misery.

Aisquith felt the same way about architecture. Countless times he'd been on the site of a half-completed building that was dogged by problems and wished he could snap his fingers and there'd be a completed building before his eyes. If he wanted his museum, he had to endure the hell of construction. He would lecture Barton tomorrow on the great care that must be given to choosing the best contractor for the job.

The next morning Aisquith waited about two minutes before Barton came into the reception area to greet him. Barton truly respected Aisquith unlike his predecessor who basically treated him as one would a secretary. He seemed to really admire the architect's efforts. He never kept him waiting very long. Aisquith thought this had to do with the fact that Barton at one time in his life had wanted to be an architect.

"Good morning, Allan. Good to see you," Barton boomed, offering his hand for a hearty handshake. "Come with me. Can I get you some coffee or juice? What would you like?"

"Nothing, thanks. I already had breakfast," Aisquith said as he followed Barton down the paneled hallway. Barton's office was remarkably similar in design to Carrollton's. The same foxhunting pictures, he noted. When they got to the sliding mahogany doors, he was convinced Barton had used the same plans as Carrollton to build the office. Barton slid open the doors and beckoned Aisquith to enter. Smiling, and with great confidence, he strode through the parted doors and stood face to face with Paul Wiggs.

It was as though his dead mother was standing before him. The words spat out before his brain could stop them.

"Wiggs. What the fuck are you doing here?" Aisquith blurted. He instantly realized his faux-pas. Out of the corner of his eye he saw the entire committee sitting around the conference table staring at him in total silence. He shifted his eyes back to Wiggs, who wore an impish grin from ear to ear. Not knowing what to expect, Barton quickly stepped between them like a referee. "Well, I see that you two have met before, so no introductions are necessary," he said nervously.

"Yes, I have had the pleasure." Aisquith's reply dripped with sarcasm.

"Mr. Wiggs will be the general contractor on the job, Allan."

"And what job would that be?" said Aisquith with a smile to Barton.

"Ah . . . well. The museum, your museum Allan." Barton was totally befuddled.

Aisquith laughed so loudly that the committee members nearly jumped out of their seats.

"You've got to be shii . . . " Aisquith caught himself in time. He knew that every man in the room probably swore like a longshoreman but it looked bad for him to do it. He took in a gulp of air and composed himself. Before he could go on, Barton interrupted.

"Allan, the committee has decided that Mr. Wiggs will be the general contractor."

"Really?"

"Mr. Wiggs has done quite a bit of work for Mr. Addington's company in the past and he was very pleased with the results. And so was Mrs. Addington." Barton sounded like a prissy schoolmarm. The last sentence explained who was now calling the shots.

"But all he did was a bunch of gas stations, right? Those brick things that looked like little Mount Vernons."

"Yep, I did lots of 'em. On time and under budget. Mr. Addington had a great appreciation for my concern about his bottom line," Wiggs interjected. His smirk could have cracked a mirror.

"That's absolutely true. When I think of you, Wiggs, the bottom certainly comes to mind," Aisquith said, almost sotto voce.

The smile evaporated from Wiggs's face. He took a step forward.

Barton, sensing fists could fly any second, again stepped between them, using his ample girth as a de-militarized zone.

"Allan, we felt there was no need to put the job out to bid. We can negotiate a fee with Mr. Wiggs after he has looked at the construction set. Mrs. Addington has great faith in him. Anyway, the bidding process is quite taxing as you well know, so why go through it?"

Aisquith already knew the answer to his next question but he had to ask it anyway.

"Is this an irrevocable decision on the committee's part?"

"I'm afraid it is, Allan," Barton whispered.

Aisquith turned to Wiggs.

"Irrevocable means they aren't going to change their minds," he explained as if he were talking to a kindergartner. He turned back to Barton.

"Wiggs here had to drop out of the tenth grade under some cloudy circumstances," he said with a wink. "Did you ever go back for that GED?"

Barton pretended not to hear the comment and cleared his throat as a prelude to another official pronouncement. "Well, then, it's understood that Mr. Wiggs will be running the show."

Aisquith received this statement with a scowl that could bring down a moose. Barton reacted instantly to correct his gaffe.

"Of course you'll be running it with him, Allan. After all, we all agree it's a wonderful design. Don't you, Mr. Wiggs?"

"A masterwork." This was dunked in sarcasm, prompting the evil eye from Aisquith.

"I know you both have a lot to go over. Mr. Addington was generous in his bequest but we still must be cost conscious from the beginning. In fact, Mr. Wiggs already has some suggestions on how to cut costs."

"I'll bet he has," said Aisquith. "Has he suggested using a prefabricated metal building to house the museum yet?"

Barton seriously feared violence was imminent. If it were to happen, it should be taken outside his paneled conference room. He didn't want blood on the specially made carpeting. Placing a meaty hand on each of their shoulders, he gently guided Aisquith and Wiggs into the corridor.

"Well, we won't keep you any longer, gentlemen. I'll give you a call to schedule a meeting to kick off construction." Barton didn't bother showing them to the door. He retreated back into the conference room and slid the doors shut, happy to be out of harm's way.

Aisquith and Wiggs were alone in the hall. They eyed each other like two bantam roosters about to begin a cockfight. Aisquith knew compromising with such a creature was foolhardy. Like a buck in mating season, he quickly set out to establish his dominance.

"I can't believe an animal like you getting a job like this. There's only about two million contractors better than you who should have gotten it."

"But unfortunately they didn't. I did," said Wiggs. He was enjoying the moment immensely and decided to throw some gas on the fire right off the bat.

"And, oh, by the way . . . I'm gonna have a lot of input when comes to the design."

"The hell you are."

"Don't get too attached to that airplane hanger of yours, especially that copper roof. They don't know how fuckin' expensive that's gonna be. Old lady Addington's running the show now that Carrollton crash landed off the Cliffs. And the old girl really counts her pennies." Wiggs laughed.

"Don't even change one goddamn bolt on that roof. You just build it the way it's drawn and we'll get along just fine," Aisquith growled.

Wiggs howled with laughter. This was like tormenting a helpless child. "You fuckin' architects. Always building monuments to yourselves. You bastards never learn." He abruptly turned and walked down the hall, still laughing.

Aisquith watched him go. His back made an inviting target for a knife. Shaking with rage, he needed to compose himself. He waited until he knew Wiggs was out of the building to go down the elevator. By the time he made his way down to the lobby, he felt dizzy and nauseous. He sat in one of the overstuffed leather chairs in the waiting area and held his head in his hands. As usual when stress grabbed him, his stomach gurgled and hissed, a signal his spastic colon was about to erupt like Mount St. Helens. He hurriedly looked around and gratefully found the men's room in time.

Some men read, but Aisquith reflected on his life and troubles when sitting on the toilet. The gods had obligingly smitten one enemy, then sent another, an even more evil adversary to plague him. Worse (could it get worse?), Wiggs had the confidence and trust of Addington's widow. The committee knew this and would never overlook it. Wiggs would make Aisquith's life a living hell and more--he'd change his design into God knows what. The pain in his stomach and the thought of his building being violated made him double over.

17

Two weeks passed. Aisquith had not heard from Barton. Maybe he was letting the dust settle after the little tiff at his office. Or maybe he was meeting with Wiggs and going over the drawings, chopping things out of the design left and right. Because the drawings were under review by the local building inspector and the fire marshal, he could only wait. Construction couldn't begin without a permit. He didn't mind the delay; he needed time to figure out how to deal with Wiggs. He considered trying reason, threats, even kicking back part of his fee for Wiggs's cooperation. Of all the options, buying him off seemed the best bet. It would be like a child giving a bully his lunch money so he'd be left alone.

On a rainy afternoon, Aisquith was preoccupied with preparing a set of drawings of the museum for publication in *Architectural Review* when he heard Grace's unmistakable knock on the door. It sounded like a prisoner beating on a dungeon door. Without waiting for him to say come in, she opened the door a few inches and shouted through the opening.

"Building inspector's on the line. Should I tell him you're in or give him a secretarial white lie?"

"Let's do something different. Let's go with the truth this once."

"Line two."

Aisquith was expecting a call from the building inspector. There was always some question even on a small building, let alone a museum.

"Hello, this is Allan Aisquith."

"Well, how are you getting along today, Allan?" a folksy voice asked.

This jolted Aisquith. He was totally unprepared for such unabashed courtesy. He expected the usual bureaucratic monotone.

"I'm doing just great," he replied in an effort to reciprocate the homespun tone.

"Allan, this is Nat Quill down in Calvert City. How about coming down here tomorrow to discuss your permit for your museum up on the Cliffs?"

"Is there anything wrong?" Aisquith braced for bad news.

"Oh hell no, nothing we can't iron out tomorrow, say about two-thirty?"

Aisquith realized Quill sounded like Andy Griffith. Growing up, he never missed the "Andy Griffith Show" on Channel 2. His own father had taken off when he was six so as a child he had searched constantly for a surrogate father. Television in the early sixties provided a wide selection. Hugh Beaumont. Robert Young. Carl Betz. But mostly he fantasized about having a dad like Andy Griffith, whose warm understanding voice put him at ease. He envied Opie even though he didn't have a mother on the show. Aisquith was loathe to admit that he would have liked to have had Aunt Bea as his own mother instead of the one he was given.

He looked down at his appointment book and saw a 2:00 penciled in. But it was a cardinal rule in architecture practice to suck up to the building inspector. Like judges, they were gods on earth and wielded a great deal of power. It was always best not to keep them waiting.

"I'll be there," he cheerfully replied.

"You know where we are, right? At the corner of Johnson and Birch," Quill said, then abruptly hung up.

Aisquith hung up his phone and walked out to the studio. He found Garrett at the photocopier. Garrett had done the building code analysis with a code consultant from New York who was experienced in museums and airports. Aisquith was confident they had covered every obscure code requirement in existence. Considering the fee that he paid the consultant, he expected no less.

"Garrett, I have to see the building inspector tomorrow. Think there'll be any problems getting the permit?"

"Nope. The only complicated part is the atrium in the lobby, but me and Alteri did a real careful analysis."

"Maybe you should give me a copy of what you guys did so it'll look like I know what I'm talking about." Aisquith returned to his office with the code analysis and stretched out on his sofa to read the document. Reading the building code was as much fun as watching paint dry. He soon fell asleep, dreaming that Barton was making love to Taylor in the meadow atop the Cliffs. The hawk perched on Barton's head, watching.

The next afternoon, Aisquith sat alone in the hallway outside the building inspector's office in the Calvert City town hall. To his surprise, or rather his ignorance, this little town of 5,000 had jurisdiction over the Patuxent Cliffs and thus would issue the building permit. But he had dealt with podunk towns all over Maryland and never had a problem getting a permit. When one inspector in Western Maryland found out he was a real live architect he cheerfully told him to do whatever he wanted.

It was past 2:30. Aisquith had just started reading a brochure about the town's landfill regulations when a man in his sixties with a full head of white hair came strolling down the hall. He wore a plaid lumberjack's jacket and puffed on a pipe.

"Howdy, there."

"Mr. Quill, I presume?"

"You presume right, Mr. Aisquith. Come on in."

Aisquith followed him into his office. To his amusement, Quill reeked of folksiness all the way down to his L.L. Bean boots. He was about six feet tall and very lean, the kind of person who can eat all he wants and never gain an ounce. Aisquith took a seat while Quill hung up his coat.

"Might fancy building you got up there. Mighty fancy. Is this the first time you've done work in this neck of the woods?"

"Yes sir. Hope there's no problem."

Quill sat down behind his cluttered wooden desk and re-lit his pipe.

"Oh hell no. Just this atrium that has me concerned. But we can work it out."

Alarms went off in Aisquith's head, signaling his spastic colon to go into action.

"But it's according to code." This prompted a smile from Quill.

"Not the way I see it, son."

"No?"

"Nope, doesn't meet section 23.5.5.7.3-2 of the code. But all you have to do is just change the drawing a little bit."

"Change it? How?" Aisquith tried not to sound panicked.

"Can't be all open like that. The four floors that overlook the lobby have to be enclosed with wired glass or fire shutters. These skywalks should be enclosed too. Code says you can't have open atriums. Creates a chimney effect when there's a fire."

Aisquith suppressed the urge to leap over the desk and throttle the old man. He chose the diplomatic approach.

"Well, Mr. Quill, that isn't exactly quite the look I 'd envisioned for the museum," he chuckled in a folksy manner of his own.

Quill's bushy grey eyebrows rose in puzzlement.

"Ya think that'll make a big difference? Still will be a damn nice lobby, Mr. Aisquith. I wish I was creative like you guys."

"I've been to plenty of museums that had tall open lobbies."

"But they're not in Calvert City."

Aisquith looked down at the worn wooden floor. Next to dealing with a stupid client and an ignorant contractor, reasoning with a building inspector was the worst experience in architecture. It was a maddening experience that Aisquith never understood. Here was an architect with an expensive education who had to pass a rigorous licensing exam under the thumb of a man who was essentially a building contractor with possibly a high school education. The latter held absolute power over the former.

Since there was only one building inspector in town, one couldn't go to a competing inspector if they didn't like the first's opinion. An architect had no choice but to seek a compromise that wouldn't destroy his design. But the building inspector had even less respect for the design than the contractor. His only concern was for the safety of the building's occupants. He didn't give a damn if a revision changed the look of the building. If a fifty-foot-high concrete block wall had to be built around the museum, so be it. The code is the code. Just like those fundamentalists who believe every word of the Bible is literally true, the building inspector reads the code as gospel. But surely patience and tact would work with this Quill. Just a quid pro quo situation. What would the quid be this time?

"My office did a thorough code review of the museum, Mr. Quill. We even hired a code consultant to help us. We came to the conclusion that the atrium could be open if we installed sprinkler heads above it " Aisquith spoke calmly as he thumbed through Garrett's comprehensive notes. "Section 23.5.7.4.4-1 allows us to do that."

"Yep, I saw that section, son and I don't believe that applies to what you have here," Quill said in fatherly tone.

"But it says you can have an open atrium." Aisquith now sounded like a petulant child.

"It surely does, if that's the code you used." Quill smiled and puffed away on his pipe.

"What the hell are you talking about?" Aisquith shot back, forgetting diplomacy.

"You used the wrong code, son."

"But this is the State of Maryland Building Code for 2001. Of course we used the right code," Aisquith barked.

"Not entirely. It seems you didn't consult the Calvert City supplement."

"What supplement, goddamn it?"

"There's a city supplement that amends the current code," said Quill as he fished around the pile of papers on his desk until he found a slim yellow-covered pamphlet. He thrust it toward Aisquith, who stared at it for a few seconds before taking it from him.

"This tiny little town has its own building code? I don't believe it," said Aisquith with anger.

"We do indeed. All incorporated towns in Maryland can have one. Look up Section 23.5.7.4.4-1 and see what it says."

Aisquith fumbled nervously through the pages. He started reading Section 23 and looked up in astonishment at Quill, who just smiled and nodded his head slowly.

"That's right, son. If memory serves me correctly, Section 23.5.7.4.4-1 says, "Delete 2001 State Code provision, refer to 1995 provision."

"But the 1995 provision doesn't allow open atriums."

"Nope. They have to be enclosed with wired glass or steel fire shutters."

Aisquith felt Quill's bony fingers grabbing his testicles and started to panic. He was sinking in the quicksand again and desperately tried to grab at anything that would save him.

"The fire marshal will allow it if we install extra sprinklers," Aisquithhe blurted. "I'm sure he would."

"That's an idea. Why don't we ask him." Quill rose from his seat and walked across the office. He sat down at another desk piled high with papers and re-lit his pipe. He looked up at Aisquith who was still seated across the room watching in sheer bafflement.

"The fire marshal concurs with the building inspector's findings," said Quill in an exagerrated baritone as he pushed aside some papers at the corner of the desk, revealing a gold nameplate: "N.F. Quill, Fire Marshal."

Aisquith slumped in his seat as if he had been shot in the chest. Quill started laughing.

"I love that joke. You're the fourth person I've played it on. And I always get a hoot out of it, too," he said, still shaking with laughter. "Damn handsome nameplate, don't ya think? I have a matching pen set to go with it."

Aisquith felt rage gathering force in his stomach. He was not amused and thought the nameplate was tacky beyond belief. It was time to get tough.

"Mr. Quill, I could go to the state inspector on appeal."

Quill's homespun expression turned into a scowl that would have made a dog yelp in fear. "You certainly can, son. But that would be one mighty big mistake, one mighty big mistake. First, by going over my head like that, you'd piss the hell out of me and I'd have your college-educated balls for breakfast. And second, by counter-appealing to the state I could hold up your permit for months maybe years. I got a lot of friends in Annapolis. One of them's an Elk just like me. And Elks stick together."

With a Herculean effort, Aisquith fought back his rage and tried to reason with the bureaucrat.

"It's only the question of the atrium," he said in a quiet voice.

"That's where you're wrong, son. The state will go over these drawings with a fine tooth comb and find a ton of things wrong. Stuff that I'd let slide. No, Mr. Aisquith, you're better off dealing directly with me."

Asquith gave up on the diplomatic approach. "Goddamn it, you stupid old fart. What makes you qualified to tell me what I can and can't do. Are you an architect or an engineer?"

Quill puffed on his pipe and studied the architect's face carefully for a few moments. He then leaned back in his chair and propped his feet on the desk.

"Hell no, I'm not an architect or an engineer. Been a building contractor for thirty-five years. But I know the code and the Calvert City code says no open atriums."

Flames now shot out from Aisquith's mouth and nostrils.

"Bullshit. I bet you never graduated from high school. And you're telling me what to do."

Quill seemed to have skin as thick as a rhino. He was unfazed by the insults.

"Don't say anything you'll regret, son," he advised in a voice Andy might have used with Opie. "Come on, it's not such a big change. You're one of those creative types. You can think of something to make your design work."

Aisquith had been patronized like this before. He saw red.

"That atrium will be built AS DRAWN. It meets the goddamn code."

Quill threw back his head and roared with laughter. He was enjoying himself immensely.

"It doesn't meet *my* code, I'm afraid, and that's the only one that counts around here."

"Changing it means changing the whole concept of the lobby. I'll lose the ephemeral quality of the entire space," Aisquith bleated.

"You can still be femeral."

"How can I do that with the whole thing wrapped in wired glass and fire shutters? "Goddamn you old man, I'm telling you this meets the code."

Quill got up from the chair, reached into his back pocket and pulled out his leather tobacco pouch. He carefully refilled his pipe, then looked Aisquith straight in the eye.

"I'm afraid our meeting's over, Mr. Aisquith. But to show you I'm not an unreasonable fella, I'll give you the go-ahead for the foundation work and you'll come back with the revision I want. If you don't, your building's dead in the water. I'll see that it never gets built. Are we clear on that point, son?"

Quill strolled over to the other desk and sat down. Pulling out a blank permit, he picked up his gold pen and started to fill it out. After signing the bottom line, he stamped the paper, "For Foundation Only," and handed it to Aisquith. The architect slowly reached out to take it from him.

"All right, Mr. Quill. We'll do it your way," he said in a defeated tone.

"Ya see. It all got straightened out. I'm an easy old bird to deal with." Quill cackled like a turkey.

Aisquith walked out of the office into the corridor past a mural honoring the town's dead of World War I. A butch-looking angel holding a large sabre in her right hand floated up toward the heavens while soldiers in the muddy trenches below gazed up at her in awe. Rays of sunlight projected downward from the blade. He wondered what would happen if the angel came to life and handed him the sword. Would he use it on himself or go back into Quill's office and use it on him?

Aisquith walked out of the town hall to his car, which was parked along the curb. As he unlocked his door, he glanced across the street. A balding man sat in a light blue Chevy Cavalier watching him. A flicker of recognition passed through Aisquith's brain and vanished. He slipped behind the wheel and turned on the ignition, then stopped to look at the permit on the seat next to him. Aisquith could start construction, but his problems were not about to go away. As he pulled out of his parking space, the image of the man parked across the street came back into his mind. He suddenly realized where he'd seen the man before. It was the IBM nut who complained about his cubicle. What the hell was he doing here? He abruptly stopped the car in the middle of the street and looked behind him, but the car was gone. In all the museum euphoria and the confusion of Carrollton's death, he had never called the client at IBM to tell him about the man's visit to his office. Aisquith drove on slowly, insisting to himself that he was seeing things.

18

The contemplative quiet of the Cliffs was shattered, to Aisquith's delight. Despite all his troubles, he watched with great pleasure as the yellow Komatsu cut through the rich green grass of the meadow. The gigantic hole in which his museum would sit grew deeper by the minute.

Standing with a roll of drawings under his arm, he imagined his creation rising from the ground. The sight of the earthmover made him forget his child was in danger until he felt a tap on his shoulder.

"How's it goin', Ass, old boy? Things are really moving along, aren't they?" Paul Wiggs bellowed over the noise. Aisquith turned away and continued watching. Wiggs expected the silent treatment and knew how to end it.

"You know, a straight slanted roof would look just as good and cost almost sixty per cent less to build," he said to the back of a brown Harris Tweed coat, which he knew he'd be seeing the front of in a milli-second.

Aisquith whirled and shouted, "Keep your goddamn hands off that roof, you bastard."

"Hey, don't get excited. It's only a suggestion . . . a suggestion I made to Barton and the committee."

Aisquith dropped the roll of drawings and stood nose to nose with Wiggs.

"You made that suggestion without consulting me first? Let me guess, your contract calls for you to get a percentage of any cost savings, right?"

"Let's just say there are some incentives in my contract."

"What did I tell you, you sonofabitch, keep your hands off my design."

Wiggs laughed so hard that Aisquith felt the spray of saliva on his face.

"You really think you're running the show here, you stupid shit," Wiggs said with a huge grin.

Aisquith gathered himself. Contractors despised architects, sure, but they usually showed a modicum of respect for them, especially in front of the client. He liked "This Old House," because it presented a fantasy world where the contractor actually listened to and respected the architect. But because Wiggs had the client in his pocket, he could walk all over Aisquith. With no control over Wiggs, Aisquith shuddered to think how his museum would turn out. He decided to try reasoning one more time.

"Come on Wiggs, you're getting paid what you want for doing this job." Actually Aisquith didn't have the foggiest idea of what Barton's committee was paying him. Architects automatically assumed the contractor received at least twice what they got.

"Relax. We haven't even poured the foundation. We've got plenty of time to figure out what to do with the roof. How about a roof like the one I did for the K-Mart over in Linthicum?" Wiggs sounded conciliatory.

Aisquith saw that the idiot was dead serious about his suggestion, but offered no rebuttal. He leaned down to pick up the drawings, then walked away. He stopped at the edge of the excavation and looked down into the deep void. The construction crew was already erecting the formwork for the columns and the massive concrete walls that would hold back five stories of earth. Aisquith watched intently for a few minutes, then left the site.

At the office the next day, Aisquith sat alone at a vacant workstation drawing on the computer. It was Saturday and he had the entire place to himself. He liked working on the computer in privacy because he didn't want others to see how slow he was. He knew he had to work on it once in a while. Computer-aided drafting was like learning a foreign language. You had to practice it occasionally or lose it. He had to admit he enjoyed the sensation of drawing with the mouse, all the pointing and clicking. You didn't have to sharpen pencils all the time and you could erase with the click of a button instead of rubbing away at the drawing, getting all the tiny pieces of rubber all over you.

He heard the front door open and twisted around to see who it was. It was Kurt. He hadn't expected anyone to come in on a Saturday morning, not even workaholic Kurt. He discouraged the staff from coming in on weekends, telling them to enjoy their weekends, especially now that the push to finish the museum drawings was over. He decried architects who browbeat their workers into coming in, making them feel guilty for not pulling their weight. Marehdi had done that to her staff while she went to the Hamptons for the weekend to party.

"Kurt, you're an unexpected sight this morning," said Aisquith, with clear annoyance in his voice.

Kurt picked up on the terse greeting and lied.

"I just had to pick something up I forgot last night. So what are you up to?"

Aisquith felt like brushing him off but patiently explained what he was doing. He would have told him on Monday anyway.

"The museum committee wants a cornerstone to put a kind of time capsule in. Part of this millennium bullshit."

"What kinds of things are they going to put in it?"

"Some small pieces from the collections, video tapes, books, and a set of the construction drawings," Aisquith said.

"Cool. Thousands of years from now they'll know we did the building."

Aisquith laughed. "So, to get all this stuff in, I'm enlarging one of the column footings. Making it a lot deeper and wider."

"I see. When are they pouring the foundation?" Kurt peered over his boss's shoulder.

"They've already started, so first thing on Monday I want you to personally deliver this revision to Wiggs at the construction trailer. And tell the jerk I know it's a change order and he'll get paid for the extra work. The schedule says he's to pour the footing on Wednesday morning, so he has to redo the formwork as soon as possible. I want it done by Tuesday afternoon."

"I'll take care of it."

"I'll put the drawing and the change order on your desk," Aisquith said and then fell silent to let Kurt know he was excused.

"See ya Monday, Allan." Kurt had to follow up on his lie and went to his workstation to pick up what he'd supposedly forgotten. He grabbed a book off his desk and turned to leave. Instead he returned to Aisquith.

"Allan, I was meaning to ask you. What happened with your meeting with the building inspector last week? You never said anything about it."

"It was nothing important. He had a few questions but everything was taken care of. He's a pretty good guy to deal with."

"Great. Have a good weekend."

Aisquith waited for Kurt to leave, then backed his chair away from the computer screen and stretched his arms above his head. He reached for the mouse and pulled down the file menu, selecting Print, which sent the drawing to the plotter. He walked over to the plotter and watched as the lines appeared on the blank drawing sheet. He smiled to himself. This was a first change order he didn't mind approving.

19

On Tuesday morning, Aisquith waited until 9:30 to make the call. He knew Quill wouldn't be in until then. Municipal employees were never in by nine and never around after four. He was actually jealous of them because they would retire with a pension. Aisquith had barely saved anything for his retirement, but the museum commission would hopefully change that.

"Is Mr. Quill in? . . . Allan Aisquith."

"Why hello, Mr. Aisquith. Good to hear from you. Things seem to be moving along up there. I was there about a week ago," said Quill in his homespun manner. Aisquith was relieved that he seemed to have put aside the harsh words he had hurled at him in their meeting.

"Yes, I know. But the reason I'm calling is that I have the atrium revision for you."

"That's great, son. Just mail it to me and I'll sign off on the permit right away."

"Well, there's one other thing I have to talk to you about." Aisquith spoke in a secretive tone.

"And what's that?" came a curious reply.

"I have reason to believe the contractor removed a lot of the reinforcing in the column footings you inspected last week. You know how those bastards are. Anything to put a dollar in their pocket."

"Goddamn him. He better not have," Quill shouted. This was the reaction Aisquith wanted so he continued on.

"I really believe he took it out the day after you were out here. Listen, why don't you meet me at the site today at around five. Everybody'll be gone and we can inspect it ourselves without him getting wise," Aisquith said, his voice now almost conspiratorial.

"That's good for me. I'll see ya at five. Goddamn that Wiggs, he better not have taken out one re-bar."

"I'm pretty sure he did. He's going to pour the concrete first thing tomorrow morning so you and I will never know. Say, when I see you tonight, I can give you the atrium revision and you could give me the permit."

"That'll be fine," Quill barked as he slammed down the phone. Aisquith hung up the phone. He gazed out his window at the other mill buildings in the complex and smiled.

Aisquith was waiting by the formwork of the footing when he heard Quill's Buick Roadmaster roar up to the edge of the excavation. He had always liked the Roadmaster because of its carrying capacity but, because it was an American car, he would be embarassed to buy one.

Quill got out of the car and shouted down into the deep hole.

"Mr. Aisquith?"

"Down here, Mr. Quill," he shouted back. Aisquith had amused himself all day thinking of Quill waiting anxiously to see the footings. In his little universe of Calvert City, probably no one ever dared to defy or deceive him. He must have clawed the walls of his office all day.

Quill ran down the temporary road that led into the excavation, surprising Aisquith with his spryness and agility. He envisioned the bumpkin as always in slow motion, never in a hurry to get anywhere.

"Can I show you the atrium revision?" Aisquith tried to sound naïve.

"Christ, can't that wait?" Quill growled. He then paused and reconsidered as Aisquith held out the drawings.

"All right, let's get it over with. Here's your permit. I signed it before I left." He thrust the paper at Aisquith. "Hold on to that drawing for me until we're finished here." He stalked to the edge of the footing with his hands on his hips. "Okay, show me."

Aisquith pointed to the formwork that he had Wiggs enlarge. It was a wooden box four feet wide and eight feet deep, lined with steel reinforcing rods. It was growing dark and the bottom was now difficult to see.

"Right down there at the bottom. It's sort of hard to see. Maybe we have to climb down into it to get a better look."

"That's no problem. I brought a flashlight with me," Quill snapped. He pulled out a yellow Eveready flashlight from the pocket of his lumberjack coat. Then with the agility of a mountain goat, Quill swung his wiry body over the edge of the box and climbed down, using the grid of the steel reinforcing as a ladder.

There was silence, then Quill shouted in a puzzled voice, "Looks like everything's here."

Aisquith picked up the four-foot length of a one-inch thick reinforcing bar he had found by the formwork before Quill arrived. He stood silently by the edge of the box.

"Who told you Wiggs took out the re-bar?" Quill shouted.

"No one. I made it up."

There was another silence. "What the hell are you talking about?"

Aisquith leaned over the edge of the box. In the dim light he saw Quill standing at the bottom. He averted his eyes from the glare as Quill beamed his flashlight at him.

"I said what the hell are you talking about?" Quill shouted again, now as mad as a hornet.

"I said I made the whole thing up," replied Aisquith in an icy tone.

"Why the hell did you do that?"

"Because you're making me change my atrium and I just can't do that, Mr. Quill. You simply don't understand how important it is to my design."

"This is all about your goddamn atrium? You just wait 'til I get up there, boy." Quill began to pull himself out of the box by climbing back up on the reinforcing.

"Mr. Quill, I've decided to make a change to the concrete section of the specifications. I'd like to add a special coarse aggregate to my concrete pour tomorrow," said Aisquith as the inspector made his way up.

"What the hell would that be?" barked Quill.

"You."

As his head appeared over the edge of the box, Aisquith swung the heavy reinforcing bar down on the building inspector's white head splitting it in two as if it were a watermelon. Quill groaned and fell backward, landing with a thud at the bottom of the box.

With the bar in hand, Aisquith climbed down into the box to assess the results. Quill rested on the bottom like a sack of potatoes. His right arm was twisted behind him and the top of his head was soaked with blood. Using Quill's flashlight, he examined the old man's head, debating whether to hit him again. But he felt his pulse and pronounced him dead.

"Thanks again for my permit, Mr. Quill," Aisquith said in a quiet voice and climbed out of the formwork box. He slowly poked his head over the edge and looked back down into the abyss to see whether Quill was moving. He had seen too many horror movies where a body considered dead suddenly lunges up unexpectedly, adding another two minutes to the film.

Satisfied that he had a corpse on his hands, he walked over to a pile of gravel ten feet from the box. Behind the pile was an old coal shovel he had purchased from an antique store in downtown Baltimore years ago. Scooping up a shovelful of gravel, he quickly walked back to the box and dumped the load on top of Quill, then returned for another load. The gravel, about the size of golf balls, was normally spread at the bottom of footings and the basement slab to serve as a solid base for the concrete pour.

It was past six. The guard at the gate by the road came on duty around seven, so Aisquith worked quickly to blanket Quill with the gravel. At last the building inspector was completely covered with a two-foot thick layer. After the last shovelfull, Aisquith leaned against the shovel and examined his handiwork.

"Just think what the archeologists will say when they dig you up 1,000 years from now. A hundred dissertations will be written on why you're there. Some will say you were a sacrifice to some god. And in a way, they'd be right. You *had* to be sacrificed."

Satisfied that Quill wouldn't be noticed when the workers placed the chute of the concrete into the formwork to pour the next morning, Aisquith picked up the roll of the now unnecessary atrium drawing and his antique shovel. As he started out of the excavation to his car, he realized that during the entire operation, he had felt no emotion. His armpits weren't soaked with sweat as he thought they would be, his spastic colon hadn't exploded because of the stress, and his hands weren't shaking at all.

Aisquith loved to watch movies about the Mafia like "Goodfellas" because he was fascinated by Joe Pesci's or Robert DeNiro's total lack of feeling or remorse when it came to shooting someone in the back of the head. It seemed as commonplace to them as flushing a toilet. But that's exactly how it seemed to him. He was exhilarated. Murder didn't bother him at all. He was proud that he didn't feel guilty. He wasn't a simpering weakling like Raskolnikov in *Crime and Punishment*, but a cold-blooded killer. Homicide could indeed be justifiable.

During the shoveling, one part of his brain kept reminding Aisquith that what he was doing was wrong, but it was like a faint voice way off in the distance, easily ignored. He suddenly realized that he was a bona fide sociopath. Had he been one all his life? Or like menopause or erectile disfunction had it come upon him in middle age?

The main task completed, Aisquith walked quickly out of the excavation. He threw the flashlight and drawings into his car, then went over to Quill's Roadmaster. To his relief, the old man had been in such a hurry that he had left the keys in the ignition. Before covering Quill up, he hadn't thought to check his pockets for the keys. It was now 6:20 and dark out. He had plenty of time for phase two, getting rid of Quill's car. The large, deep pond within the wetlands along by the entrance would be a convenient hiding place. Was it fate that he had channel-surfed the other night and caught the very end of "Psycho," when they discovered where Norman Bates hid the cars of his victims?

That night Aisquith slept like a log and felt quite refreshed when he woke the next morning. He looked at his bedstand clock and saw that it was 9:30. By now Quill would be under a nice warm blanket of concrete. He rolled over and slept for another hour.

Instead of going to the office, he stayed home until it was time to leave for his biweekly progress meeting with Barton. When Barton's secretary led him into the conference room, he was surprised to see only Barton and Wiggs sitting at the long mahogony table. Usually the meeting was a progress report to the entire committee. Barton stood up and came forward with his hand extended. Wiggs remained seated. From the grin on Wiggs's face, Aisquith could tell he was walking into an ambush. His body immediately tensed up, bracing for a blow to the groin.

"Allan, please sit down. We're not having our usual meeting today as you can see," Barton said, his tone grave. He had dispensed with his usual pleasantries so Aisquith was certain something was up. As he sat down he glared at Wiggs. The contractor continued his mega-grin.

Barton, who had always looked directly at Aisquith as he spoke, now had trouble making eye contact. Aisquith purposely zeroed his eyes into Barton to make him feel even more uncomfortable.

"Allan, we'd like to discuss some . . . uh, uh . . . value engineering ideas with you today." Barton said, stumbling over an obviously unfamiliar term.

"Ah, value engineering. Isn't that another term for chopping some unnecessary design element out of the building to save money?"

"Yea, that's about right," Wiggs blurted.

Barton shot the contractor a sidelong glance, then smiled at Aisquith apologetically. "We wouldn't do anything drastic to your design, of course," he said anxiously.

"I'm relieved," said Aisquith, looking amused.

"But Paul says we can save a substantial amount of money by revising the roof, Maybe simplifying the form a bit." Barton was exceedingly cautious, braced for an explosion.

"What kind of revison do you have in mind?" Aisquith asked, feigning interest as he turned to Wiggs.

"The roof doesn't have to curve up like that. And it doesn't have to be covered in copper which is damned expensive." Wiggs spoke in a deep, stern voice, trying to impress the client.

Aisquith thought out loud. "Mmmm. Maybe a straight shed roof like that K-Mart you did, huh?" He held his chin as if he were seriously pondering. "Well, maybe we *could* straighten it a bit. Make it easier to build." He nodded vigorously.. "Yes, that could work out."

Wiggs flashed Barton a triumphant smile. Aisquith had backed down. Nothing was more satisfying for a contractor than to show up the architect, especially in front of the client. Wiggs had just won a major skirmish in the class war between architect and contractor. With blood in his eye, he was eager for the kill.

"And that window wall in the back is as wide as the moon. We have to cut that down."

"We can talk about that too. Maybe it is a bit over done. Hamilton, Wiggs and I could set up a time to go over some of these changes between us."

Happy that no fists had been thrown, a delighted and relieved Barton jumped up from his chair and was his jolly old self again. "That's great Allan. Mind you, these changes will in no way affect the integrity of your design. I can assure you of that," he blustered as he glanced at Wiggs, who merely nodded.

Aisquith got up from his seat and shook Barton's hand.

"We'll work together on it. Let me do some drawings and see what I come up with."

"Don't take too long now. I don't want it to hold up the steel order," said Wiggs in a fake whine. Now that he was in the driver's seat, he would cut the architect no slack. He enjoyed giving orders to Aisquith. It was like having a classy servant.

"You'll hear from me in a few days," Aisquith assured Wiggs in a quiet voice as he walked through the door.

Wiggs beamed, itching to get back to the construction trailer to tell his crew of his victory over the pansy architect. They'd probably knock off early and all go out for beer this afternoon.

20

Kurt stuck his head into Aisquith's office. "You wanted to see me, Allan?"

"Indeed, I do, Kurtster," replied Aisquith, hunched over his drafting board. "The prints and drawings curator who the museum just hired reviewed the drawings and wants to add a special room to handle rare drawings that are very light sensitive. Addington had a whole collection of medieval drawings."

Kurt looked over his boss's shoulder. He knew that Aisquith was in a hurry for this because he was hand drafting instead of working on the computer, which would have taken him hours longer. Although Aisquith was slow as molasses on the machine, the intern respected him for learning computer drafting. It made him seem like one of the guys in the trenches. On days when he really hated being a computer jockey, Kurt dreamt of a nationwide strike in architectural offices. Everybody would walk away from the workstations. Management would be helpless, unable to find even a single drawing on the computer.

"It's just a windowless room?" Kurt asked, ending his reverie.

"Yep, sort of like a darkroom. We'll put it in the north corner of the upper basement level right next to the drawing and print department's storage area. It'll need special humidity control so we'll have to get Jenkins to design a small system to serve the room."

"Shall I take care of that?" asked Kurt.

"No, I'll talk to him about it. I want you first to take this sketch and put it in to the computer. Plot it out and then take it to our favorite ass-hole contractor. Tell him to go ahead and build it now. It's just a four-by-six concrete block enclosure. We'll fur out the outside and drywall it. It has to have a thirty-two-inch-wide masonry opening. And here, take this change order form along with you. He won't touch it without it. It should cost about $3,000 but I know he'll charge $6,000."

Kurt took the sketch and left. Aisquith got up from the drafting board and stretched out on his leather sofa. Gazing up at the exposed wood joist floor of the mill, he thought of his grandfather again. He died the year he started Columbia. Half of his grandfather's weekly salary had gone to his mother to help put him through prep school. They were both totally supportive of him and never let him down. His grandfather didn't want him to feel ashamed in front of his more affluent classmates at Cambridge so he made sure his only grandchild had money to enjoy himself. He once told Aisquith never to reveal that his grandfather worked in a factory for it would bring shame on him. He was fond of Joseph Kennedy's advice to his sons that it isn't what you are but what people think you are that counts. Aisquith had never told the old man that the money he gave was still a pittance and that he was always ashamed of his background.

Just the fact that he was going to be an architect had been enough for his mother and grandfather. They never knew what a professional failure he'd been. If still living, they probably wouldn't understand his explanations of why he was so second-rate. They'd just say he was being too hard on himself.

As Aisquith slowly dozed off in what promised to be a very blissful sleep, the pounding of Grace's fist on his door woke him up.

"Yessss?" he called out groggily.

"Paul Wiggs in on the line. Is a secretarial lie in order?"

"Nah, he'll just keep calling back. Let's get it over with."

"Yea, what is it?" he barked as he picked up the phone next to the sofa.

"Ah, was the baby having a nappy?"

"How can I help you?" This with mock civility.

"We've been shut down," Wiggs blasted into Aisquith's right ear.

"What the hell do you mean? Who shut you down? Barton?"

"Hell no. Some skinny little bitch with glasses with a court order in her hand telling us to stop work."

"Who is she, for Christssakes?"

"Hold on, she gave me card. Mabel Marston, State Environmental Protection. Said the job was in violation of the law."

"You're kidding me, you sent the guys home?"

"I had no choice. She even had a state trooper with her," Wiggs said, annoyed that Aisquith would think he made something like this up.

"What else did she say?"

"All she said was the environmental permit was all fucked up. Said that you had to call her to clear this all up."

"What the hell do you mean?" Aisquith shouted, instinctively looking for someone besides himself to blame.

Wiggs's voice was like thunder. "I dunno. You guys took care of all the permits. Why the fuck are you asking me?"

After taking down the number Aisquith slammed down the phone and slumped into the sofa. He covered his eyes with his hands and remained motionless for five minutes. His enemies were multiplying exponentially.

21

    As Aisquith sat in the environmental protection office he killed time memorizing a Trees of Maryland poster in the waiting area. He had great sensitivity for the environment, he felt, but he was secretly ashamed that he didn't know an ash from an oak. The poster conveniently listed the leaf shape and silhouette of each common tree type. The environmental office was just what he had expected. The walls were covered with the usual flora and fauna prints and U.S. Geological Survey Maps. There was a small Greenpeace poster off in the corner by the coat rack that troubled Aisquith. It meant there was a radical on the premises. Just as he started memorizing the shape of the European Beech, he heard footsteps behind him. He turned and faced another expected sight.

    Mabel Marston was mousy and bespectacled, just as he had envisioned her when speaking to her on the phone the day before. Only in a movie would an environmentalist look like Julia Roberts. They nodded at each other and muttered hellos. Aisquith followed the back of her bunned hair and white cable-knit sweater to her office. Her space was crammed with papers, maps, and more Greenpeace posters. She motioned for him to sit down in the molded plastic chair next to her desk.

    Aisquith was in no mood for pleasantries and threw the first punch. "I thought all the permits were in order."

    "Not the environmental permit I'm afraid," she replied in a quiet voice. She took a sip of what smelled like herbal tea from her Save the Redwoods ceramic mug.

    Although he felt his museum showed great respect for the environment, Aisquith hated environmentalists on principle. Self-righteous, zealous, and inflexible. Every one of those traits seemed embodied in the woman sitting across from him. He had immediately called her to try to arrange a meeting that very afternoon. Marston had enraged him by saying she was busy for the next two days and couldn't meet with him. Aisquith had breathed fire into the telephone receiver and she relented. She could give him twenty minutes.

Marston, he found to his surprise, was the chief environmental official for the entire Chesapeake Bay region, someone who wielded great power though you'd never know from looking at her.

He studied her closely, trying to her gauge her mettle. She was a homely creature, someone who probably never had a date in high school and assuaged the pain of being an outsider by overachieving as a student. When a ten-page history paper was due, she turned in forty. The plaque on the wall over her desk testifying that she had a Ph.d. from M.I.T. showed that her hard work had paid off, though he'd bet she was incredibly unhappy. Now she put all her emotional energy into saving bog turtles from extinction. She could be a lesbian or she could be like one of those uptight secretaries he had seen in 1950s movies. The type who, alone with the boss in his office, would unpin their hair and take off their cats-eye glasses, revealing a beautiful woman. The boss in those movies always responded the same way. "Why, Miss Higgenbottom, you're gorgeous." But his child was in danger. He had no time for erotic thoughts about its attacker.

"So the environmental permit was wrong?"

"It was done incorrectly. And under the law all work must stop at once."

"And how did that happen?" Aisquith tried for a matter-of-fact tone.

"It's because of a mistake by the local environmental officer. Look at this map."

Marston rolled her chair toward a side table piled high with large topographic maps. Aisquith rose and looked over her shoulder as she drummed her index finger on a squiggly line on the map.

"See that line?" she snapped.

Aisquith saw Marston was pointing at a map of the coastline of the Patuxent Cliffs.

"Which one?"

"Right here," she barked impatiently as she stabbed the line with her finger.

She smelled like wildflowers. Aisquith smiled. That's the way an environmentalist should smell. All natural, with no artificial preservatives.

"Ah, yes. I see now. And what am I looking at?" he said in a cheerful tone, hoping to annoy her.

"This is the coastal conservation management boundary. And your building crosses it. It's in violation of the law."

"It doesn't. I saw the site plan and the edge of the museum is at least ten yards behind it. I knew we weren't supposed to cross it" Aisquith spoke with patient calm as if he were dealing with a recalcitrant child.

"That's probably true. But I found out that you were looking at an out-of-date map." Marston unrolled another map that seemed to be an exact copy of the first.

"Here's where the line used to be." With the maps side by side, she pointed to a line that was far closer to the edge of the Cliffs than the one on the first map. "And this is where the line is now. It was pulled back in the latest revision of the coastal conservation management map."

She unrolled the site plan of the museum. "See, you used the line off the out-of-date map."

Aisquith saw how much closer the boundary was on his site plan and how indeed his museum crossed over the new line. "But we complied with the one that was given us. We assumed it was correct," he continued in his soothing voice.

"But it's the wrong boundary line. The right one's almost fifty yards from the edge of the Cliffs which puts the edge of *your* building about ten yards over it."

"And what do you propose I do about it?"

"Move the foundation of course!"

Aisquith started laughing loudly. Marston frowned and put her hands on her bony hips. The sight made him laugh even harder. "You're pulling my leg."

"I'm absolutely serious, Mr. Aisquith. You can redesign the end of your museum so it's within the boundary. Just revise the site plan and I'll sign off on the permit. Then construction can resume. That's all there is to it."

The smile evaporated from Aisquith's face. He looked into her mouse-like eyes and saw the iron resolve in them. "That would mean changing the entire end of the building and that's out of the question."

"Oh really." She spit out the words like venom.

He felt at that instant like throttling her but kept his hands to his sides. He braced for an all-out nuclear exchange.

"Damn it. I complied with the map I was given. That building stays the hell where it is," he fumed.

"The boundary line was changed."

"When?"

"About four months ago, I believe."

"Right before we applied for the permit."

"It seems that way. The local official went by the wrong map and never should have given you the permit."

"So he screwed up. Call him and get it straightened out. He can issue a modification."

"That's going to be a trifle difficult," she said with a wry smile.

"And why's that"," he lashed back.

"Because Nat Quill has vanished."

"Quill? What the hell does he have to do with all this?"

"Quill is . . . or was . . . the local environmental official."

Aisquith felt chills up his back. The hair on the back of his neck stood up. All of a sudden he had stumbled into an episode of "The Twilight Zone." He could swear he heard the show's theme song in his head. "But, but.... you can correct the mistake," he stammered.

"I can . . . but I won't." Her answer was like a stilleto plunged into his chest.

"And why the hell not?" he shouted, clenching his fists and teeth.

"There's a nesting area for ring-tailed hawks all along the edge of the Patuxent Cliffs. No other place along the eastern seaboard has such a habitat and we're not going to disturb it. It's all part of a very delicate ecosystem, you know."

Aisquith stared down at the green-and-brown tile floor. It looked very old. He wondered if the tiles contained asbestos and what Marston would say if she found out she had a toxic substance right beneath her feet. Her words reverberated through his brain. Delicate. The hawk that knocked Carrollton over the edge hadn't seemed so delicate, more than capable of protecting its ecosystem, in fact. He raised his eyes and met Marston's stony gaze.

"You damn well know that the museum is fifty yards from your goddamn birds. They can mate and lay their eggs in complete privacy. I'll design a special sign that says, "Hawks Having Sex. Please Stay Away. I'll even put one up in Braille to meet the disability code."

"I'm afraid you have a very limited knowledge of wildlife, Mr. Aisquith," Marston said with a wicked smile.

"Bullshit. I watch all those nature shows on Public Broadcasting. I just saw one about the red-ass baboon."

"There are no red-ass baboons living in the state of Maryland."

"I can think of one right off hand!"

"Insults will get you nowhere, Mr. Aisquith. The building must be moved behind the conservation boundary and that's all there is to it," Marston said, smiling again.

"That's going to be a bit difficult."

"Only the foundation's been poured. You can jackhammer it up or bury it."

"You're bloody mad, woman," Aisquith murmured. An Anglophile, he liked using "bloody."

Marston leaned back in her chair and grinned. She was enjoying this to the maximum.

"I am the state's environmental officer for this region and that's my final ruling," she pronounced, without a shred of emotion in her voice. "Good day, Mr. Aisquith. My next meeting is about to start."

Aisquith stood up and stared her straight in the eye. Design had no meaning to a contractor or a bureaucrat. Another ape trying to appreciate a string of beautiful pearls.

She was enjoying the stare-down and without batting an eye said, "I know what you're thinking Mr. Aisquith. But don't do it."

"And what I am thinking, Ms. Marston?"

"You're going to ask one of those rich bastards on the Addington board to make a call to the Governor."

"And if I did?"

Her impassive face broke into loud laughter. "You'd fail miserably, I'm afraid." Aisquith was clearly startled by her unexpected response and that amused her even more. "Hey, wake up, pal. Think the governor will overrule a key political appointee with a distinguished environmental record who helped him get out the women's vote last election? Fat chance."

"I want to . . .," Aisquith began, but she cut him off.

"Our legal department will wait until you comply before we lift the court order. Once I get the revised site plan, I'll sign the permit. And only then."

"All this because of some goddamned birds," Aisquith muttered under his breath as he turned to leave.

"Let me know when you're ready. And have a nice day," Marston called after him.

Aisquith walked out of the state office building and sat on a wooden bench by the front doors. He was breathing hard and tried to calm himself by pressing his hand on his chest. Across the street a young man emptied parking meter coins into a strongbox. The man moved from meter to meter in complete acceptance of the monotonous chore. He would probably empty scores of meters the rest of the day, go home, watch TV, and come back the next day to empty scores more. For the next thousand working days he'd do the same thing. Aisquith wanted to trade places with him. To do something completely mindless and just accept that's all he was capable of doing. He hated having an artistic bent, the innate urge to have to do something creative. He detested his craving to be published or be respected in his profession. It was like an addiction he couldn't control. He felt like running across the street and asking the man how to get such a job.

Aisquith lowered his head and stared at a crack in the concrete sidewalk. A pair of Hushpuppies suddenly appeared next to the crack. Aisquith stared at the soft brown loafers for a couple of seconds, then his eyes followed up the pants legs they were attached to until they came to an IBM identification tag clipped to a plaid shirt pocket. He didn't need to go any further, because he recognized the laminated photo. It was the disgruntled worker he had feared would go postal in his office over an office cubicle. Then an image flashed in his mind. The day he left Quill's office and saw a familiar face in a car across the street. It was the same guy. Aisquith's head jerked up and met an intense expression. The man was simmering with rage.

"Why... hello Mr . . . " stammered Aisquith helplessly.

" Kelly. Chet Kelly," was the icy reminder.

"You came to my office one day and . . ."

"You were mistaken. Middle management doesn't get real offices. They get cubicles. You said I'd be getting a real office with real walls and a real door," Kelly said in a menacing tone.

There was no choice but to lie. "Well, I talked to your boss, but he didn't want to follow my suggestion."

"But you're the architect. They'll listen to you."

"But IBM is my client and I have to do what they ask," Aisquith bleated, with an air of desperation.

"You said I'd get an office. I've been with the company for sixteen years. I can't sit in a cubicle. I can't even make a private telephone call. I can hear other people talking. The walls are only four feet high."

"Yes, I know. It takes some getting used to, but you'll see. It won't be that bad."

"Yes, it will, goddamn it. You just can't put me in one of those things. You thought up the design. It was your idea to stick us in these goddamn cattle pens." Kelly was shouting now.

"Hey, calm down." Aisquith looked up and down the street for a policeman. "Believe me, I'm not the one who decided to stick you in a cubicle. I'm really sorry."

"That's fuckin' easy for you to say. I bet you have your own office. With a door, huh? Am I right?"

Aisquith dodged the question and frantically searched his mind for something to say to placate him.

"I know how you feel. I had to sit in one myself and I hated it. But working for IBM has a lot of advantages like a generous pension plan and all that personal leave."

"Don't patronize me, you bastard. I created the XG-333 main frame that every goddamn insurance company in America uses and this is all I get? A cubicle?"

Aisquith remained seated as Kelly hovered over him. He could smell the man's bad breath as he harangued him.

"Listen, I'm really sorry. It's no way for a man with your abilities to be working."

"You're damn right. And I swear you're not going to get away with this." Kelly's face was beet-red and contorted with anger. Then, before Aisquith could say more, Kelly suddenly pivoted and walked hurriedly away, muttering to himself and gesturing with his arms as if talking to some imaginary person. Aisquith watched in amazement as he stomped down the street and turned the corner out of sight. He looked back down at the crack in the sidewalk as his mind gradually returned to his problems with Marston. Then another chill went up his spine. He realized that Kelly didn't just run into him down here by accident but that he had followed him here. It *was* Kelly he had seen outside Quill's office that day. How long had he been following him and what had he seen? A surge of panic almost seized him, but he kept control of himself. He had to be extra careful from now on.

22

"Is Wiggs there? Tell him it's Aisquith."

After an interminable two minutes, the hated voice came on the line.

"Hey Ass, old boy. What's going on with these tree huggers. When can I get back to work? You know this delay means a change order. I'm entitled to compensation for the inconvenience, you know."

Aisquith rolled his eyes. "Yea, yea. You'll get paid, don't worry."

"So when can I get back to work?"

"Real soon. I'm working on it. I need to talk to you tomorrow, around five."

"That early?"

"No, for Chrissakes. Five, in the afternoon, at the site. That's when I'll be free tomorrow."

"Goddamn it. Can't you make it another time?"

"Nope. Has to be tomorrow. I'll bring a change order that'll start to compensate you for the delay. The museum committee won't have a problem with that."

"All right, all right. I'll see you then."

Aisquith put down the phone and rocked back and forth in his leather executive chair, lost in thought. The world wanted to crush him, but he wouldn't let it. He was pleased with his resilience. Grace suddenly opened the door to his office and stood in the doorway with a grave expression. He knew something was amiss. She always pounded on the door before entering even when it was open.

"There's a policeman here to see you," she hissed at him, looking over her shoulder.

Aisquith smiled at her and rose from his chair.

"Show him in, Gracie."

With every muscle and bone in his body, Aisquith fought a panicky urge to dive out the window behind him. He tightly clutched the edge of his desk with both hands, then relaxed his body. He took in a deep breath and waited. In the next five minutes his life could come crashing down.

A small voice deep within his brain kept telling him that the police would come around but he had ignored it. Right after Quill's demise, Aisquith rehearsed his answers in preparation for the police. But as the weeks passed, no one contacted him and he doubted that anyone would ever show up.

A well-dressed man well over six feet tall strolled confidently through Aisquith's office doorway. Aisquith was surprised by the detective's appearance but made sure to keep his body neutral. He knew the policeman would size him up the second he walked in.

"How do you do, Mr. Aisquith. I'm Phillip Packard. Maryland State Police Criminal Investigative Division," the visitor announced in a loud but friendly voice as he quickly flashed a gold shield at Aisquith.

"Pleased to meet you," said Aisquith in a clear, strong voice. "Have a seat."

"I'd like to ask you a few questions. I'm investigating the disappearance of Nat Quill, the building inspector from Calvert City. I won't take much of your time."

From the hundreds of movies he'd seen, Aisquith automatically expected a very overweight, badly dressed policeman who had barely made it through high school. This man's accent was more Yale than South Baltimore. And his forest green tie was from Brooks Brothers. Packard was probably in his late thirties and had a trim athletic build. With his high cheekbones and strong jaw line, he could have been a model in a fashion ad. Aisquith sensed trouble.

"Well, I don't know how much help I can be, but I'll try," Aisquith replied, smiling.

"You do know Mr. Quill?" As he asked this in a pleasant tone Packard pulled out a notepad the size of a paperback book from the breast pocket of his natty sport coat.

"Not personally. Just as the building inspector on my museum."

"So you'd never dealt with him before applying for your building permit?"

"No, that was the very first time."

"And when was the last time you saw him?"

"At his office … I believe that was around May 6."

"His secretary remembers him saying he had an appointment with you out at the construction site. This would be about six weeks ago, June 2. About the time he was last seen."

"We did have an appointment but he called toward the end of the afternoon to cancel it. Said an emergency had come up and we'd have to re-schedule it. But he never called me back."

Aisquith flipped open his appointment book, shuffled through some pages. "Yep, he cancelled."

"And what day was that?"

Aisquith didn't want to pinpoint the date, but he was cornered. "Mmm . . . looks like June 1."

"Did Quill say what the emergency was?"

"No, he didn't." Aisquith made sure all his answers were short and to the point. Any extra explanation could cast suspicion upon him.

"What were you supposed to meet about?"

"He had a couple of questions about the foundation?"

"Was something wrong?"

"No, not at all. He just wanted to make sure they were being done correctly."

Packard looked up from his notepad and frowned. "Had he any reason to believe they weren't?"

Aisquith realized he shouldn't have opened that can of worms. He tried redirecting the line of questioning.

"No one's heard from him at all? Not even his family?" said Aisquith in a very concerned voice.

"No, his secretary said he was very upset about something the day he was supposed to meet you at the museum." Packard obviously wasn't easily diverted.

"Can't think of what it could've been . . . you know, come to think of it, Quill mentioned something about going fishing."

"Did he say where?"

"I think he said Western Maryland. You know, ah, Garrett County."

"Mmm. That's the first I've heard about that."

Aisquith's sense of danger was now even more pronounced. Packard's questions reminded him of a rodent patiently gnawing away at a thick electrical cable. It would take a long time, but eventually he might snap the cable of Aisquith's life. Packard gazed into Aisquith's eyes. It was almost as if Packard had x-rays emanating from his eyes into Aisquith's skull, searching for the truth. Aisquith looked him straight in the eye and simply smiled. "Quill said something about fishing when I visited him at his office."

"This was back on May 6? So what makes you think he went fishing on June 1? Did he say something about it when he cancelled the appointment?"

"No. It was just something I remembered. Thought it might be of some help."

"Quill seemed to be a guy with very steady, predictable habits. It wasn't like him to take off like that, even to go fishing. He would've told people where he was going."

"Colombo" had been one of Aisquith's favorites TV shows when he was growing up. The audience already knew who the killer was but Peter Falk didn't. The show featured a cat and mouse plot in which Colombo solved the crime because of a slipup in the murderer's alibi. Aisquith had wondered many times what would happen if he were in the same situation. Could he outsmart a real live policeman? But instead of being soaked with sweat, he had the same sense of exhilaration he'd had on the drive back from Carrollton's funeral. Still, he wasn't dealing with a normal policeman. Those guys always had low reading scores in school. He looked at Packard's hand as he wrote in his notepad and saw a college ring that signified Johns Hopkins.

"You never know what goes on in someone's head. They could have the most bizarre desires," Aisquith said with a horse laugh.

Packard didn't see the humor. "Did Mr. Quill ever mention anything like that to you?" he asked in a deadly serious tone.

"You mean did he tell me he had a secret desire to run off to Las Vegas and become a showgirl at the MGM Grand?" Aisquith bellowed with laughter. "No, we only talked about exit lights and sprinkler heads."

Packard allowed himself a wan smile, then looked down at his notepad and scribbled for a few seconds. Aisquith thought he had better shut up before he blurted out something incriminating. To his relief, the detective stood up, signaling the end of the interview, as the police politely call an interrogation.

"Here's my card, Mr. Aisquith, if you happen to think of anything that could be of help," Packard said. He must be saying in his mind that this visit was an enormous waste of time, Aisquith thought. He had seen this scene many times in the movies and knew exactly how to reply.

"If I think of anything, I'll be sure to call."

"Well, thank you for your time, Mr. Aisquith." Packard headed for the door. "This is a very odd case. The man seems to have been swallowed up by the earth."

Aisquith remained silent. Then the detective suddenly turned back to Aisquith, who was following him to the door.

"That's quite a beautiful building going up there on the Cliffs. I saw a rendering of it in the *Sun*. Blends in beautifully with the landscape."

Aisquith was taken aback by the compliment and stammered a bit before he got out a a simple thank-you.

"Congratulations on your design, and thanks again. I can find my way out," Packard said as he went out the door.

Like all architects, Aisquith lived for praise of his work. Even though the only praise that counted came from colleagues and the right architectural publications, he was flattered by a sensitive compliment from the average guy in the street. He snapped out of his fantasy. Anyone who could make such an observation was sharp and intelligent and a genuine threat to him. Packard would be back.

23

Wiggs was late for their appointment, but Aisquith wasn't bothered in the least. He enjoyed walking the construction site at dusk by himself. The foundation was finished and the steel columns that would make up the skeleton of the building were in place. The steel for the second floor had been erected just before Marston stopped work on the project. With the superstructure starting to go up, it was easier for Aisquith to visualize the entire museum. At the southeast corner of the foundation, he paced off the ten yards the building extended over the conservation boundary. He shook his head in disgust. The museum was still quite a distance away from the edge of the Cliffs. What impact did the extra ten yards have on the nesting area? Moving it back wouldn't make a damn bit of difference. The thought of Marston's intransigence made his blood boil. She had to know it didn't make any real difference. His rage was interrupted by the roar of Wiggs' Mercedes coming up the hill.

Aisquith felt it a travesty that Wiggs owned a beautiful machine like a Mercedes. Like a chimpanzee owning a Stradavarius. This was just unadulterated jealousy. He hated Wiggs for owning an expensive vacation home on the Eastern Shore, too.

Wiggs popped out of his car like a wound spring. He always had a smile on his face when he saw Aisquith. If he had total control of the project, he'd be smiling, too, Aisquith thought.

Wiggs had a roll of drawings under his arm as he approached Aisquith. "So when can I get back to work?" he snapped.

"In a couple of days. I just have to make a revision on a drawing and get the permit. It won't be long. You should keep ordering your material."

"I intend to do that," Wiggs said in a churlish tone. "I have to talk to you about your sky walks or whatever the hell they're called."

"Sky bridges. Now let me guess. You convinced the committee to get rid of them. You're substituting ropes so the people can swing across the lobby to get to the other side."

"Nah. They'd never get rid of those fuckin' things. That's where they're putting that statue of that naked Greek guy. I just made a little revision on the shop drawing of it that I want you to take a look at."

"Sure," said Aisquith, distracted. " I can look at it later."

"Bullshit. Just look at it now. It'll only take a second."

Wiggs unrolled a drawing of steel fabrication drawings. Aisquith held one end of the sheet. Wiggs pointed to a small detail at the bottom of the drawing.

"I'm just simplifying the hanger detail. Instead of one thick threaded rod to hang both skywalks, I'm gonna use two thinner ones. I'll use one to hang one bridge from the ceiling and use the second rod to hang the bottom bridge from the top one. It'll be easier to set the lower one in place."

"That's smart thinking, Wiggs. It'll really simplify things. Go ahead and do it." Aisquith barely glanced at the detail. He realized it was getting dark.

"I already went ahead and gave the fabricator the change," Wiggs growled.

"I want to talk to you about a couple of things. First, I want to take a look at the rare drawing room we added," Aisquith said.

" What the fuck is that thing anyway?"

"It's a room for storing light-sensitive drawings. Some of the drawings in the collections are a thousand years old and even one ray of light can destroy them." Aisquith spoke as if he were talking to a thick-headed child.

"No shit? All that for a bunch of old drawings. All right, I'll show you the damn thing,"

Wiggs led the way down a set of concrete stairs into the deep basement, which now was completely poured with a floor slab. Aisquith followed behind, staring at the back of the contractor's forest green Ralph Lauren polo shirt. They made their way through a maze of storage and maintenance rooms constructed of gray concrete block. The steel deck of the floor above was already in place, cutting off all light to the basement level. Bulbs strung along the underside of the floor provided dim light for them to make their way to the corner of the basement. The plumbing lines had been installed beneath the floor with groups of pipes popping up through the floor at different intervals. Aisquith stumbled over one of them.

After a four-minute walk, they finally reached the corner of the basement and the concrete block enclosure.

"Christ, it's like walking across the entire state of Texas to get here," Wiggs bitched. "You know this was an $8,000 change order."

"It probably only cost $4,000, but that's okay," Aisquith replied calmly.

Wiggs, who knew the comment was absolutely true, still turned to Aisquith and gave him the evil eye. Aisquith roared with laughter, annoying Wiggs and making him eager to retaliate.

"I was going to wait, but it's best to get bad news over with. Bad news for you. Good news for me," Wiggs said with a smirk.

Smiling, Aisquith stood with his hands on his hips. "You know, I believe in getting bad things over with, too. So what's your bad news?"

"The committee's on my side, Frank Lloyd Wrong. They want you to change that fuckin' dumb roof of yours and save a few hundred thousand dollars. Oh yea, the rear window wall's gone too."

"Gee, you've really got me by the balls, Wiggs," said Aisquith said, in a mock dramatic tone that Wiggs didn't catch.

"I do indeed, asshole, and it feels great. I saved old lady Addington some real bucks. Anyway, it was a horseshit design. People want to come out here and look at the art, not be distracted by a lot of weird-ass angles and curves."

"You're absolutely right, Wiggsy. Fuckin' architects are always building monuments to themselves. We never fuckin' learn?"

Wiggs was disappointed that Aisquith was taking all the bad news with such good grace. It annoyed the hell out of him. He realized that it was a class thing. The Ivy League-educated jerk was taking it like a well-bred gentleman instead of erupting into a violent rage as a blue collar worker would.

Aisquith changed the subject when he saw Wiggs' reaction.

"I want to take a look inside the room."

"It's pitch dark in there," Wiggs protested. "You can go in yourself."

"You have to come. I want to show you where the electrical will go. There're some special requirements for this room. I didn't show them on the sketch I gave you. It'll only take a second. Look, I brought a flashlight."

The room was a concrete block box four by six feet in size with one opening into it. Aisquith switched on his flashlight and motioned for Wiggs to go in ahead of him.

Wiggs frowned and stayed put. "I'm telling you, there's only room for one person in there."

"Come on, don't be a goddamn baby. Just for a minute. I'll be right behind you and I'll shine the light so you can see."

Wiggs cursed under his breath and went through the narrow opening. Aisquith held back a second, then in one fluid motion bent over and picked up a concrete block next to the wall and smashed it into the top of Wiggs' skull. The forty-pound block squashed Wiggs's head like a pumpkin. Wiggs let out a long baritone grunt and fell forward onto the concrete floor with a dull thud. In delivering the blow to the head, Aisquith had let go of the heavy block. He picked it up to finish off Wiggs, but saw in the dim light that the contractor was out cold. Blood streamed from the gash. He felt through Wiggs pants pockets and pulled out his cell phone.

Aisquith walked over to a small concrete block room about 20 feet away and came out carrying a white plastic bucket full of wet mortar. Setting it down by the opening to the room, he looked at Wiggs' motionless body and took off his sportcoat and laid it carefully to the side. He pulled a trowel out of the bucket and proceeded to spread a bed of thick grey mortar the full width of the entry of the room. Laying down the trowel, he walked to his right to a nearby stack of concrete blocks, brought one back, and placed it firmly on the bed of mortar. With the trowel, he deftly applied mortar to the side of the block and returned to the stack for another one, repeating the task over and over. Without pause, he laid block after block until two-thirds of the seven-foot-high doorway was filled in. Returning with still another block, he heard a low moan from inside the room.

"Goddamn it, what the hell happened?" Wiggs groaned. "Shit, I'm bleeding. Aisquith, where the fuck are you?"

Wiggs was still on the floor, writhing in pain with his hands holding the back of his crushed skull. Aisquith was surprised to hear from him given the severity of his wound, but now was glad he had a chance to talk to him.

"I'm right here, Wiggsy. But I'm a little busy at the moment," he said cheerfully. He put the block up on top of another then scooped more mortar on the trowel and slathered it on the side of the block and the top of the one next to it. The blocks were now above his eye level so he put his hands on them and pulled himself up so he could talk into the room. It was pitch black in there now.

"I'm almost finished though." Aisquith who let himself down and shoved another block in the opening.

"What the hell's going on?" Wiggs croaked. Just four more blocks would seal Wiggs' tomb. He suddenly realized what was happening.

"Goddamn you, Aisquith. Let me out of here. What the fuck are you doing?"

Wiggs heard a burst of laughter from the other side of the wall and saw another block fill in the doorway. Only a small stream of light now shone through the gap at the top. He felt small clumps of mortar falling down on him as Aisquith laid another bed of mortar for the next block to rest on. He crawled over to the doorway and tried to pull himself up but fell down clutching his head in agony.

"You bastard, lemme outta here," he wimpered. Aisquith could tell he was starting to cry, which made him happy.

" I'm doing a damn good job laying up block for the first time, don't you think? I know it's getting dark in there, but I think you can see that the wall's pretty plumb. All these years, seeing masons put up block walls, I must have picked up the skill just by watching. Isn't that amazing?"

"For God's sakes, man, get me out of here. Are you fuckin' mad? What have I done to you?"

The question resonated in Aisquith's mind. What had he ever done to him? He smiled as he replayed every insult and threat Wiggs had ever made.

"Why, you're going to take my roof away, for one thing."

"Your roof? This is all about your fuckin' roof?"

"Yes." Another block was hoisted into the opening. Lifting forty-pound blocks above his head was beginning to wear Aisquith out. There was only one block left to put up. Wiggs couldn't escape, so he sat down on the last block and took a short break.

"Come on. The joke's over, lemme out. I swear I'll never touch your design. I'll tell 'em your roof doesn't cost that much. I swear," pleaded Wiggs in a pathetic voice.

"Ah, come on, Wiggs. You know you're lying. You'd say anything to get out of here. Besides, it's in a contractor's nature to destroy the design. You couldn't help yourself."

"I'll die in here, you bastard," Wiggs whimpered. "This is a fuckin' tomb."

"That's the whole idea, dumb ass. Did you ever happen to read "The Tell-Tale Heart" by Edgar Allan Poe in English class? Ooops, I'm sorry. I forgot that you only took auto shop in high school. They wouldn't have had Poe in those Dick and Jane books you were assigned"

"You're fuckin' crazy." Wiggs was sobbing now.

"You just never understood that beauty belongs to the cultivated and educated. People who can appreciate the importance of art and culture. Can you imagine what would happen to civilization if guys like you were responsible for art and beauty? There would *be* no civilization. We'd be back swinging in the trees. Can't have contractors being designers."

"Help ... someone help me," Wiggs screamed in panic. Aisquith was surprised he could muster the strength to shout so loud. He had read that in the face of certain death, people summon up superhuman strength to save themselves. Maybe that was Wiggs now. But it didn't matter, Wiggs could shoot off a shotgun and no one would hear.

"It's okay to scream, Wiggs. Get it all out of your system. You'll feel much better. Go ahead and vent that anger."

"Help me, for God's sakes."

"You're out of luck. With work stopped here, there isn't going to be anyone around to help you for a while."

There was no more screaming, just a constant sobbing coming from behind the concrete block wall. Rested, Aisquith stood up.

"I have another change order for you Wiggs. You're being deleted from the job, which means big cost savings for the client. You won't be around to rip them off anymore."

"Aisquith ... I'm begging you!"

Aisquith picked up the roll of the steel shop drawings Wiggs had left outside the room and shoved them through the remaining opening.

"Here, I won't be needing these. It's a tad dark in there and you may have some trouble reading them, but it'll pass the time for you." Aisquith hoisted the last block into place abruptly, cutting off Wiggs' sobbing. He was pleasantly surprised by the soundproofing quality of the block. He would make a note to himself to use more block on future jobs. The block would also seal in the smell of Wiggs body as it started to rot. He had heard of neighbors summoning the police when they smelled something dead in the apartment next door.

He stepped back a few paces to admire his handiwork. Using the rounded end of the wooden handle of the trowel, he forced it along all the mortar joints to compress them and give them neat concave profiles.

"Important to tool the joints. Good workmanship is a must," he chuckled to himself.

Aisquith threw the trowel into the almost empty plastic bucket and reached for his sportcoat. He was relieved that he hadn't dropped any mortar on the front of his pleated khaki trousers. Aisquith put on the jacket and, with the bucket in hand, turned to leave. He stopped to take a last look at the wall. He smiled broadly and walked over to it and gently patted it as if it were the rump of a horse. Putting his cheek right against the wall, he spoke in a loud voice.

"Sleep tight, Wiggs. And keep in touch."

Aisquith walked back through the basement, swinging the bucket back and forth like a happy child and whistling "The Toreador Song." Always glad to discover talents he never knew he had, he decided then and there to design a small brick shed in the rear of his Roland Park home and actually build it all by himself.

24

Aisquith had a date to meet Paul Griffin at the Owl Bar in the Belevedere at six. Aisquith's own career had been a major disappointment, but it hadn't hit the rock bottom of the profession--designing tract housing, which is how his friend Griffin made a living. He produced countless variations of vinyl-clad colonial houses, some with two-car garages, some with three. All of his projects had waspy names like the last names of the guys on the Addington board--the Kensington, the Carrollton, the Middleton. Even if the entire subdivision were populated by Jews, the models bore Waspy names. There would never be a subdivision home called the Zuckerman or the Cohen.

Each model home offered an amazing range of optional choices. Big bay windows, porches, walk out basements, family rooms, French doors. Griffin cranked out model after model without complaint. To Aisquith's amazement, he seemed to take a real pride in them even though he knew the rest of the profession denigrated what he did.

Aisquith was at the bar drinking a beer when Griffin came strolling in. He gave Aisquith a big wave. He might have been the grand marshal of the Rose Bowl parade. Aisquith stood up to meet him.

"Grif, how's it going?"

"Same old shit, just a different day, Al. But what can I do? I had the chance to go to law school twenty years ago. Could've followed the dark side of the force and become wealthy."

Aisquith laughed heartily. "I'm glad you stayed an architect and took a vow of poverty."

"So how's the museum going? Heard from my structural engineer the steel's going up."

They walked over to a table, sat down, and motioned for the waiter.

"We were into the steel, but now's there's a hang up with the environmental permit."

"So how long will it hold you up?" Griffin asked.

"Can't tell yet. So what are you up to?" asked Aisquith.

"Just finished sixty townhouses at Cromwell Farms up in Bel Air. Now I'm starting Wellington Square in Towson."

Aisquith took a drink of his beer and looked at Griffin. There was a warm, clubby feeling in the bar that made him feel unusually loquacious.

"You like residential work, don't you?"

"Let's say I've learned to like it," Griffin said with an air of resignation.

Aisquith had correctly imagined that Griffin had once had high hopes for architectural greatness but had thrown in the towel for the sake of earning a steady living.

"I give 'em what they want, Allan. And they want closet space and a formal dining room they never use," he said jovially. "The Wellington looks like a billion other colonial houses but it pays for my kids' college tuition." Griffin sipped his beer and popped a couple of peanuts into his mouth. He then raised his glass in a mock toast to Aisquith.

"Here's to your success, Allan. You know, I envy you."

Aisquith was taken back by the compliment. He had never heard Griffin say anything so touchy-feely. "Thanks,' he said uncertainly.

"I never look at the architectural magazines anymore. I don't want to know what's current. Used to make me feel ashamed of what I was doing. The Hampton doesn't quite have the creative spark of Gehry's Guggenheim in Bilbao," Griffin said, laughing.

Aisquith smiled and suddenly felt ashamed of the way he treated Griffin's work. Who was he to judge? Griffin accepted his fate with grace and good humor. He knew he wasn't capable of that himself.

"Back in '76, I designed a house that looked like Mies' Barcelona Pavillion--all glass and steel. It was beautiful. I spent hours detailing every square inch of it. It was supposed to be a prototype for a house in an upscale subdivision out on Long Island. The developer, an old man named Dugan, looked at the design and practically laughed in my face. I still can remember the stink of his breath. He said that either I come back the next morning with something a banker would want to live in or don't come back again."

"And what happened?"

"The next morning, I came in carrying a design for the Rockingham, a four-bedroom colonial any banker in America would love to live in."

They both laughed at once.

"Allan, I give them what they want. I let others put up the creative fight. What you're doing out there on the Patuxent Cliffs is pretty special. You stood your ground and got a terrific design. You must be proud."

Aisquith lowered his eyes and stared at his half-finished mug of beer. "No, not so proud, really."

"You're going to be remembered for that building for a long time to come. And deep down, that's what every architect wants. Just one great building that carries on for him after he's turned to dust. Like a son or daughter would."

25

Aisquith spotted Mabel Marston about 200 yards away, a speck in the distance. She reminded him of the scene in "Lawrence of Arabia" when Omar Shariff appears on the horizon of the desert, then gets closer and closer. Aisquith was waiting by the corner of the foundation that hung over the conservation boundary. He could make out Marston's green cardigan sweater and sensible rubber-soled shoes. He turned away and gazed out onto the bay. It was a magnificent day, another cerulean blue sky without a cloud in sight.

When he heard Marston a few feet behind him, he wheeled around and, with an enormous grin, bellowed a jovial hello.

"So great to see you, Ms. Marston, on such a beautiful day."

His greeting literally knocked her over. She skidded to a stop on the wet grass and her feet almost went out from under her.

"Hello Mr. Aisquith, it's nice to see you again," she stammered as she regained her balance. Marston was taken aback by his friendly manner. Since leaving her car, she had been bracing for all-out war.

"Allan, call me Allan. Glad you could make it today. I thought it would be best to meet here to work things out."

"I hadn't expected to hear from you so soon."

"Time is money and the building committee wants to me to resolve this as quickly as possible."

She was visibly pleased by his friendly response. "That's very sensible. So what have you decided?" she asked cautiously.

"To move the building back behind the new boundary line, just as you wanted."

Marston would have been no less dumbfounded if some man declared she was the most beautiful thing in the universe. She looked over at the corner of the building and back at Aisquith.

Marston thought she might have misunderstood him. "You are or you aren't moving the building?"

"I *are*," he replied with a horse laugh.

Marston smiled brightly and relaxed her scrawny body. She could let down her guard now that she had won the battle. Aisquith read her body language and continued. He held up a roll of drawings as if it were the Olympic torch.

"We can look at the drawing right here. It's already been changed."

Aisquith unrolled the drawing and stepped next to Marston. He was so close to her he could smell her organic herbal shampoo. She set her environmentally correct cloth briefcase on the grass and stared intently at the drawing, holding one end while Aisquith held the other.

"Yes, I see. That's much better," she said like a teacher complimenting a seven-year-old on a drawing of a cow. She turned around and pointed to the imaginary line behind her. "See, now it won't be such an encroachment on the flora and fauna of the Cliffs. It's absolutely imperative that the birds be given as much space as possible."

"You're absolutely right. And I want to apologize for the things I said to you. Things were going bad for me that day and I took it out on you. I'm very sorry. I didn't treat you like a professional."

Marston looked down at her sensible shoes and shyly said, "It's all right, people get angry, especially when they have to comply with environmental regulations. They just don't understand the enormous impact man has on the natural environment."

Aisquith nodded. "Again I apologize. See, I redesigned the rear of the museum so it's way behind the line. He sounded almost boastful as he pointed back to the drawing. "Even further back than the law requires. As soon as construction can start up again, we'll rip up the foundation and repour."

"That's terrific," Marston gushed and looked up into his eyes.

Aisquith bent his head down to her ear and asked roguishly, "And when can construction start up again?"

"Right away. I have the permit in my briefcase and I can sign off on it right now."

"Grrrrrreat," Aisquith exploded, imitating Tony the Tiger. He folded up the drawing and handed it to her. "I know you'll want this for your records."

"Yes, I do. Thank you very much," she said as she knelt on the grass and unzipped her briefcase and fumbled for the permit. Marston was in a state of bliss. She thought she'd be fighting in court over this for months, but she'd won a swift victory. She couldn't wait to sign.

Aisquith snatched a blue rollerball pen from the inside pocket of his tweed coat and handed it to her. Still kneeling, Marston took it and quickly scribbled her name and date at the bottom of the sheet. She stood up and handed Aisquith the permit and the pen. He folded it and jammed it in his side pocket, then extended his hand to help her up. "Again, I apologize for the way I acted," he said in a humbled voice.

Marston smiled and looked straight into his eyes. "I know changing the design was hard for you, but the law is the law. The environment is a fragile entity that must be protected at all costs. Especially here. The Cliffs have been part of the migratory path for many species of birds for centuries."

"You're absolutely right. You know man is a disrupting force. Wherever he plants his foot, the harmonies of nature are thrown in discord, " Aisquith said, shaking his head sorrowfully from side to side.

Marston stared at him for a few seconds. She sensed chemistry and immediately started daydreaming he would ask her out. It was hard to find a man with a sensitive nature. In truth, it was hard for her to find a man, period.

"There are few landscapes in America that have remained untouched," she said in a mournful tone. "It's crucial that we preserve this ecosystem. I never wanted to see any building up here at all."

Aisquith lightly placed his hand on her shoulder. He sensed that she was warming up to him but still didn't want her to start screaming rape. You could never tell about eco-feminists.

"You wouldn't have budged on the permit would you?" he asked gently.

"No, I wouldn't have let you build," she said as she picked up her briefcase from the grass. "I just couldn't. You can understand that, can't you?"

"Of course." Aisquith started walking away from the Cliffs towards a field that had just been bulldozed and regraded. Marston followed him like a puppy. Like DeMille's Moses gesturing toward the promised land, he waved his arm in a 180-degree arc at the field before them. "Our landscape has been completely transformed since the arrival of the Europeans. Our virgin prairies became wheatfields and towns. Our wetlands were drained and filled. Forests were cleared for lumber." He gently took Marston by the elbow. She felt a surge of excitement shoot up her spine.

"Rivers dammed for power," she chimed in, now really getting a rush. She thought of what she would wear on their first date. Maybe her peasant blouse made by Bolivian peasants at non-sweatshop wages.

"Suburban sprawl eating up our farmland," Aisquith moaned.

"Habitats swept away, every day."

"Destruction of the entire planet," he lamented.

She couldn't hold back now.

"It's the wetlands that are so critical. They're so important to the ecosystem. You know without them, the migratory paths of thousands and thousands of species of birds are so . . ."

In mid-sentence, Marston dropped straight into the ground, literally sucked through the earth as if the underworld had reached up, grabbed her by the ankles, and pulled her down. A fraction of a second later, Aisquith heard a loud splash.

He looked down expressionlessly at a two-foot diameter hole in the earth, then suddenly jerked his head around to see if anyone was watching. The construction site was still deserted. He then knelt down by the hole and peered into the darkness.

"Mabel, old girl, are you down there?"

Seconds passed until he heard a low moan drift up from the darkness.

"God, what happened?"

"You've fallen into a septic tank." He spoke matter-a-factly, as if that occurred all the time.

"My God, how'd that happen?" Marston cried out. "I think I broke my ankle."

"Well, that's easy. You see Mabe, there's no public sewer way out here, so we had to install this gigantic septic system to handle all the waste from the museum. "You know, all the shit from all the patrons. So I covered up the hole to one of the tanks with a piece of tar paper and then I covered it with dirt so it looked like the rest of the earth. You walked on it and then, plop. I guess you can surmise from that smell, that some of construction workers have been testing the system."

"Why the hell did you do that?" Her voice was close to a scream.

"I had to, my girl. It's what you were going to do with my building."

"Your building?" she yelled in absolute amazement, momentarily forgetting about the excruciating pain in her ankle.

"I just couldn't move it back. That meant changing the design and I couldn't do that."

"This is all about your goddamn ugly building?" she shouted in a voice that was a mixture of disbelief and impending doom.

"Now you've hurt my feelings."

Marston was in a frenzy. Aisquith could hear her trying to stand up but falling back down with a splash. She tried again and again with the same results. He laughed when he heard her cursing her head off.

"You still there," he asked with a laugh.

"Your museum looks like a fuckin' airplane hanger. Now, you shit, get me out of here," she replied from the stygian darkness.

"Come on, now," Aisquith said in a mocking tone. "Doesn't it merge with the site?"

"Fuck no. All you architects say that bullshit. It destroys the site, you asshole. It's a crime to put a building there at all."

Aisquith roared with laughter. He really admired unvarnished honesty in a person.

"At least it'll have a real nice view of the bay out the back. It'll only be fifty yards from the edge of the Cliffs."

"What do you mean?" she shrieked.

"The building stays where it is."

"You'll never get a permit to build it."

"You mean . . . *this* permit?" he said as pulled the folded paper out of his pocket and waved it in the air. "The permit which I'll fax to the museum's attorneys so they can get the your court order lifted?"

"You shit, you goddamn shit. You can't get away with this."

"Can't I?"

"You changed the drawing. I saw it."

"Yea, I know but I won't be needing that anymore. Here, you can have it." Aisquith picked up her briefcase and with both hands flung it down the hole.

A yelp of pain rose from the hole. He smiled. He couldn't see her because of the great depth of the tank, but he knew she was right beneath the opening.

"You can't put that building so close to the Cliffs," she yelped.

Aisquith laughed hysterically. He actually had a great deal of respect for her. A true environmentalist to the core. Here she was about to be entombed and all she cared about was her ecosystem.

"You know, I admire you. I really admire your dedication."

"You bastard, get me out of here," she shrieked. "Right now. The joke's gone far enough."

"Joke? I'm afraid you're quite mistaken. This is no joke."

"Let me out, goddamn you."

"You know, old girl, everytime I flush a toilet, I'm going to think of you. A septic system as you know, is very environmentally friendly. You'll slowly decompose into a liquid with the rest of the waste matter, then percolate harmlessly into the soil. You'll become one with the earth. What a perfect way for a tree hugger to die."

Aisquith walked about ten feet from the hole to a mound of dirt. He pushed the dirt aside with both hands, uncovering a concrete plug about two feet in diameter. He lifted it and carried it back to the hole. Marston was still screaming at him. Instead of pleading for her life, she kept cursing him up and down about his building. He had to admire her courage and conviction.

"Well, I don't mean to cut you off but I got things to do today. So I'll just say goodbye and good luck. Don't worry, you'll get used to the smell after a while."

Aisquith dropped the heavy plug into the hole, obliterating Marston's screams. He covered the plug, which was a few inches below the level of the ground, with dirt. In a year when they started using the system, there would be little left of her. By then the bugs would have had her for dinner. But at least it was an all-natural way to go.

He rubbed his hands together to shake off the dirt, then smoothed out the dirt over the plug with his Land's End boots so it blended in with the surrounding earth. Satisfied with his handiwork, he put his hands in his pockets and walked briskly to Marston's car. He smiled to himself. She wouldn't have liked what he was about to do with her car. Dumping it in the pond in the wetland was ecologically incorrect. It could destroy the delicate ecostructure of the spotted tadpole.

26

The steel for the entire building was in place. Aisquith loved this part of the construction. He could really see the whole building fleshed out now. This was the point when he could judge whether he had made the right design decisions. He had always found the whole process magical. His lines on paper had been transformed into this huge swooping structure. He walked around the building a dozen times, savoring every angle.

There had been times when the structure of a building was up that he realized the design was a flop. He cringed when he looked at it. He wished he could snap his fingers and his mistake would vanish so he could start all over. Yes, he would say, I could make this part lower next time. But there wouldn't be a next time. This was it and he would just have to live with it. There wasn't a tarpaulin big enough to cover his artistic misjudgment. It would stand there for the next fifty or a hundred years. There were some buildings he had screwed up that he never laid eyes on again.

But not this one. He had taken his time and didn't give up until he had what he wanted. He knew deep down that his talent was real and he could produce a first rate building. The nineteen years of mediocrity and failure were fast becoming a distant memory. His whole life seemed to spring from this very moment. He stayed next to his creation the entire afternoon like a mother who could not leave her child.

Aisquith's legs were tired from the constant walking. He sat down on the grass. With his knees pulled up to his chin, he gazed out at his museum.

"What a beautiful sight." The stentorian voice came from directly behind him.

Aisquith twisted his body around and came face to face with a pair of twill pants. He jerked his head up and saw Packard towering over him like Gulliver over a Lilliputian. Embarassed, Aisquith jumped to his feet, almost butting the policeman's chin with his head.

"Inspector Packard," he wheezed. He was dizzy from standing up too fast.

"Detective Packard, Mr. Aisquith. You've been watching too many of those British mystery series on PBS."

Aisquith liked his sense of humor. Most cops would think PBS meant policeman's bowling society.

"Yep, I watch them religiously. Inspector Morse is my idea of a police detective."

Packard laughed. " I'm afraid he's a bit refined for the Maryland State Police force. But he does drink a lot. He does have that in common with a lot of state cops."

"Well, what brings you here, detective?" Aisquith replied, impressed by his wit but anxious to get rid of him.

"Your office said you'd be out here, and indeed here you are, admiring your creation. I don't blame you a bit. It's very special."

"Thank you, I appreciate that. You seem to know a lot about architecture."

"Not much really. I took a general architectural history course in college."

"Don't tell me you wanted to become an architect." Aisquith laughed, trying to keep this discourse light.

"Nope, I always wanted to be a cop. But art and architecture always fascinated me."

"So where'd you go to school?"

"Hopkins."

"That's interesting."

"You mean it's unusual for a cop to be college-educated at all, let alone graduate from Johns Hopkins." Packard grinned as he said this.

Aisquith smiled back with delight. The guy was sharp. He should be scared to death of him but he was enjoying his company.

"Touché, Detective."

"Must be great to design something like that," the policeman remarked as he turned to face the building.

"Yes, it's been a great experience for me, the high point of my career so far."

"I bet. You'd do almost anything to see it built, I guess," said Packard in a quiet voice.

"You better believe it. I've never worked so hard on anything in my life. I was extremely lucky to get such a commission. You know, I . . . " Aisquith realized he was rambling on and stopped himself. He knew Packard was there to ask questions and he wanted to get it over. "Any news of Mr. Quill?"

"No, all dead end leads. But I'm afraid I've another problem."

"What's that?" asked Aisquith sheepishly.

"Paul Wiggs, your general contractor, has disappeared."

"I haven't seen him in a couple of weeks. I always deal with his superintendent, Dan Topolewski, but that happens all the time with contractors. Once a job is under way, they're racing around to other job sites and you don't see them very often."

"We thought he might have taken a vacation when the job was shut down over that environmental permit. But his wife said he didn't have anything planned like that. He had other jobs going on. We've checked all the airports and haven't found his Mercedes."

"He never said anything about taking a trip to me."

"Did he know the environmental thing was going to be settled so quickly?"

"Not when I saw him last. That was during the shutdown."

"I see. Did Wiggs ever discuss any problems with his subcontractors? Did any come to you saying that they weren't getting paid?"

"No, I never get involved with that side of the job. He handled all that."

"Did you two get along?"

Aisquith sensed a trap although he couldn't imagine Packard had connected him with Wiggs' disappearance.

"Listen, Detective, architects and contractors are like lions and hyenas. Natural-born enemies."

"I can guess who the lion is," said Packard with a broad smile.

"RRRRRiiiight," Aisquith exclaimed in a mock roar.

Packard threw his head back and laughed heartily.

"You can look it up. Hyena and contractor are synonyms *in Roget's Thesaurus*."

Packard laughed even harder. "Okay, I get it. Wiggs could've had some money problems and maybe had to skip town."

"He is always trying to cut corners on a job and put the money in his pocket. Maybe it finally caught up with him."

"I thought you said no subs came to you about nonpayment."

Aisquith paused and tried to squirm out of the corner he had just painted himself.

" I meant to say these were just rumors."

"Did he ever try to screw you?"

"No, I'd worked with him on one other job before this one, so I knew what to expect. You just have to be tough with him." Aisquith made sure he used have instead of *had*.

"How tough?"

"You have to stand your ground with him, that's all."

"Like your roof?"

Aisquith was startled but didn't show it. He knew that Packard had done his homework by talking to Barton.

"Yes, that's a good case in point. He wanted me to change it completely, but I worked it out with him so it wouldn't cost as much to build."

"You worked it out before he disappeared?"

"Yes, I believe it was about two weeks ago."

"I see. Well, thanks for your time Mr. Aisquith. You have my card if you hear anything from him."

"I'm sure he'll show up sooner or later."

Let's hope so. But that's what we said about Quill. Well, so long."

Aisquith watched Packard walk away, then suddenly turn around.

"Your building seems to have a curse on it," he called out.

"Like King Tut's tomb?" Aisquith laughed with mock nervousness and waved goodbye.

Packard cheerfully returned the wave and walked away. Aisquith watched until he was out of sight. He knew the tweedy figure disappearing over the horizon could put him in the electric chair or whatever means of execution the state of Maryland was using at the present. No way. He wouldn't let that happen to him.

27

The museum was in its sixth month of construction. Aisquith rarely went to the office anymore, leaving the rest of the office's projects to Carlos, including all of the design responsibilities. He knew that made Carlos happy. Aisquith rode a wave of praise and garnered new work before the Addington was even half finished. As a result of the museum commission, two new jobs, both small museums, were about to start the preliminary design phase. It was like winning an Oscar for a role as a madman; all parts offered after that would be madman roles.

It didn't bother him a bit to be typecast. Museum work was the professional pinnacle, where the greatest creativity could be unleashed. One museum was in Texas, the other in Nevada. The museum committees had seen his beautiful renderings in the architectural magazines along with the articles praising the building. If the right magazines said he was brilliant then it must be so. Aisquith milked the drawings for all they were worth, allowing more than one publication use them. He even finagled another article in the the *New York Times*, to let the general public in on the status of his Addington project.

But this morning he needed to attend to some administrative matters. There was one important if personally unpleasant chore to attend to. Carlos pestered him constantly about an even larger share of the partnership. The twenty per cent deal didn't satisfy him. Aisquith's natural instinct as an only child was to hog everything for himself. But if Carlos made good on his recurrent threats to leave, the office would be like a ship without a first mate. Aisquith would have to turn his attention to the smaller, less aesthetically challenging work he didn't really give a damn about, like the expansion of the Hecht Company department store in Towson.

Aisquith almost invariably showed up alone to meet new clients, giving the misleading impression that he personally would handle the design when, in fact, it would be handed off to Carlos the minute he returned to the office. An owner had to hang on to one reliable person to run the show. And if that meant offering Carlos a bigger piece of the pie, so be it. If projects kept coming through the door, there would be plenty of money to go around.

Aisquith asked Grace to fetch Carlos. He didn't want to ask him in personally. It was bad enough that he had to take on a partner. He wanted to summon him like an office boy.

Carlos walked into the office without even knocking, putting Aisquith in a bad humor right off the bat.

"Yes, padrone?" the surly Latin growled.

"Carlos, muchacho, you can have a forty-two per cent share. And that's as high as I'm going. You notice whose name is still on the front door," Aisquith said in a brusque businesslike manner that surprised even him.

Carlos was caught off guard. He hadn't even time to respond to the muchacho slur.

"Well, Allan, I accept your . . . belated offer," he said with a snarl.

Aisquith looked at him impassively. Viscerally, he wanted to piss him off and make him quit.

"And my name on the front door. Aisquith & Ricardo?"

"Aisquith & Partners"

Carlos stared at him for five seconds, an eternity to Aisquith.

"Then my name goes on the letterhead as partner."

"No problem. It'll be in bold type."

Carlos smiled and walked out of the office without a word. Aisquith slumped back into his chair and breathed a sigh of relief that the encounter was done with. Aisquith & Ricardo. He started laughing to himself. He hated ethnic-sounding names, especially if linked to his by an ampersand. Even though it would help his chances of securing government work because he had a minority partner, he wouldn't do it. Hearing the name, most clients would automatically think of Ricky banging on bongos at the Copa with Lucy, Fred, and Ethel cheering him on.

Grace knocked and poked her head through door. "Mr. Barton's on the phone."

"Thanks." Aisquith swiveled around in his chair, pressed the blinking button, and snatched up the receiver.

" This is Allan, how are you?"

" We finally found him, Allan. It took a long time but we did it."

Aisquith thought he might lose control of his bladder. He looked down at his crotch to see if there was a spreading wet spot. His grip on the receiver could have snapped it in two. He swallowed hard and forced the words out of his throat. "Who did you find?"

"Our new museum curator, Dirk Dannon. He used to be with the Brooklyn Museum, but not anymore. He's all ours. He starts in two months, but he's willing to do some coordination and consultation right away. That's why I'm calling. He wants to meet you out at the site tomorrow."

The preceding twenty seconds had been sheer, blind terror. Aisquith looked down again to see whether he'd wet himself. Seeing that he hadn't, he breathed a sigh of relief and cleared his throat.

"That's great Hamilton. I've heard of Dannon, of course, he's done some wonderful things in Brooklyn."

"He singlehandedly arranged the Manet and the John Singer Sargent exhibits at the same time. No one had ever run two blockbusters like that at once."

"Yes, I heard."

"Can you meet us tomorrow morning at ten? Dirk has a few comments about the plans and wants to talk with you."

Aisquith flipped open his appointment book and saw the one o'clock slot filled in but it was only Gavone, his guinea developer. "No problem, I'll see you there."

Aisquith hung up the phone, leaned back in his chair, and looked up at the ceiling. "He has comments about the plans" was always a bad omen.

28

Work on the building had greatly accelerated. The interior was still just a shell, but the copper cladding and all the glass had now been installed, giving the outside a completely finished look. Aisquith arrived at the site at 9:30 and walked twice around the building. Usually he could nitpick a hundred things he wished he could have done differently, but this time all was seemingly perfect.

At five minutes to ten he didn't have time to walk around the building again, so he just stood there gazing at it like a proud father. He walked toward the rear of the museum. The workmen had started constructing the sculpture garden, which was sited between the building and the edge of the Cliffs.

Aisquith was very pleased with the progress. Now that Wiggs was gone, everything ran smoothly. Wiggs' replacement, Dan Topoleski, was honest and easy to work with. He built from the drawings without comment. The perfect subservient contractor.

Aisquith watched the men set the thick granite pavers for the garden in a herringbone pattern. Set in a wet mortar base on top of a concrete slab, the pavers would stay in place for a long time. Wiggs would have set them on an unstable sand base and charged for the concrete nevertheless.

The gravel base on which the concrete slab would be placed was being prepared. A six-inch bed of gravel was compressed by an enormous roller with a front wheel six feet in diameter. The stones were crushed into a perfectly flat plane by several tons of pressure. The paved sculpture garden would extend about thirty yards from the glass-wall at the rear of the museum, then a lawn would gently roll down to the edge of the Cliffs. Sculptures on pedestals would dot the lawn. It was all part of a carefully planned circulation path Aisquith had designed to lead the visitor from the lobby to the cliff edge to enjoy the view.

Focused intently on the rolling operation, Aisquith didn't hear Barton and Dannon come up behind him. He jumped when Barton tapped him on the shoulder. He turned to face a distinquished looking man in his late forties.

"Allan, meet Dirk Dannon, our new director." Barton almost shouted the name.

Aisquith could see Dannon was amused that he was startled. It was a bad first impression. He was embarrassed by his reaction, but made no apology for it.

"I'm very glad to meet you, Mr. Dannon. I've heard great things about your work in Brooklyn and also the Toledo Museum."

"Thank you very much. That's very kind of you to say," Dannon replied in a pronounced Princeton lockjaw accent. He was impeccably tailored in an Armani suit and Gucci loafers. His full head of blond hair contrasted nicely with his deeply tanned face. His good looks mesmerized Aisquith.

"It took us a while, but we got the man we wanted," Barton blustered jovially, snapping Aisquith further out of his trance. Dannon, flattered by the praise, shyly looked down at his expensive shoes.

"You'll be in charge of quite a collection,"Aisquith said, with sincerity and admiration.

"I know. It will be quite a challenge, but I'm sure I'm up to it." The arrogant reply instantly erased the admiration. Aisquith almost grimaced. This jerk is very full of himself, he thought. That could mean trouble. He tried to ignore the egocentric remark and resolved to carry on an intelligent and friendly conversation with Dannon. "The interior spaces of the galleries are just starting to take shape. Did you get a chance to walk through them?"

"I just did and I'd like to . . ., Dannon began with hauteur, but Barton's cheerful voice cut him off.

"Allan, Dirk has a few questions about . . ."

Dannon obviously wasn't accustomed to being interrupted, even by the man who was probably paying him an enormous salary.

"The exhibition spaces. I've got a few problems with them. But because we're in the construction stage we certainly can rectify some of the most serious ones."

"Which spaces did you have a problem with?" said Aisquith calmly. He sounded like a pediatrician asking a six-year-old where does it hurt?

"All the spaces, actually. I have problems with all the spaces. They all have to be redone."

Although he felt the old rage welling up inside of him and about to fly out his mouth, Aisquith's brain quickly sent out a signal to stand down.

"I know when I started to design the interior there was no director on board to work with but the committee told me to proceed, so I . . ."

Barton's portly figure came between the two like a referee. His 250 pounds separated them and defused the iminent battle of words.

"Allan, maybe you and Dirk should schedule a meeting to go over all this."

"Well, that's what we're doing right at this minute, Hamilton," Aisquith said, staring straight into Dannon's eyes.

"Please, old boy, no need to get your back up. It's not as if the galleries have all been finished. Changes can be simply made," Dannon said in a seriously patronizing manner.

"Changes?"

"Certainly, old boy. Some parts can be reworked without much additional cost. I've already talked to Barton here about it."

Aisquith shifted his gaze to Barton, who smiled meekly and looked down at his shoes.

"I guess you feel the design should be subservient to the collection?" Aisquith said, now grinning.

"There you have it, old boy," Dannon exclaimed, as delighted as if he had finally made sense to a dimwitted child.

"Well, I see you two can sort this out without me, so I'll be off," said Barton in a relieved voice.

"I think we can work this out. Can't we, Dirk?" Aisquith said as graciously as he could manage, for Barton's sake.

"Absolutely. You go on, Hamilton. We drove separately, so I don't want to keep you any longer. I'll call you first thing tomorrow at your office."

"Great. I'll schedule a committee meeting after you both have settled on the design." Barton, who despised confrontation, spoke almost gleefully. Eager to get out of the line of fire, he practically trotted back to his car. Aisquith had never seen him exert himself so. He half expected to look up in a moment and find Barton dead on the ground from a heart attack.

"Okay. What would you like changed?" asked Aisquith, like a waiter asking, "What will you have?"

"First the hanging bridges with the statue of the Spartan on it."

"That's the main focus of the entry lobby. I thought it was the collection's most prized piece."

"It is, it is. Even though it's a second-rate piece in my opinion. The angle of view of the damn thing is wrong. The bridges are okay. I know that's *your* big aesthetic interior statement so we won't touch them."

That crack really irritated Aisquith, but he kept calm. "So what's wrong then?"

"The statue should be moved to the upper bridge. It's so damn big. It seems cramped on the lower bridge."

"The committee thought that's where it should go."

"The committee doesn't know shit. They'd stick the thing on the roof over the front door if they could."

"And what else?" Aisquith inquired patiently.

"The gallery for the Courbet paintings shouldn't be ramped like that. It's too distracting for the visitors. It should be all on *one* level."

"Is that it?"

"And then there's the gallery for the nineteenth-century American paintings. There's hardly any wall space for the size of collection we have. And that design to let natural light in won't work. I saw something like that in St. Louis. It was an absolute waste of money."

"Finished?" Aisquith began to write down the director's criticisms in his pocket sketchbook, again, like a waiter taking down a customer's order.

"Not quite, old boy. The worst space is for the most important part of the collection, the French Impressionists. Does it have to be one big curving space like that? Why do you guys always have to throw curves in, huh? Can't it be a series of small intimate spaces?"

"Okay."

Aisquith seemed to have an out-of-body experience. He watched a calm, cool, collected man withstand a tidal wave of abuse without blinking an eye or throwing a punch.
He was quite pleased with himself that he stood steady as a rock. He smiled and pulled out his appointment book from his inside jacket pocket.

"I've got my book right here, so let's schedule a meeting."

"They're working on the galleries as we speak, so let's do it as soon as possible," Dannon whined.

"That's all right, I'll tell the G.C. to shift the crew on to something else for a day or two.

"Tomorrow at five?" Dannon asked, looking at his Palm Pilot.

"Fine. The construction crews will have gone home by then and it won't be so noisy. I'll meet you right here in the garden."

"Good. There're some things that need to be redone here as well."

"Such as?" Aisquith took out his sketchbook again to take down notes.

"The placement of all the outdoor pieces will change, so your paving patterns will change too."

"We'll have a working meeting. I'll bring the drawings and some tracing paper and we can rework the spaces. "

"That would be wonderful. The sooner we redesign all the galleries, the better." Dannon seemed delighted to find such a subservient architect.

"Fine, I'll see you tomorrow, right here," Aisquith said over his shoulder as he walked away.

"Oh yes, the conservation labs need to be redone," Dannon shouted after him.

Aisquith nodded his head and rolled his eyes as he walked on. His head throbbed from Dannon's browbeating by the time he got back to the office. He threw open the reception area doors and stormed past Grace as she tried to hand him his pink message slips. Grigor was coming toward him, but stopped when Aisquith glared at him. Now, for sure, was not a good time to ask for Thursday and Friday off.

Aisquith headed into the studio, stopped, and yelled for Kurt, who popped his head over the top of his cubicle like a gopher peeking out of his hole.

"Kurt, bring me the quarter-inch exhibition gallery drawings. *Now*. There's a revision I want you to make."

29

Dannon and Aisquith found a stretch of meadow in the sculpture garden that hadn't been bulldozed. They sat on the ground with the drawings unrolled in front of them. The site was deserted since all the crews had left at four.

Aisquith had determined to be cordial to Dannon but it was getting harder by the minute. A man like Dannon, continuously successful and constantly reminded of his "greatness," was bound to have an ego the size of Mount Everest. But even though he was a bastard through and through Aisquith still admired guys like Dannon who were tops in their field. He even envied Dannon's incredible good looks and had to stop himself from staring at him. Dannon had already noticed the stare and was hoping Aisquith wasn't going to start hitting on him. His looks probably brought lots of unsolicitated attention from both men and women, which got quite tiresome.

"I'm glad we can go over all this out here after quitting time. I couldn't hear myself think with all that noise here yesterday," Dannon whined.

The persistently bitchy manner made Aisquith wonder whether Dannon practiced the unspeakable vice of the ancient Greeks. "I know. It's hard to shout over all the noise," he said consolingly.

Dannon shifted smoothly from civility to his bossy, arrogant style. He continued his withering critique of the sculpture garden. "As I said yesterday, the layout of all the pieces has to be changed. The small Rodin piece must go over to the right. There are too many pieces on the north end. We have to spread them out a bit. Then the Henry Moore figure has to be shifted down about ten yards or so. Are you with me?" Dannon sensed his architect's mind was wandering.

"Why, yes," Aisquith said, his annoyance barely contained.

"Well, you aren't writing any of this down. It's going to be a lot to remember."

A rich and successful guy like Dannon probably had a personal assistant. Aisquith pitied the poor devil."If you want all the pieces rearranged, then that means all the paving must be torn up," he said.

"Fine. Just do it. The committee won't have a problem with it. Then there's the problem with the fountain."

"What's the problem? That's where the Calder piece is going. The piping has already been laid." Aisquith knew *he* now sounded like a whiner. Be careful, he reminded himself.

"The Calder can still go in the center of the fountain, but the fountain should be at the end of the garden instead of smack in the middle of the whole damn thing. You made the building completely assymetrical, so why all the symmetry in the garden for Chrissake?"

"I thought it would be a nice counterpoint, producing a sort of duality and . . .

"Please Allan, I've heard every bullshit, convoluted, theoretical explanation for a design from an architect there is in the universe. You made the garden symmetrical because you felt like it. That's what it comes down to. If you fuckin' architects were just honest about your aesthetic decisions, there'd be ten billion tons less bullshit in this world."

Aisquith was furious even though every word this Princeton-educated twit said was true. He wanted to smash him in the mouth and cure his lockjawed diction. Instead he smiled graciously and nodded what he thought was a patrician-like nod. Although he had a Harvard degree, he knew he wasn't part of Dannon's social class. It was Chaucersburg all over again. He knew that Dannon knew this, too.

"All right, we'll move the fountain. So where would you like it?" Aisquith knew exactly where he would like to put it in relation to Dannon's anatomy.

"Right before the lawn slopes down to the Cliffs. See where that roller is parked?

Aisquith looked behind him at the huge piece of equipment and grimaced.

"That means all the piping will have to be re-routed. And the slope will have to re-graded to make a level area to set the fountain."

"I told you once," Dannon snapped, "the committee won't have a problem with that."

Aisquith was glad he hadn't chosen to be a servant as his life's work. He would have been a complete failure. But, for now, he played the part.

"As you wish. We should start marking up the prints to note all these changes. My staff will need the notes to revise the drawings on the computer." Aisquith pulled a red marker out of his side jacket pocket and handed it to Dannon, who proceeded to draw on the plan of the sculpture garden.

"All right, we should also shift the Brancusi over about twenty feet. Could I use your scale?" He stretched out his hand like a surgeon asking a nurse for a scalpel.

Aisquith stood up and searched the pockets of his jacket and pants for his six-inch scale. "Damn. I must have left it in the glove compartment of my car."

"I'd think an architect would always have a scale on him," Dannon said testily without looking up from the drawing.

Aisquith stood silent for a few seconds restraining himself from kicking the kneeling director in the face. Dannon noticed the pregnant pause and looked up.

"Well, are you going to get the scale or not?"

Aisquith looked out across the bay and then back at Dannon. His policy of appeasement was about to come to an end. He couldn't stomach the bastard any longer.

"Yes, I'll be right back."

Dannon returned to studying the drawings while Aisquith slowly walked up to the granite-paved patio. He passed the roller and the shoulder-high stacks of pavers. He decided to walk through the museum to get to his car, which was parked out in front. Let the prick wait, he grumbled to himself. When he got to the glass doors of the window wall, he heard a curious rumbling sound. Immediately thinking it was an oncoming thunderstorm, he turned away from the building and looked up to the sky. There was nothing but a brilliant blue, cloudless sky. The rumbling continued. As he lowered his eyes, he noticed something yellow moving very slowly off to his right.

Transfixed, he walked slowly toward the moving object, which was getting smaller and smaller. In an instant of terror, Aisquith knew it was the paving roller. His eyes widened while his brain frantically tried to remember the spot where he'd left Dannon. When he pinpointed Dannon sitting directly in the path of the roller, he broke into a sprint.

"Dirk, get out of the way," he screamed at the top of his lungs. He tripped and fell to the ground, but quickly picked himself up and continued running.

Dannon, absorbed in the drawing, heard a high-pitched sound, far off. He looked up from the drawing toward the bay and saw a hawk swooping high above the edge of theCliffs.

"What a beautiful sight," he murmured. Then he heard an odd rumbling sound. He looked directly above him to see if there was a thunderstorm brewing but realized the sound was coming from behind. He turned around and saw a wall of steel rolling toward him.

Aisquith sprinted down the slope directly behind the runaway machine, screaming Dannon's name. The roller blocked his view of Dannon. In a second he heard a simultaneous crushing and squishing sound and stopped dead in his tracks. Aisquith watched in horror as the roller continued on, going faster and faster down the slope until it disappeared over the edge of the Cliffs like a toy truck.

Aisquith started running again, but skidded to a halt when he got to the spot where Dannon had been sitting. His eyes widened in horror and he doubled over and violently threw up. When the heaving stopped, he straightened up but couldn't look at the splatter that had been the brilliant young Dirk Dannon. He walked slowly up the slope through the museum to the front entry where his car was parked. There was no need to hurry. Even if he had a giant spatula to scrape up the museum director and rush him to the emergency room, he couldn't be saved. Not even the heroic doctors on *ER* could save Dannon now.

As Aisquith walked to his car to get his cell phone, he looked up and saw a cloud of dust about fifty yards away. Through the haze he thought he recognized the rear of a blue Chevy Cavalier.

30

Packard glared at Aisquith for almost twenty seconds before saying anything. He was sitting in the upholstered chair across from Aisquith's desk.

"An accident, huh?"

"I've told you a thousand times, it *was* an *accident*," said an exasperated Aisquith.

"The roller just started rolling down the hill, all by itself?" Packard's question was drenched in sarcasm.

"You know the operator left it parked on a slope when he quit work yesterday," Aisquith protested angrily.

"Yep, I checked that out. The guy with Naparilla Brothers admitted he left it partially parked on the slope. But he said it was impossible for the braking system to fail like that. You need to squeeze two handles simultaneously to release the brake on that thing."

"Then it was defective. It was an old piece of equipment, you know that."

"Yea, it was pretty worn out, but the brakes seemed fine. We have an investigator checking it out."

"Listen. I was walking back to the car to get my scale when . . ."

"Scale?"

"A scale." Aisquith picked one off his desk and held it up for Packard to examine. "It measures distances on architectural drawings."

"Funny you didn't have it on you. You knew you'd need it to go over the drawings with Dannon."

"Goddamn it, I forgot it. I left in the car," Aisquith shouted.

"So the roller just started moving by itself? That's your explanation?"

"I told you. I walked past the roller. When I got to the rear of the building, I heard something, turned around and saw that the roller was moving. I ran after it, yelling at Dannon to get out of the way. A freak accident, that's what it was . . . an *accident*."

"Like Carrollton's death was an accident?"

Aisquith froze and glared at Packard. "What the hell do you mean by that?" he growled.

Packard looked at him without a trace of emotion and folded his hands in his lap. "He could have been pushed off the edge."

"He lost his balance when that hawk swooped down on him. The police saw the hawk and the nest of fledglings the mother was trying to protect. You know all that."

"He could've been looking at the birds and you could have been given him a shove over the edge."

Aisquith shook his head vigorously from side to side in frustration. Packard was reminded of his own six-year-old when he accused him of drawing on the dining room wall.

"Sorry, Detective. The medical examiner found a cut on his scalp from the hawk's talons."

"There was no lab analysis to confirm the cut was made by a hawk."

"Bullshit. You know there was. You're trying to bluff me. The guy had just given me a commission with a fee of over five million dollars. Why would I then go and throw him off a cliff? Like they say on PBS, what was the motive for the murder, Detective?"

Packard leaned back in his chair and placed his right hand on his chin and squinted at Aisquith.

"The PBS inspector would guess that you felt your fee was insultingly insufficient for the amount of work required. I hear architects are always bitching they're never paid enough. You argued and you lost your temper. Simple manslaughter."

"Forget it. The contract had been signed. And let me tell you something. I would have done a building like that for one-tenth of the contractual fee and blown every guy on the whole building committee. It was an opportunity of a lifetime."

"I admire dedication to one's profession."

"I'm glad to hear it."

"You won't be glad to hear that I'm a dedicated guy. One of those cops that never rests until they get their man."

"Packard of the Royal Canadian Mounties?" said Aisquith sarcastically.

Packard laughed. "Yep, call me Dudley Do-Right."

Even though he was practically accusing him of murder, Aisquith still admired Packard's quick wit.

"Plus," Packard continued, "three people who were connected to this project are missing. Quill. Wiggs. And . . . here's a news update for you--Mabel Marston, the environmental official who held up your permit."

"I barely had any contact with her."

"But you were one of the last people to see her alive. That's what her appointment book on her desk says. You met her out at the construction site."

"That's true, but I don't know anything about her after that."

Aisquith got up from his chair and noticed a large sweat stain on the seat of his leather chair. He knew there could be a corresponding stain on the seat of his khaki trousers so he stood behind his desk. "So what are you hinting at? That I'm responsible for all three of them disappearing? Then what did I do with all of them and most importantly--why?"

Packard gazed at a piece of marble on the desk. Aisquith had stolen it from the Acropolis on a trip to Greece twelve years before.

"I didn't say you did anything to any of them," Packard said, still studying the purloined marble.

"Well, I didn't. So put that thought out of your mind," Aisquith snapped.

This brought a smile to Packard's face. He shifted his eyes from the marble to Aisquith. "I will. For now."

Aisquith frowned. He didn't like where this was going. He needed time to think, but kept defending himself vehemently. "Dannon got in the way of a runaway roller. The poor shit didn't see it coming. Like getting hit by lighting."

"This is my first murder by roller, " said Packard dryly.

"Accident," Aisquith protested brusquely. "It was an accident!"

"Accident. I remember cartoon characters flattened by rollers on Saturday morning TV when I was a kid. Like on *The Road Runner*.

"The mess I saw wasn't anything like a cartoon," Aisquith replied. "The poor bastard was flatter than a tortilla."

"Yep, the medical examiner's office had to gather him up with a snow shovel." Packard shook his head. "No open casket for old Dannon. They could put him in a jar and just set it out at the funeral parlor."

He had grown to despise Dannon within twenty-four hours of meeting him, but the crack annoyed Aisquith. "It was too bad. He was the very best in his field. Dannon could've made the Addington one of the most famous museums in the world," he said with a long sigh.

"You didn't say he was a nice guy."

"He wasn't. He was a first-class prick. Arrogant, mean, and a real shit."

"Not a reason to kill him?"

"Hey, if I killed all the pricks I came across in my practice, I'd never have time to design any buildings." Aisquith strained for a laugh, but he knew instantly what he said wasn't the least bit funny.

Packard slowly rose out of his chair like an old man with arthritis. He faced Aisquith, who was still standing behind his desk.

"What if he changed all of your design? That's what Barton told me the meeting out there was all about. And that kid in your office."

"Kurt?"

"Yea, Kurt. He said you don't like making changes in general."

With both arms outstretched, Aisquith leaned against the edge of his desk and looked directly into Packard's steel-blue eyes.

"If you knew anything about architects, Packard, you'd know that no architect likes to change anything. Not even a toilet-roll holder. We all think our designs are perfect."

"But people say you get real pissed when you have to make them. Kurt told me you burned a model because the client didn't like the design and made you do it over again."

"Like I said, Pack. You haven't been around architects so you don't how it enrages them to change anything. But we all do it because it's the client's money paying the freight and in the end we do what the client says. Or we don't get paid."

Packard walked to the closed office door and opened it halfway, then paused. "Be careful Mr. Aisquith. Your building has a curse on it. It's almost as if the earth has swallowed three people up. *You* could be the next to go."

Aisquith hated the curse analogy, but smiled amiably. "Thanks for the advice. I'll be sure not to let anyone suck me underground." Careful, careful, he thought.

"For now, Dannon's death will be ruled an accident. But something isn't right. I'm going to keep poking around. I'll find something sooner or later," the detective said, shifting to his official police voice.

"Like a body? Doesn't the inspector have to find a body before he can bring a murder charge? That's what Inspector Morse said to his sergeant last Thursday."

"Yea, I saw that episode. But in special cases, you don't need to produce a body." Packard turned to leave.

"Wait. You're not going to tell me not to leave town?" said Aisquith with a boisterous laugh.

"Packard smiled. "Don't have to. I'll probably put a tail on you," he said as went through the door.

Aisquith's smile lingered on his face as he wondered if Packard was putting him on. He waited until Packard was out the front door before he paid a visit to the studio. He sneaked up behind Kurt and pulled his Walkman headphone off.

"Kurt, my young cohort, come see me in my office," he hissed.

"Sure Allan." Kurt leapt up to follow behind him.

Aisquith closed the door the second Kurt was across the threshold. "So Kurt, you've been questioned by the authorities and didn't tell me anything about it," he said, trying to conceal his irritation.

"The detective said you knew about it, so I didn't think there was any need to mention it."

Aisquith decided to hold him blameless due to his youthful naivete and pathetic ignorance of black-and-white detective films. "So what did he ask about?"

"Just about the revisions you mentioned that Dannon wanted."

"Anything else?"

"Nope. That was it, Allan."

Aisquith was about to launch into a lecture about civil liberties and police interrogation when a knock came at the door.

"Yea?" he barked in annoyance to no one in particular. "What the hell is it, Grace?"

Sensing he was in one of his foul moods, she didn't dare open the door but shouted the message through the stained wood door.

"Mr. Barton just called. He said it's very urgent and he has to speak to you right away. He's holding on line two."

"All right, all right. Thanks Grace."

He turned his attention to Kurt again. "Listen, Kurt, the next time Packard comes sniffing around, please tell me, okay?"

"No problem, Allan. Do you think he will?" he asked with a frown.

"Yep, he'll be back."

There was silence. Kurt realized that was his cue to leave so Aisquith could take Barton's call. He nodded and quietly slipped out.

When Aisquith snatched up the receiver, the first thing he heard was Barton wheezing away. He knew only a crisis made the old man wheeze like that.

"Hamilton, whoa, take it easy. What's wrong?" Aisquith realized it was a stupid thing to ask. The man's newly hired museum director had just been squished by a paving roller.

"Allan, Mrs. Addington's returned from her home in England. She saw the CNN report on Dannons's death before I could call her about it." Barton sounded panic stricken.

Aisquith himself had refused interviews with the media about the accident on the advice of the museum's legal counsel. He had never been on TV and secretly wished he could've granted the interviews. But he knew that after the museum's completion he'd get on TV, at least on a local Baltimore station.

Barton wheezed on. "She's upset about Dannon and also Wiggs being missing for so long. She's mad as hell about everything getting so screwed up."

"Hamilton, everything's going fine. The museum's on schedule. "Relax for god's sake."

"Allan, a world famous museum expert's been flattened by a ten-ton roller. The story made the national page of the *New York Times*. How can you say everything's fine? She wants us to meet at my office tomorrow morning at eleven to straighten all this out."

"You tell the old girl, I'll be there," Aisquith replied with a slight chuckle. "I'll settle her down. You can count on it."

"For god's sake Allan, you're taking this all too lightly! You've never met her. I'm warning you, son, this woman's a demon from hell!" Barton sounded like a terrified man in a science fiction movie, warning the town about invading aliens.

31

As he recounted the happenings of the past week to Mrs. Addington, Aisquith couldn't help being amused by Barton's warning about "the demon" the day before. Here she was, an eighty-nine year old woman about four feet-ten-inches tall, seated at the end of Barton's shiny mahogany conference table. Dressed in a crimson dress and a green woolen cardigan, she looked like a combination of Queen Victoria and a pixie. Her appearance gave Aisquith, the quintessential Anglophile, great pleasure and comfort. He was tempted to look under the table to see if she was sitting on a telephone book.

Throughout his presentation, a sweet, almost cherubic, smile lit her heart-shaped face, which was framed by snowwhite hair. When Aisquith finished, he sat down next to Barton, the only other person in the wood-paneled room. There was a deafening silence. At first Aisquith thought Mrs. Addington might be deaf and hadn't heard anything he said.

"Horseshit," were the words that finally broke the silence.

Aisquith looked at Barton, who returned an equally incredulous look.

"I beg your pardon," Barton blurted.

"Pure, unadulterated horseshit is what I said, Mr. Barton." Mrs. Addington said this in a soft melodious voice, the kind a granny would use in reading a bedtime story to a gaggle of grandkids.

Barton jumped up from his seat and started gesticulating wildly. "You mean . . . about what happened to Mr. Dannon? I can assure you, Mrs. Addington, that it was an accident." Barton's face was beet red.

"No Mr. Barton, I'm not talking about that poor devil, Mr. Dannon. I was talking about Mr. Aisquith's design."

Barton and Aisquith exchanged wild-eyed looks as if in a vaudeville routine. Aisquith stared at the tiny person at the end of the table for a moment before he could force words out of his mouth.

"But you . . . approved the design. You saw all the drawings right from the very beginning. How can you say you don't like it after all this time. The museum's almost half built. What part of the design don't you like?"

"The whole kit and kaboodle," she said with a bright smile.

"Could you be more . . . specific?" Aisquith said, as cowed as he had ever been in his life. He hoped he was hallucinating.

"The building looks cold and feels cold."

"But with all due respect, why didn't you say something before? We could've changed it while it was still on paper," said a flabbergasted Barton.

Mrs. Addington adjusted her little hat that looked like a bellboy's cap, and her cornflower blue eyes seemed to brighten.

"I probably should have. But a lot of these fancy big museums all seem to be to be these weird designs that look like space ships right out of Buck Rodgers. So I thought if that was what they're building nowadays, then so would I. Like that theatre in Los Angeles by that guy whose buildings all look like exploded beer cans."

"I'm so sorry you don't like it," Aisquith murmured.

"Well, to be honest. I thought Mr. Carrollton would make some changes but the damn fool fell off a cliff looking at some goddamn bird. It's my fault. I should've come back to the States to look after things. It's not what Angus would've wanted either. But he's dead and who cares about what he wanted. *I* don't like the design."

"Mrs. Addington, we took great care in designing the right building to house your late husband's collection," beseeched Barton. "It's too late to change anything."

"Nonsense, man. It's never too late to change anything. Especially when you're filthy rich like me. So the building is delayed. It's not the end of the world, you know," she said with a big smile that made her resemble an elf.

"Mr. Addington wanted the museum to be built without delay," Barton countered.

"I told you a couple of minutes ago--who the hell cares what he wanted. Let me set you straight about a few things, son. I met Angus at the 1929 debutante's ball at the St. Regis in Manhattan. I drank too much, we went up to a room, and he knocked me up. The ballgame was over. In those days you had to get married. None of that pro-choice crap in those days, let me tell you."

"Mrs. Addington, this is all very personal. You don't have to . . ."

She let out a huge laugh that seemed too explosive for her little body and cut Barton off in mid-sentence.

"Heavens man, I'm too old to be embarassed. He was an idiot. I woke up the next morning knowing that I'd be stuck with this lump the rest of my life. Thank God he was loaded. The money made life bearable. You know, that man had hair growing out of places you couldn't imagine. He was . . . oh dear, I'm afraid I've gone off on a tangent," she exclaimed with a schoolgirl giggle.

Aisquith shot a look of defeat toward Barton, who mustered a wan smile in return.

Mrs. Addington suddenly slammed her shiny black aluminum cane on the mahogany table, making both men levitate from their high-backed chairs.

"Well, Mr. Asquith, what can you do to gussy up my building?" she shouted.

This time Aisquith sprang up from his seat on his own. "You're serious about changing it, aren't you?"

Mrs. Addington slammed her cane on the table again and let out a whoop.

"I like you, Aisquith. You're not scared by a rich old bag like me. You've got a set of testicles on you and I respect that. But I'm paying the bills here and you'll follow my direction or I'll have what's been built knocked down tomorrow. Am I making my self clear?"

Aisquith fell back into his chair if he had taken a bullet in the stomach. He rubbed his forehead and temples with both hands, then looked down the table at her.

"We're going to change the entire building?" he squeaked, cringing in fear at what the answer would be.

"Goodness no, Mr. Aisquith. I mean just the outside of the building. Some brick and marble to warm it up a bit. What do you say? Mmmm?"

Aisquith was beaten. It was as if the old woman had rammed him in the groin with her ergonomically designed cane. There was none of the usual rage welling up within his chest, but he sensed a stream of last ditch arch-speak was about to pass from his lips. He made no effort to hold it back. It was a dying man's last gasp.

"Mrs Addington." He paused for dramatic effect. She smiled sweetly at him. She knew she had him at bay.

"The design is perfect for that site. It is a precise and reciprocal relationship between built architecture and the natural topography. A harmony of . . ."

Her piercing shriek of laughter almost punctured his eardrums.

"Oh, Mr. Aisquith, do talk English," Mrs. Addington said, her face bright red from laughter. "Why do architects speak such gibberish. They always have to intellectualize why they design such godawful things."

Undaunted, Aisquith picked himself off the mat and tried one last desperate punch before he went down for the count. "There's a concern for proportion, rhythm . . ."

A shriek twenty decibels higher than the first knifed through the air of the conference room. "Please stop, Mr. Aisquith, if I laugh any harder, I'll have a stroke," she pleaded, waving both hands in the air.

Spent, Aisquith dropped back into his seat and stared into space. Barton stared at a pencil on the table, not daring to look up. The old woman's laughter continued like a broken car horn until Aisquith thought she would keel over. A brilliant idea suddenly flashed through his brain. He considered launching a barrage of arch-speak that would bring on a coronary and finish her off, but he thought better of it. Packard would probably charge him with murder by rhetoric.

After a minute or so, Mrs. Addington managed to get her laughter under control. She pulled out a white lace hanky to dab at her eyes, now filled with tears.

"Don't worry, Mr. Aisquith. Together we'll fix this turkey. And I'll make sure you get compensated handsomely for your extra efforts."

She then picked her enormous handbag, the size of a shopping bag, off the floor and set it on the table. "Wait until you see what I've done for you, Mr. A. This will make things a lot easier for both of us."

Mrs. Addington started pulling things out of the bag. A hair brush, a tube of Preparation H, amber tinted prescription bottles, a stapler remover, envelopes of all sizes, a flashlight-- all were strewn across the mahogany surface.

"Hold on. It's in here somewhere, I know it. I put it in here last night so I wouldn't forget it this morning. Ahhh, yes, here we go."

She waved some pages torn out of magazines. "I thought you'd want to see some idea of what I want."

Aisquith rose slowly from his seat. Like a condemned man walking to the gallows, he shuffled toward her. He already knew what the pages contained. He just knew. She thrust them eagerly into his hand and beamed a wide smile at him.

He carefully unfolded them. They were from the type of home decorating magazines that are displayed at checkout stands in supermarkets. All the photos shared a theme or, as Aisquith felt at that very moment, the lowest common denominator.

"Williamsburg," he said.

"Yes, Mr. Aisquith, Williamsburg's what I want. Ever been there?"

"No, m'am, I haven't."

"Well then these clippings can start you off in the right direction." Then another idea sprang into her into white-haired head. "You know what we could do?" she chirped excitedly. "We could go together to Williamsburg. Like a field trip, what do you say? We could stay overnight."

"I think I know the direction you want just by looking at these pictures, Mrs. Addington. It's very kind of you to offer, but let me get to work and do some sketches for you."

"All right, if you say so, Mr. Aisquith. I'm really looking forward to seeing what you come up with. Call me as soon as you have something. If you need more examples, let me know. I have tons of magazines at home."

"Yes, m'am, I'll be sure to," he answered in a defeated tone.

"Hamilton, let the work continue on the interior for now. Some paint and wallpaper can spruce things up in the galleries. Don't worry, I've got plenty of ideas about the inside," she gestured with her bony little hands toward Barton, who sat silently in shock.

The old woman started to put back the junk she'd removed from her bag. She was giddy with joy. "Oh my goodness," she exclaimed as shoved in the last of of a dozen or so prescription bottles. "I'm too worn out from all this. I haven't laughed this hard since Angus was almost indicted for tax fraud. I'm going home and take a nice long nap."

Barton was now standing next to her. "Mrs. Addington, let me help you to your car."

"That's very kind of you." She looked over the table. "I think I have everything."

Aisquith, emotionally drained, was leaning against the wall by the door for support. He felt nauseous and prayed that he wouldn't vomit right then and there in front of the old lady. With Barton's arm interwined with hers, Mrs. Addington slowly walked to the door. She stopped and playfully poked Aisquith in the stomach with her scrawny index finger. "You take care Mr. Aisquith. You'll see, we'll make a heck of a design team."

He nodded meekly and managed a smile. Barton's eyes locked on Aisquith just then. He was alarmed at how dead the architect's eyes seemed, like a great white shark's.

Aisquith knew it would take an hour for Mrs. Addington and Barton to walk to her car in the adjacent garage, so he bade them goodbye and quickly walked down the hall into the elevator lobby. When he reached the main floor he shuffled like a zombie through the revolving door into the street, which bustled with lunch-goers and shoppers. He looked to his right and saw Chet Kelly standing there glowering. Aisquith's shock was quickly overwhelmed by anger. He strode up to him.

"What the hell are you doing here?" he barked.

"See what happened for trying to stick me in a cube? I hope they throw you in jail for killing that guy. You're going to get what you deserve."

"You're mad!" Aisquith screamed so loudly that passersby paused to see what all the fuss was about.

"I hope they fry you in the electric chair," Kelly said with glee.

"Stay the hell away from me, you nut. You don't belong in a cubicle. You belong in a padded cell."

Kelly laughed in his face, spraying Aisquith with a fine mist of saliva. "I'm not finished with you. Not by a long shot, you shit." He turned and strolled away as if nothing had happened and quickly faded into the stream of pedestrians.

32

It was dark by the time Aisquith dragged himself back to the office. He had stopped at the Owl Bar and spent the rest of the day there. He wanted to go home but he had to make some calls tonight and needed some files from his desk.

To his annoyance, Kurt was still there. Evidently he had no life outside of his work. He kept telling the intern that these were the best years of his life and he should be out drinking and getting laid. But there he was, always at the office until all hours of the night.

Aisquith knew that Kurt felt lucky to be working in his office. Kurt's classmates, who worked only on townhouses or cheap speculative office buildings, probably were envious of him. He worked for a hot architect who was doing museums, the best kind of commission an office could get. He had fallen into a dream job and probably loved the museum as much or even more than Aisquith.

Kurt had been an enormous help to him during construction. He knew every detail of the museum no matter how small or insignificant. He knew exactly how the paper towel dispensers were fastened to the tile walls in the restrooms and what type of hinge was used on a door on a storage closet deep in the bowels of the sub-basement. As Aisquith recalled all the help he'd received from Kurt his annoyance faded. He wanted to say goodnight to him.

Kurt saw Aisquith come in and immediately sensed something was wrong. He hurriedly cleaned up his workstation and gathered his jacket to make a quick exit the moment the boss went into his office. But Aisquith headed straight to the studio, blocking his escape route.

"Kurt, my man, prepare yourself for some revisions," said Aisquith in a world-weary voice.

"Revisions?"

"Revisions. Major revisions, I think you'd call them."

"Why?"

"In architecture, as in life, we must compromise. Even if it means sacrificing our principles."

"What do we have to change?"

"I'll tell you tomorrow. Go on home and get some rest."

Kurt nodded and walked away but stopped and turned back to Aisquith. His sense of duty compelled him to speak up even though the moment was clearly inappropriate. In a quiet voice he said, "Allan, something odd happened today that you should know about."

Aisquith's annoyance returned instantly. "Well, what is it?" he snapped.

"I got the as-built drawing of the sky bridges from the steel erector, today and there's something that makes no sense at all."

"And what's that?"

"The original detail you worked out had both bridges suspended from thick rods fastened to the steel floor beams above. The rods would carry the weight of both bridges with ease. Now, the lower bridge is suspended by thinner rods just attached to the higher one that's held up by rods attached to the ceiling."

"I don't recall authorizing any change like that. They just installed the bridges yesterday. Did the structural engineer change it?"

"I called Roger Carney right away and he said he didn't."

"Don't worry about it. I'll check it out," Aisquith murmured in a distracted manner. The events of the afternoon ran over and over in his brain. It was the old movie projector again, and he couldn't shut it off.

"Carney said the top bridge can't support the lower one, it's too heavy a load. The lower bridge could bring down the upper one. Even an impact load could bring it all down, he said."

Aisquith was staring out the window at the lights in the adjacent mill building. He saw the night janitor emptying wastebaskets in the offices. He wanted a job like that. A simple task he could do at night when nobody was around.

"I said I'd look into it," said Aisquith tersely, still staring through the window.

The tone of Aisquith's voice robbed Kurt of all courage for what he wanted to say. He was now too scared to tell him that Packard had visited earlier this evening and asked him more questions. Questions about revisions Aisquith had made to parts of the building, especially odd, last-minute changes. Kurt hadn't had the guts to tell Packard to take a hike as Aisquith had told him to do. Instead, he had felt intimidated by Packard and meekly obliged when the cop asked him to plot out some of the revisions.

Aisquith turned abruptly to Kurt, almost surprised to still find him standing there.

"Well, is there anything else?"

Kurt was silent for a moment. "No."

"Then on your way, lad."

33

Aisquith had the office to himself the next day. It was Saturday morning and his drafting board was encircled with wads of yellow tracing paper. For the past two hours he had tried to clad the museum in brick without much success. At the top of his board there was a pile of books, none of which had provided fresh inspiration. He hoped he could trick Mrs. Addington by applying brick while not compromising the modernistic design, but was disgusted at the results and ashamed of himself.

"Christ, this doesn't work," Aisquith muttered to himself. As he looked up at the rendering of the museum he had framed on his wall, he let the soft lead pencil slip from his fingers. It rolled off the board onto the floor, breaking its point. He kept gazing at the rendering, admiring the strong curve of the building springing out of the earth. He loved especially the towering glass window wall in the rear.

The rendering included the landscape plantings, which in five years would spread from the meadow onto the sloping copper roof and make the building literally part of the earth.

Finally, Aisquith couldn't bring himself to do it. Abraham might have killed Isaac, but Aisquith couldn't put his own child to death. He stood up and walked to his desk.

"I'm gonna have it out with the old hag," he muttered as he dialed the phone.

"This is Allan Aisquith," he proclaimed in a stentorian voice. "I'd like to speak to Mrs. Addington."

I'm sorry she isn't here," the housekeeper said in a monotone.

"When will she be back?"

"I don't really know. She left to go to the museum to meet with the architect. She might be gone all afternoon."

He was totally befuddled. It took him a few seconds to gather his thoughts.

"But *I'm* the architect and I don't know of any appointment with her today," he stammered.

"Well, Mrs. Addington said she had an appointment for today. She left about fifteen minutes ago in the Lincoln to go down to the Cliffs where they're building the museum. Doctor Grant told her she shouldn't drive, but she gave Ralph the day off to go to Pimlico this afternoon, so she just took the keys and went. She hasn't been behind the wheel of a car since she drove through the front window of the Hallmark shop at the Monkton Shopping Center, about eleven years ago. There was nothing I could do to stop her."

"But I don't remember setting anything up for today," Aisquith protested.

"She just received a call from the architect about thirty minutes ago, asking her to come out and look at the new sketches he'd done for her museum."

"But I'm the architect, goddamn it."

"Then you're supposed to be at the museum now," the housekeeper scolded. "The way she drives, you'll be able to get to the museum about the same time she will."

Aisquith thought that made no sense at all and slammed down the phone in a rage.

He glanced over at the wads of yellow tracing paper around his drafting board, then at the rendering on the wall. A spasm of anger shot up through his chest.

"I don't give a damn what happens. I'm going to have it out with her."

Aisquith ran through the reception area to the parking lot and jumped into his Volvo.

He raced around the beltway and in twenty minutes was on Route 2, heading south to the Patuxent Cliffs. The ride gave him time to rehearse what he would say to her. He had faced that nasty crossroads again and again in his career. This time he *would* turn *left*. He was glad that he'd have Mrs. Addington all to himself. He would browbeat the old bat into sticking with his design. Barton wouldn't be there to interfere.

He turned off Route 2 onto Calverton Road and was only ten minutes from the Cliffs when he ran straight into a traffic backup. Cursing and pounding the steering wheel, he joined the line of cars that was traveling about twenty miles an hour. After five minutes, the steady but slow speed of the cars in front of him made him guess he was at the tail end of a funeral procession. He craned his neck to see ahead of the cars. After another painstakingly slow five minutes, the road, more or less straight until then, began to curve through the countryside. Then, on a wide bend of the road, he finally saw the cars ahead. The lead vehicle, a long black car, was about a quarter of a mile ahead of him. It appeared to be moving about twenty miles an hour. Suddenly the drivers ahead of Aisquith started honking their horns with a ferocity seldom heard in Baltimore. The car still proceeded at a snail's pace.

It was just some old geezer crawling along the highway at a third of the speed limit. Why do they let these fossils drive? Aisquith fumed. Over the years he had seen many an old woman peering through the spokes of the steering wheel of a big Cadillac or Lincoln, the length of a battleship, clogging up the fast line. Wait a minute--hadn't the housekeeper said Mrs. Addington had taken the Lincoln. At another bend in the road, he saw it was indeed a Lincoln Town Car at the head of the line. He started laughing uncontrollably. He would arrive at the museum just minutes behind her.

Aisquith turned off Calverton and raced up the road that led up the hill to the museum. When he got to the temporary parking lot that the construction crews used, he saw the Lincoln parked there. Next to it was an overturned blue plastic portable toilet. Aisquith parked his Volvo next to the Lincoln and lept out into a foul-smelling brown liquid. Cursing his head off, he quickly realized its origin. It oozed from the toilet and puddled under Mrs. Addington's Lincoln. After taking a minute to scrape the mess from his Topsiders, he sprinted down the spiral entry ramp to the lobby. He ran up to the front doors and peered in. The natural light from the lobby skylights made it easy to spot Mrs. Addington.

She sat on the concrete blocks, looking up at the skybridges above her.

When Mrs. Addington had finally made her way into the lobby she was greeted with what she considered a wonderful surprise. Both hanging bridges were in place. She looked up and saw with great satisfaction the statue of the Spartan on a pedestal on the upper bridge.

The second century AD statue of an ancient warrior brandishing a sword had been in the main foyer of her English mansion for years. She hated most of her husband's collection of modern art. Despite the praise he received, she thought Picasso drew like a child. But she had approved of the Spartan from the first day Addington brought it home. The beautifully modeled face under the magnificent helmet sent chills down her spine, and his muscular nude body had inspired many an erotically charged dream. She had more and more such dreams as Angus's body gradually turned into an amorphous blob. It made her very happy to see the Stud, as she called him, in so prominent a place in her museum. She walked under the bridges to view the Spartan from different angles. She had walked around the Stud many times in her mansion, but here the high perspective gave her a new appreciation of the ancient sculpture, especially the groin area.

She circled under it so many times, she became dizzy and had to go sit on a low stack of concrete blocks directly below some scaffolding. The masons used the rig to build the five-story concrete block wall of the lobby and fasten a veneer of red granite to it.

Aisquith opened the specially hinged lobby doors he had designed and called out Mrs. Addington's name. The old woman waved happily. "Yoo hoo, Mr. Aisquith, I'm here. I'm ready to start designing," she said with giggle.

She quickly struggled to her feet. The second her bottom slid off the blocks, a single concrete block came crashing on the exact spot where she had been sitting.

The smashing sound startled her and she turned quickly to see what was happening. On the spot where she sat only a second before there was a pile of shattered gray block. Aisquith had looked up to see the block in the last eight feet of its descent and froze in his tracks. He tried to yell, but the words stayed inside his throat.

"Oh dear me, Mr. Aisquith. You should tell these workmen to be more careful where they put their material. Look, this block can't be used, it has a crack in it."

Aisquith's knees almost buckled under him but he placed a hand on the doorjamb of the entry to steady himself. He slowly looked up at the scaffolding above her to see where the block had come from. What he saw paralyzed him with fear.

"Oh Christ," he screamed so loudly that an echo bounced off the tall lobby walls.

"Careful, Mr. Aisquith. Remember about using the Lord's name in vain," Mrs. Addington scolded with a frown.

"Yes, Allan, don't use the Lord's name in vain--at least not in front of the client."

Carlos stood defiantly on the scaffolding directly above them.

Aisquith was thunderstruck. He just stared at Carlos in disbelief. Carlos smiled and returned the stare.

Aisquith slowly gathered his wits and his heartbeat slowed down to 1,000 beats per minute. He walked slowly toward the scaffolding, looked up at Carlos, and smiled.

"Carlos, I know you're new at being a partner, but killing the client isn't good business practice. It's specifically stated in the AIA handbook of practice."

"That's a hoot. You lecturing about me not killing people. Kind of like the kettle calling the pot black, mmm?'

"Really?" said Aisquith in an icy tone. He was beginning to piece things together. Now it was plain who had set up the appointment with Mrs. Addington today.

"Mr. Aisquith, is this young man a friend of yours?" asked Mrs. Addington, gazing up at Carlos. She didn't seem the least bit surprised to see him up there.

Aisquith had momentarily forgotten about the old lady, but knew he had to get her out of there.

"Not exactly, he's more like an employee, but I'm about to let him go. Would you mind waiting for me outside in the parking lot? I won't be long. There's something we have to discuss."

Mrs. Addington's bright blue eyes widened in rage.

"Well, goodness. You call me out here, then you make me wait. Very well, but be quick about it! There's a lot we have to go over." She picked up her pocketbook and cane and waddled to the door. She stopped and turned around.

"Mr. Aisquith, I think I may have damaged that Johnny-on-the-Pot in the parking lot. You'll see to it, won't you? The men won't have a place to go to the bathroom on Monday. It's unfair to ask them to hold it in all day."

"Yes, m'am. I'll take care of it right away," Aisquith answered like a schoolboy.

"Good. I'll meet you by the bottom of this ramp out here, then," she said with a smile.

Aisquith and Carlos watched until she was outside, then turned to face each other.

Carlos spoke first. "Allan, in my new capacity as partner, I've made a business decision. I decided *I* don't need a partner."

Aisquith with his hands on his hips, smiled and looked up at Carlos. "What an incredible coincidence. I just realized *I* don't need a partner either."

"Things haven't worked out as planned," Carlos lamented. "I was very disappointed when I squashed Dannon and Packard didn't arrest you. But sooner or later he would find out you killed Wiggs, Quill, and Marston. I know damn well you did, but I still don't know what you did with them. Unfortunately I'm an impatient sort, as you know, and I couldn't wait. So I asked the old lady out here today with the expressed purpose of killing her and framing you for it.

Packard would have no choice but to arrest you. A weak-willed weasel like you would certainly break down under interrogation and confess. But you've shown up quite unexpectedly and complicated my plans."

Aisquith started to climb the aluminum ladder attached to the side of the scaffolding. "I'm awfully sorry to mess things up for you," he said. "Here, let me come up there and make it up to you." Carlos walked to the end of the scaffold to watch him climb up.

"You know, I think I can find some room in the basement for you. Wiggs would love to have a roommate. The accommodations are a bit cramped, but you won't mind."

Carlos suddenly picked up a concrete block off the stack next to him and threw it down on Aisquith who dodged the block and kept climbing. Carlos grabbed another block and raised it above his head with both hands, then hurled it down on Aisquith like a caveman repelling an invader. The block hit a rung on the ladder just above Aisquith and bounced off, striking him in the shoulder. Aisquith screamed in pain and clutched his left shoulder with his right hand, clinging to the rung with the left. His rage, pumped him full of adrenaline, giving him almost superhuman energy to bound up the last rungs to the level where Carlos stood.

Carlos retreated along the scaffold to reach another stack of blocks, but Aisquith was right behind him. As he ran past the stack, Carlos dislodged a block, pushed it in Aisquith's path, and smashed him in the ankle. Aisquith let out a yell and fell heavily on the wooden boards that made up the floor of the scaffold. Carlos, with a lead on Aisquith, ran off the scaffolding through an opening in the wall at the fourth floor.

Cursing and writhing in pain, Aisquith rubbed his ankle but got back on his feet and limped after Carlos, following him through the opening.

Now about thirty yards ahead of Aisquith, Carlos ran into what was to be a gallery space. He stopped when he saw a metal storage locker the size of a steamer trunk. It was padlocked. Carlos swiftly searched for something to break the lock with. He spotted some concrete blocks holding up a plank with bags of mortar on it. He pulled a block out from under the plank, raced over to the locker, and pounded the lock off.

Flipping open the top, he frantically rummaged around through hammers, putty knives, and screwdrivers until he found a portable nail gun. He smiled at his find. The gun had the same power as a 22-caliber rifle. He yanked it out of the box, saw that it had a battery attached, and sprinted through a doorway at the far end of the gallery that led to the upper sky bridge.

Though his pain was excruciating, Aisquith kept limping in the direction he last saw Carlos. He hobbled through the opening, passed the open locker, then stopped to get his bearings. Because he had spent countless hours designing the museum, he knew exactly where he was. He saw that the opening at the end of the room led to the bridge and knew that Carlos must be out there. He couldn't allow him to leave the museum alive now. But he realized that when he caught up with Carlos, he had no means of finishing him off. Aisquith hobbled over to the locker to look for a weapon and pulled out a circular saw. He deftly took off the nut that held the round saw blade in place and pulled the blade off. Then he continued his pursuit of Carlos out onto the upper sky bridge.

Carlos was waiting for Aisquith on the bridge just to the right of the opening, out of sight. He let Aisquith limp by him until he was almost in the center of the bridge.

"Hello, Allan." he shouted at his back.

Aisquith twisted his body around, but his leg collapsed underneath him and he fell onto the steel plate floor of the bridge, smashing the knee of his good leg. Carlos, holding the nail gun at his side, walked slowly toward him.

"Allan, I hereby dissolve this partnership." Carlos raised the nail gun in his right hand. Aisquith recognized the weapon and knew what was about to happen. Carlos was now twenty feet away. He knew he couldn't make it to the other end of the bridge. With the saw blade in his right hand, he raised his arm and flung the blade at Carlos. It spun through the air with a hiss, just missed Carlos's ear, and bounced off the sheetrock wall behind him.

"Allan, you've been watching martial arts films, haven't you? I thought that would be beneath a Harvard man," said Carlos with a vicious laugh as he walked toward Aisquith and slowly took aim again.

Aisquith frantically looked around for cover but there wasn't any. Then with every ounce of strength he had left, he suddenly grabbed the railing and pulled himself up. To Carlos' astonishment, Aisquith swung his body over the railing.

Carlos dropped the nail gun, ran and looked over the railing, expecting to see Aisquith dead four floors below but he was lying on the lower bridge ten feet below. Carlos broke out in laughter. "You lucky bastard. I'll give you credit, you know your own building."

Aisquith had landed on the lower bridge with an enormous impact. The pain in both legs was now ten times worse than before. He thought he must have broken both legs. In desperation he tried to drag himself across the bridge.

Carlos, directly above him, leaned on the railing of the bridge and watched, amused, like a child looking at the seals at the zoo. "Go on, asshole, try to crawl away." Carlos then looked to his right and was surprised to see the statue of the Spartan on his marble pedestal, standing about ten yards away in the center of the bridge. He trotted back to pick up the nail gun, then walked back to the statue. With the help of the Spartan's muscular right thigh, he boosted himself up on the pedestal to get a clear shot at Aisquith.

After dragging his lifeless legs ten feet, Aisquith collapsed, lying flat on his back looking up at the rows of sawtoothed skylights in the roof of the lobby. At that instant his mind drifted away from his predicament. He admired the beams of sunlight streaming through the skylights. What a beautiful shot for the architectural magazines. The light streamed down on the Calder mobile, which was slowly turning, changing position every hour. He had done it! He had finally designed one great building in his life, a life he knew was seconds away from ending. With this one wonderful building, Aisquith knew he didn't have to be ashamed anymore of all the second-rate work he'd done. He wasn't afraid. He felt very much at peace. He just closed his eyes to wait for the end.

With his arm around the Spartan's waist, Carlos took aim with the nail gun. "As I said before, I hereby dissolve this partnership."

A gunshot rang out, echoing through the cavernous lobby. Carlos' eyes opened wide and he stared out into space as if witnessing an apparition. Aisquith, expecting to feel pain at the sound of the shot, felt nothing. He knew Carlos would have to pump him full of nails to kill him, so he expected another shot but there was only silence. Aisquith opened his eyes and saw Carlos still standing above him. The hand holding the nail gun dropped slowly to Carlos' side. Puzzled, Aisquith raised himself on his elbow. Through the geometric pattern of the balusters on the bridge he had so lovingly designed he saw Packard on the ground floor below the bridges. He had a pistol in his right hand that was pointed at the upper sky bridge. Aisquith looked back at Carlos who was slumping against the statue with his left arm still wrapped around its waist.

A torrent of laughter poured out of Aisquith, making him forget the pain in his legs. "Inspector, I thought the British never resorted to firearms," he yelled with glee. "Bloody uncivilized!"

Still barely clutching the Spartan's waist, Carlos slowly raised the nail gun. Another shot crackled through the air. The gun dropped from his hand and landed on the lower bridge ten feet from Aisquith. Carlos lurched forward, but kept a death grip on the Spartan's waist. As Carlos fell, the Spartan, not yet permanently fastened to his pedestal because the workman assigned to that task went home early yesterday, went with him, toppling over the stainless steel railing. It came crashing down to the bridge below and landing atop Aisquith, who was still looking down at Packard.

The impact instantly ignited a high-pitched screeching sound like fingernails dragging across a chalkboard. Wiggs's last-minute structural change on the hanger rods never could have accommodated the weight of the Spartan.

Realizing what the sound meant, Packard dropped his gun and sprinted back to the front doors of the lobby. The screeching increased to an unbelievable pitch, then the lower bridge suddenly dropped, yanking the one above down on top of it.

The crash sent Packard diving for cover behind a pallet of concrete blocks. A deafening roar engulfed the lobby like a tornado tearing through the building. Then came an immense cloud of dust. After two minutes, Packard cautiously peeked over the stack of blocks and saw a twisted heap of steel.

With the dust still thick in the air, Mrs. Addington waddled through the glass doors.

"Heavens, what's all the racket?" she demanded. As her eyes took in the damage, she shrieked, "Oh, my God. My Spartan, what have they done to my Spartan?"

The old woman picked her way carefully through the debris until she came to the severed head of the sculpture. She poked at it with her cane almost as if to see if it was still alive.

"Oh, good gracious. Look at him. Oh my poor Stud. What have they done to you? You were so beautiful."

She lowered her head in deep sadness, then looked about the dust-filled lobby and cried out, "Mr. Aisquith, Mr. Aisquith where are you? What have you done here? My attorney will look into this."

Packard surveyed the wreckage as he walked over to her. His eyes came to rest on the bodies on Aisquith and Carlos who were only ten feet apart. The architect looked as though he was sound asleep among the twisted steel. He almost seemed to have a smile on his face, Packard thought. Mrs. Addington noticed the policeman and banged her cane on a steel beam to get his attention.

"You there, young man. Who are you? Are you responsible for this mess? I hope you're not an architect. I've had my fill of architects for today."

34

The afternoon sky was a beautiful blue; not a cloud to be seen. Sailboats and powerboats plied their ways in all directions over the choppy waves of the Chesapeake Bay. Up on the Patuxuent Cliffs, a crowd of over five hundred persons gathered along a great spiral ramp that led down to a wide white ribbon stretched across three pairs of stainless steel-framed glass doors. Normally they would swelter in the August heat, but the weather was unusually cool for this time of year. The guests were in jovial moods, talking and joking with each other as they awaited the ceremony. All the Baltimore and Washington television crews were there to record the moment.

With no fanfare, G. Hamilton Barton IV rose from his seat by the side of the ribbon and raised his hand, motioning for the crowd to come to attention.

"Ladies and gentlemen, this is a great day for the State of Maryland and the arts. In a few moments, one of the finest cultural institutions in the entire United States will be open to view, giving present and future generations the opportunity to see the best creative work man has done." His bellowing voice needed no electronic amplification.

He then turned and nodded to Mrs. Addington who was seated next to him. She was wearing her favorite periwinkle dress with a white handbag looped over her arm. With the help of her black aluminum cane and Barton's hand under her elbow, she slowly rose from the high-backed upholstered chair provided especially for her.

Barton handed her a specially crafted solid gold pair of scissors. She smiled brightly and waved the scissors above her head for all to see. The crowd gave a roar of approval. It was a joy to see how spry she was. Many secretly hoped they would be the same at the age of ninety. With Barton's help she walked up to the ribbon and faced the assemblage. With a twinkle in her cornflower blue eyes and in a surprisingly strong voice, she addressed them.

"It's with great pride that I officially open this great museum that is a monument to Angus Addington, a man who loved art and a man I adored my entire life."

With great dexterity for one with arthritic fingers, she snipped the ribbon, prompting an even bigger cheer from the throng. Museum guards dressed in navy blue blazers and charcoal gray slacks held open the doors for her and at a snail's pace, the old woman led the crowd into the museum.

At the very moment the crowd started filing down the ramp, a ring-tailed hawk with a wing span of over six feet soared low over the festivities. As it swooped ever lower over the building, the hawk seemed to be in a flight of admiration for the red brick and white marble temple with its exquisite classical detailing. A little girl walking down the ramp tugged at her father's pants leg and pointed up into the sky. Her father looked up at the bird as it made yet another pass. "What a beautiful sight," he said.